Closing Time

The Last Elder Darrow Mystery

Closing Time

The Last Elder Darrow Mystery

Richard J. Cass

Encircle Publications
Farmington, Maine, U.S.A.

Editor: Cynthia Brackett-Vincent

Cover design by Deirdre Wait
Cover photograph © Getty Images

Author photograph by Philip McCarty

Published by:

Encircle Publications
PO Box 187
Farmington, ME 04938

info@encirclepub.com
http://encirclepub.com

For Anne, as ever

Some say the world will end in fire,
Some say in ice.
From what I've tasted of desire
I hold with those who favor fire.
But if had to perish twice,
I think I know enough of hate
To say that for destruction ice
Is also great
And would suffice.
—Robert Frost, "Fire and Ice"

1

The punk shoved his way in through the automatic door as if it were trying to slow him down. Eighteen, nineteen, oozing attitude, the circus-colored tattoos up both stringy arms glowing against the dirty white wife beater. A turquoise scarf wrapped around his head, a look only Stevie Van Zandt could get away with. Not this wrung-out junkie with the wild dark eyes, jittering in withdrawal.

Up on the raised platform with the cash register, Leon reached under the counter and rested his hand on the comforting wooden grip of the .38 Special. Another great band, now that he thought of it. He pitied the kid already. If he was about to try what Leon expected, the end of the story was as inevitable as sleep.

The fluorescent tube above the hard liquor aisle flickered, shredding the cold milky light. Leon kept the high-dollar items, the handles of whiskey and gin and vodka, on shelves near the inside wall of coolers, far enough from the entrance to discourage any grab-and-runs. The middle aisle, straight ahead, held case beer, the one closest to the door, the wines. Wine drinkers tended to be a mellower lot than the Old Mr. Boston crowd.

The punk stalked down into the far back corner of the store, under the big round shoplifters' mirror up in the corner over the black and white poster of the statue of Molly Malone Leon had bought on his last trip to Dublin. The kid reached into the cooler for a six-pack of hard seltzer, the drink you drank when you wanted to get fucked up but you didn't want to taste anything. Leon tried not to judge his customers' tastes—he used to be owned by the need to drink, too—but nothing seemed more pointless to him than a beverage with some other beverage's flavor.

He relaxed a fraction and picked up the handheld scanner with his left hand, as the kid plucked a bag of pork rinds from the rack on the end cap and strolled toward the register. Maybe, squirrelly as he was acting, he was only a customer.

Fuck. No. Because here came the big foreign-looking pistol from the back of his jeans, the seltzer and pork rinds still clutched in his other hand.

Leon sighed and started to reach back under the counter.

"Uh-uh, dad." The junkie's voice was high and shaky, but the mouth of the pistol didn't waver.

Leon felt a circle of ice on his breastbone. Still, he crawled his fingers in the direction of the .38 Special.

"Up."

He raised his hands.

"You think everyone in the neighborhood doesn't know you keep a gun under there? My question for you is how lucky you feel today."

The mangled Eastwood line almost made Leon smile. People actually watch those old movies still?

"You really don't know whose neighborhood you're playing in, do you? Does the name Mickey Barksdale ring any bells?"

Flick of the automatic. Was it Czech, maybe? Russian? Cheap shit, anyway.

"Not so much anymore. The cash, dad."

"It's mostly credit card receipts these days. But let me save you a long ton of heartbreak, son. I'll spot you a Grant, you get yourself fixed up, and we will speak of this no more."

It was a generous offer and much less hassle for Leon than shooting the junkie. Fifty bucks would buy the kid a couple of bags, blunt his need for the moment, and let him live long enough to consider how stupid he was to pull an independent robbery in Mickey Barksdale's city.

"Give me the money. And stop your yammering."

The junkie's hand twitched and Leon flinched. Token resistance was all well and good, but he wasn't going to eat a bullet over the hundred bucks he kept in the drawer to make change. Everything else slid right down the chute into the safe that was bolted to the floor.

"And don't forget what you've got in the safe."

Leon frowned. How did a clueless punk know about his safe? His paranoia ramped up. Was this a setup?

"I don't know what you're talking about."

The junkie loosed a shot at the ceiling, where the bullet rang off a metal support. Leon's ears rang.

"You want to quit fucking around with me, old man. That money's not worth your life to you, is it?"

The man was correct about that, though Leon was tired of hearing how old he was. He was only resisting because, in addition to Saturday's receipts, always the best of the week, he was storing a small package of great value for a man higher up the food chain than a man who owned a liquor store.

"OK. OK. Take it easy, youngster."

He pushed the release button on the old brass and wood National Cash Register. Unlike the newer models, it didn't record a sale unless you pushed an amount button, which was handy when he needed some walking around money. He counted out the bills, still thinking about how to finesse the safe. As long as that junkie prick stayed on his own side of the counter, he wouldn't see the package of dope.

The automatic door whirred open, startling them both. The junkie whirled and snapped off a shot in that direction, shattering the glass with a clash like cymbals. Return fire, one shot, drilled him in the middle of the turquoise head scarf, leaving a neat round black hole like a cigarette burn, smoldering at the edges. The junkie dropped to the linoleum like his strings had been cut.

Leon breathed in his relief, a long shuddering inhale, and shut the register drawer. The door, now a glassless aluminum frame, stayed open, as if whoever had shot the junkie was standing on the pressure pad.

"There wasn't but only the one of them." Leon's voice shook, which pissed him off. "You got him."

The crunch of glass underfoot preceded Leon's first sight of the pistol advancing into the store, a more serious weapon than the junkie carried. Every baby gangster in Boston knew what a 40-caliber Glock looked like.

The man holding it swept the gun and his hard focused gaze left and right as he entered the store, then down each aisle.

"Not that I don't trust your word." He faced Leon with a faint smile. "You can put your hands down now. You OK?"

Looked like a cop, talked like a cop. And he was familiar.

His savior was a middle-sized man, bulky in the chest and gut like a wrestler gone to seed. His sandy-ginger hair was thinning, his face freckled and pale, despite the fact it was the middle of summer. Irish as potatoes. He wore baggy Levis and a black T-shirt commemorating the Montreal Jazz Festival. A red furrow creased the flesh of his upper left arm where the junkie's shot must have grazed him.

Leon's eyes widened as he dropped his arms and recognized who it was. Could he be this lucky, to have this man just walk in on him?

"I'm fine." He reached under the counter.

The cop knelt next to the junkie's slack body and pressed two fingers into his neck, shook his head.

As the cop straightened up, Leon pulled out the .38 and shot him three times in the chest. If that didn't do it, it wasn't getting done.

He stepped down off the platform, moving fast in case the shots attracted attention. He walked around the dead cop, whose blue eyes were wide and empty, and bent over to remove the crappy foreign automatic from the junkie's hand, swapping it for the .38. He hated to lose an old favorite, but it was the only way his story was going to work. For the same reason, though he would have loved a brand new pistol, he left the Glock where it was in the cop's slack hand.

Then he climbed back up behind the cash register and called 911.

While he waited for the cops and the EMTs to come, he dialed another number, one he wasn't sure he was supposed to know. But he needed to stake his claim right away before anyone else tried to take credit.

"Who the fuck is this?" The snarl made him flinch.

"Leon. At the Liquor Barn?"

"Where'd you get this number?"

He talked past the question.

"The request you had out? On the guy from Charlestown?"

He didn't dare say the cop's name out loud. You never knew who might be listening.

"So what?"

"So it's filled. It should be in the paper tomorrow."

Leon hung up in a hurry. It might be dangerous to have his name out there, associated with this. But—fifty. Grand.

When the first uniforms stuck their noses in the door, Leon was standing with his hands in the air. This time, it didn't bother him half as much.

2

Francesca didn't flinch until the twenty-one gun salute went off. As the final report of Burton's passing echoed into the trees, her shoulders rounded forward as if she'd been punched in the gut. A trickle of tears escaped down her cheeks, and her throat gave up a guttural sob.

It was a cloudy, humid, charmless July day, entirely appropriate for a funeral. I almost hadn't come, knowing the focus would be on Burton's police identity, an opportunity for the law enforcement community to grieve its loss and renew its solidarity. My grief was too personal to inject into that.

Francesca had tried to convince me otherwise, as we ate dinner the night before at Pat's Pushcart in the North End.

"You'll probably be the only non-police there." She twisted linguine around her fork. "Someone needs to be there to represent the civilian part of his life."

As relatively minor a part as that was, Burton being a cop first, foremost, and always. And Francesca herself could have represented most of his current non-police life. They'd been lovers for more than a year, and I'd watched with approval as she lightened his personality. She'd accepted his depressive side, Burton once told me, asshole, elbows, and all.

She set her fork down with a click.

"Elder. You weren't his only friend. But outside of work? Maybe. What's your problem?"

Burton's work was his life, the way he measured his value in the world. He never referred to it as a job. Which meant everything else, everyone else, took a lower priority. Francesca had been all right with that. Me, not so much. At least recently.

"Not sure I want to put up with all the attitude from the blue line." I drank some Pellegrino. Pat's didn't serve liquor and I hated wine, even if the alternative was staying sober. "And Martines—his captain—doesn't like me at all. He's liable to throw me out."

"Ah, bullshit." She pointed a breadstick at me, candlelight glinting in her dark brown eyes. "No one brings their petty crap to something like this. So you shouldn't either. And it's probably not personal for Martines. He's probably remembering the times you got tangled up in Burton's cases."

"Just not sure I'd be welcome."

"It's not about how you feel, Elder. You're there to witness. For Burton. You don't come, I guarantee you will regret it. You need to see the love he's going to get."

She was as blunt as a brick in the face.

"As a cop. Not as a person. But OK. I'll think about it."

"No." She tapped the back of my hand. "Don't think about it. Do it."

And so here I was, having trailed the slow cortege from Saint Francis de Sales in Charlestown out to the Fairview Cemetery, the last several miles lined with flashing blue and red lights and police officers at attention in dozens of different jurisdictions' uniforms.

I understood the display as homage to the tragedy of an officer killed in the line of duty. It did make me wonder, through the knot in my chest, what it was like to know you were always a member of a pack. But none of these people were here to honor the person I'd known, my friend.

The honor guard finished folding the American flag that had shrouded Burton's casket. He stepped stiffly to Francesca, the triangular bundle balanced on his outstretched, white-gloved hands. He must have assumed she was Burton's wife. Burton's ex-wife, Sharon, hadn't even shown up.

Francesca held up her hands and stepped backward. The captain spoke gently. She shook her head and gestured toward me.

Formal as a general, he stepped across the turf.

"Mr. Darrow." He extended the bundle, the white stars glowing against the dark blue field. "Will you stand in for Detective Burton's family, please? And accept this flag with the profound thanks of a grateful department. Of course, with our deepest condolences."

I bowed my head and accepted the flag, holding it out from my body like an offering to memory. It was heavier than I expected, and the only reason I did not crack into a thousand shards was the thought of how Burton would have mocked me if I did.

* * *

Francesca wasn't drinking, but that didn't mean I couldn't. She'd skipped the wake for Burton, which was being held at a cop bar near the old Combat Zone, knowing it would only be an excuse for raucous hardcore drinking.

I set her up at the Esposito's bar with a pot of tea. I'd closed for the funeral and given my cook Syndi the day off. The speakers rolled out some vintage Alain Touissant—I half-expected to hear him sing "Just a Closer Walk With Thee," which would have been too much. I leaned on the back bar with a full tumbler of Macallan in my hand.

"You want something to eat? I can make you a sandwich as long as I don't have to cut off the crusts."

She smiled weakly, her graveside composure having leaked away with that final salute. She leaned her elbows on the bar, chin in her hands, the steam from the tea rising into her face. Those beautiful brown eyes were rimmed in red.

"What sucks the most about this?" She squeezed out the tea

bag with her fingers. "It was random. Burton decides he needs a six-pack, walks in on an armed robbery, and loses his life. No rhyme or reason."

"He did take the thief with him."

"I'm sure that made him feel better." She shook her head. "Sorry. It wasn't even going to be a big payday. The owner only kept like a hundred bucks in the till at a time."

I swallowed my whiskey. It was no balm.

"And a fucking junkie, to boot. Burton would have laughed his ass off. At the absurdity."

His life had been in danger many times before, for far more rational reasons than the need of an addict.

Francesca sighed.

"You're right. Goddamn it. It's just too hard to say that it ends right here."

3

Four o'clock on a Thursday afternoon, middle of July. The Esposito had been dead all summer. My laugh felt sour. Was I ever going to be able to say that word without thinking about Burton? I'd lost my mother at thirteen, my father in my forties, but neither of them had torn this large a hole.

Burton dying while breaking up a liquor store robbery was a pretty shitty story, and he would have been the first to agree. The force had given him the full line of duty funeral, the casket watch, the twenty-one gun salute, but none of it made me feel any better.

Syndi walked out of the kitchen in the white chef's coat she liked to wear. It seemed pretentious, but my reactions since Burton had died were all over the map, so I kept my mouth shut.

"I hope you're not going to close up early yet again." She ran a glass of club soda from the gun. "I need the hours."

She was clowning. I paid her a salary, not by the hour.

"I'm joking, obviously." She read my face. "You being the boss and all."

Syndi had added a few pounds since she kicked heroin and her face had color, as if she'd been spending time at the beach. She was much healthier now than when she started working here, or rather, when her father, Mickey Barksdale, placed her in my employ.

She shivered. The air conditioning was stuck on high and I hadn't been able to find anyone to fix it.

"You ever think about playing more upbeat music?"

I was listening to the Keith Jarrett Köln Concert, solo piano. It was complicated music, dark and intense. But the Esposito was empty, so I didn't have to worry about any of my customers complaining.

"I like it. And it suits my mood."

"Which has been stuck in compound low for like two weeks in a row."

"I am not having this discussion."

"OK. But look at this place."

What was she talking about, the dusty bottles, the sticky bar top? None of that seemed to matter.

"Let us not forget who works for who here."

"Whom," she said. "The second who, that is."

I leveled a look that should have shut her up. She drank soda.

"Dishwasher's on the fritz again. Did you call them?"

I'd forgotten, but I wasn't going to tell her that.

"I'll check on it. Anything else major weighing on your mind?"

She shook her head.

"Elder, I—

"Not one more word. Please. All I need is one tiny reason to shut this whole operation down."

As if I could blame it on her if I did.

She clinked the glass down on the bar top and slipped back into the kitchen. What was she doing back there, with no customers to cook for?

I was losing my heart for the business I'd run for decades: the late nights, the mouthy drunks, the endless pinprick hassles of running a business. And my own struggle, which endured. When I bought the bar, my rationale was that being around booze all the time would inoculate me, keep me from drowning in my own addiction. Magical thinking, maybe, but it had worked, more or less. Until now.

Which reminded me. It was four o'clock. For Syndi's sake, I

swapped out the Jarrett for a playlist of easier listening, but still jazz—George Shearing, Oscar Peterson—and reached for the Macallan bottle.

I measured out a four-ounce shot, corked the bottle, and replaced it on the top shelf. If I controlled the size and frequency of my drinks, how bad could it be?

The whiskey slid down my throat like warm syrup, quenching my pain as water soothed a pilgrim in the desert. I rinsed the glass and turned it upside down on the drain board as the door at the top of the stairs creaked open.

"Shit."

I was in no mood for serving today. Until Syndi made her little joke, I had been thinking about closing for the day. Most of my regulars hadn't been in these last two weeks. It was as if my grief and my rage at Burton's death were repelling people.

"Good afternoon," this intruder in my day said, as he stepped off the bottom stair.

He strolled across the black and white floor, his face pale as lace curtains, a prominent Adam's apple above his shirt collar. He was thin enough to swim in the blue and white seersucker suit he wore over a button-down Oxford, and he sported one of the few neckties I'd seen in months. If he tried to order a drink, I was going to have to card him.

A sudden memory, of Burton and his cheap suits, stabbed me in the solar plexus. He favored beautiful and expensive shirts—Sea Island cotton or Irish linen—but crime scenes were messy and dry cleaning wasn't cheap. Hence the suits from Robert Hall.

"You all right there, sir? You seemed to leave us for a moment."

"A little indigestion. What can I get you?"

If he was older than twenty, he'd taken a rough road getting there. A vertical scar bisected his right eyebrow. Whatever caused it had barely missed blinding him. A small chunk of one earlobe was missing, corrugated pink scar tissue in its place. He looked like a tomcat who'd been in one too many scrapes.

He shook his head.

"I don't drink alcohol. Though I appreciate the offer."

He gazed around the Esposito's interior, the picture of Bobby Orr flying across the goal mouth in the old Boston Garden, the signed poster from the Newport Jazz Festival, the black and white photos of Dizzy and Miles.

"Very old-school, isn't it? I like it."

He leaned on the bar, then picked up his hand, and grimaced.

"This is a tavern, you know. Maybe you'd like a Shirley Temple?"

Perched on a stool, the man eyed me the way a cat might watch a hole in the wall, patient and indifferent.

"Someone would like to speak with you."

Shearing smoothed the way through "The Nearness of You."

"'Someone.' The City Council? The Neighborhood Watch? The Home for Little Wanderers?"

"Elder." Syndi hissed at me from the doorway.

"Pardon me."

Despite his threatening manner, I turned my back on the man at the bar. I couldn't have cared less why he was here. It was getting close to my five o'clock shot.

"That's Alistair Dain." She raised her eyebrows as if I ought to recognize the name.

"Why didn't you say so? I could name a drink after him. Call it the Dain Curse."

She bit her lip, ignoring the joke.

"He's Mickey's, what do you call it? His PA?"

"Mickey has a personal assistant?" She would know, Mickey being her father. "He looks like a senior in high school."

I hated the idea of Mickey Barksdale, even once removed, in my bar. His history with Burton was one of the factors that got me in trouble in the past.

I stepped back out to the bar. Alistair was an upscale name

for a kid from a working-class neighborhood—Charlestown, I assumed, since that was Mickey's home base. His mother must have had aspirations.

"Kindly inform your boss that there is nothing in the world I wish to discuss with him. Any connection he and I might have had died with my friend."

Syndi sucked in air. I didn't care.

"So if you're not here to drink? Please remove yourself from my establishment."

Dain smirked as if amused by the idea anyone would deny Mickey something.

"It's also possible the protection your association with Detective Burton provided died along with him."

"Assuming I need protection from anything."

Dain's baby face made the threat hard to take seriously. His smirk evaporated.

"Everyone needs protection, Mr. Darrow. Especially in your business. The food, the linen, the beer and liquor? Deliveries can turn up short, or never arrive. A drunk stabs someone? A fire in the kitchen? And so on and so on."

I'd been threatened plenty of times, and by scarier people than this. My friendship with Burton had kept the more egregious threats at bay, but I'd also learned not to give an inch. The first step downhill was always the slipperiest.

"I didn't build this place up by listening to threats. Tell Mr. Barksdale thanks very much, but I don't wish to talk to him. I have a business to run."

Dain wiped his finger across the bar, looked at the other signs of my recent neglect: the dust on the liquor bottles, the smeared back mirror.

"You don't seem to be working very hard at it." He held up a finger. "One minute, please."

He stepped back and reached into his coat, watching my eyes.

Mickey probably only wanted to offer some half-assed condolences. He and Burton had been boys together in Charlestown until life forked them off in different directions. And while they might have used each other, they weren't anything like friends.

Instead of a weapon, Dain pulled out a phone. I was relieved—I might have been depressed, but I wasn't suicidal.

He poked a single key, Mickey on speed dial. It implied he occupied a higher rung on the Barksdale ladder than most. He walked off into the shadows by the stage.

Syndi disappeared back into the kitchen as if she didn't want to witness whatever came next.

As Dain emerged from the shadow, he slipped the phone into his pocket and adjusted the drape of his jacket.

"Mr. Barksdale will respect your need to further grieve. He also requests, when you feel able, that you contact him."

I doubted I would comply with the request, though the implication if I didn't hovered between us.

"My regards to Michael." Which only his intimates called him—let Alistair parse that. "But I would sooner gargle Drano. Now remove yourself from the premises. Please."

Dain's lips pinched white.

"I'm under specific orders from Mr. Barksdale at the moment. But were I not, it would be a pleasure to teach you better manners."

"Too late for that, my friend." I flicked the back of my hand at him. "Out."

Dain knocked his knuckles on the bar top.

"Until that time, then. Sir."

4

After Dain left, I decided to stay open, as much to spite Syndi's certainty she could predict what I'd do as anything else. A trickle of customers came and went, no one I knew and no one I cared to talk to. By midnight, I was exhausted, though my mind was buzzing, as if the Scotch were a mental accelerant rather than a depressant.

I leaned against the back bar, listening to Grant Green light-finger his way through "My Favorite Things." The kitchen closed at eleven—I didn't want to encourage a late-night college crowd with the munchies—and Syndi had gone home. Some nights she stayed around to talk, but not tonight.

The upstairs door squeaked open, a reminder I still hadn't managed to lubricate those hinges.

The deadbolt on the street door snapped. Only one person would assume he had the right to close me down, and as if thinking about him conjured the little bastard, here he came, stomping down the metal stairs so the taps on his boots rang. He marched across the floor like a little general on an inspection tour.

"Bartender."

He stood no taller than five and a half feet, and he'd lost some of his bulk since the last time I'd seen him, though his forearms were still Popeye-massive. His lips were a liverish gray and his breath was a broadcast of garlic and old cigarette smoke. He hopped up on a bar stool.

"What are the chances of a libation in this golden hour?" He swept a look around the room. "It doesn't appear you're too involved in serving paying customers."

He slid a crisp hundred dollar bill onto the bar, the middle three fingers on his left hand bound with surgical tape.

"I thought you were going to leave me alone for a while. To grieve, was what Dain told me."

"Needs must." He tapped the bill. "That drink? What about a White Russian? A little cream to soothe my stomach?"

He patted a nonexistent pot belly, his torso tight under the Bunker Hill Community College T-shirt.

"It's late, Mickey. And I'm tired. Can we skip the foreplay and move right to the part where you try and fuck me?"

His jaw set, and the room temperature dropped.

"Have I not asked you politely to call me Michael?"

He acted insulted, but his face was mobile enough to fake any expression.

"You did." My curiosity stirred. "And I apologize. Let me buy you that drink."

Which may have been the point of his acting insulted. He was as cheap as dirt, though he did not retrieve his hundred-dollar bill. I turned down the music and reached for the vodka on the top shelf.

"I never got the chance to tell you how sorry I was about Daniel. Obviously, I couldn't go to the funeral."

It was a statement of fact, not regret. I scooped ice into a stemmed glass and assembled the drink.

"You could have sent a card."

Mickey took a cautious sip.

"Daniel and I were always close, you know. Since the third grade at Warren-Prescott. Mrs. Ward's class."

He changed the subject when I frowned.

"How's my daughter working out for you? She taking care of herself?"

Meaning was she still an addict? Mickey and Syndi didn't talk much. He disapproved of drugs, and of her using them. She'd survived one overdose before she kicked the habit this last time.

"Why don't you ask her yourself?"

He took another tiny sip and waved his hand.

"Not what I came to talk to you about."

He paused, a ham actor about to deliver his big line. I poured myself a healthy Scotch, which stalled him.

"Back on your shit, are you?"

"Michael."

"I know. I know. It's difficult to talk about this."

"You could try spitting it out."

He placed the glass precisely in the center of the coaster.

"If this turns out to be true, people are going to die because of it. By my word and by my hand."

His naked rage jarred me. I sipped the whiskey for its comfort.

"This obviously has something to do with Burton. Why come to me if you're not ready to talk about it?"

He curled his fingers around the glass like he wanted to throw it.

"I have come to believe." His teeth grated. "I have come to believe that my very good friend Daniel Burton did not die by accident. But as a message to me."

He shoved the empty glass across, holding my stare.

"And I will have another drink. If you please."

"Very good friend, my ass." I wasn't going to let his bullshit slide. "And you cannot be serious. Someone murdered him?"

Mickey gave me a molten look.

I assembled the second White Russian, happy to have something to do with my hands. His statement shocked me, but Burton was still gone from the earth.

"OK. You are serious. You must have some evidence."

Mickey shut his eyes, as if he wasn't used to being challenged.

"I just know."

Not a helpful answer. I stirred the drink and served it. He pushed it to one side.

"My gut can barely handle one."

He reached a pack of Luckies out of the snap pocket of his shirt, shook one free, and lit it. Smoking in bars and restaurants had been illegal since 2004, but I wasn't going to remind him. I did wonder if he had anything other than an intuition that Burton's death wasn't random.

"Mickey. Michael. You must have a reason to think what you're thinking. Have you said anything to the cops?"

He scoffed.

"Did they say anything to me? All I have right now, my friend, is whispers. Intimations. But you don't get to where I am without good instincts. And my instincts say there's something rotten in the story of our good friend's demise."

And maybe those were only intimations of his own mortality. Or a worry someone had taken out a hit he hadn't approved.

"You know I saved his life once." Mickey stared into his smeared reflection in the mirror. "Of course you do. You were there. I took the shot you couldn't."

I ignored the insult to my shooting, but couldn't forget that morning at the baseball field next to the old Navy Yard, Burton zip-tied to a support in one of the dugouts, about to undergo box-cutter surgery at the hands of a demented female murderer. Mickey had killed her when I froze.

"And you know he was grateful. But you also know there were lines he wouldn't cross."

Mickey glared.

"You might be surprised, bartender. My question is what are you going to do about this?"

"I am not going to do a goddamned thing, Michael. Even if I could, what would I be working from? The evidence of your wonky gut?"

He shook his head like he was shooing a mosquito.

"You have a certain amount of leeway with me, pally. But it has limits."

I stared over his shoulder at the photo of Miles Davis and took a long breath to keep myself from saying something stupid. Mickey's temperament could rocket from placid to thermonuclear in the space of a heartbeat, not something I wanted to experience.

"If your instinct is correct, you're in a better position to find out what happened than I am. If somebody killed Burton for a reason, it happened because of something in your world. Not mine."

"Maybe yes, maybe no. And those worlds may not be so far apart. But I can't be seen chasing this down."

"Why not? You were his best friend, right?"

The sarcasm slid past him.

"You're not thinking, bartender. You know what I do, who I am, the type of people who work for me."

At least he didn't pretend he wasn't a criminal. For a time, he'd worked very hard to make his activities look respectable. Maybe Burton's death had freed him from that.

"I start poking around with my own people, their daily activities? Any more than I do? They're gonna want to know why. What do I tell them, I'm looking into whether a cop friend of mine got murdered?"

"People know you two were friends. You made such a big thing out of it." I was enjoying his conundrum. "Tell them you're outraged someone might have killed him. They'll understand revenge."

"Won't fly. No one knows that Burton and I used to talk. And hearing that we had would make people question my judgment— I'd look soft. Also, I'm involved in some delicate negotiations at the moment." He lipped a small smile. "Someone is always trying to get over on me. Which is why I need you."

I hated the idea he needed anything from me.

"I understand the problem. But there's no evidence."

"That's where you come in. You used to work with him. On his cases. You know how to look into things."

"Usually I was dragged in. Moral support, mostly."

"But you know that side of the fence. The cops, his girlfriend. Maybe it was someone he arrested once upon a time. All I'm asking is you wade in there and ask some questions. See if anyone else thinks something's not right. He was your friend, Darrow. You should care about this."

That killed any impulse I had toward agreeing. No one, least of all Mickey Barksdale, told me what to do.

"Hey, Michael. I'm sorry for your loss. It's my loss, too. But as you keep pointing out? I'm a bartender. I don't have the skills or the desire to play Sam Spade. So let's call it right there."

He wouldn't know who Sam Spade was—Mickey hadn't read a thing since SRA cards in grammar school. But he knew when he was being told no.

He dropped the cigarette butt in his untouched drink and dismounted the stool.

"If that's the best you can do for your oldest pal, bartender. I guess I'll have to accept it."

Then he swatted the drink the length of the bar, spraying a foamy trail that soaked the hundred-dollar bill. The glass fell off the end of the bar and shattered on the floor.

"Even if I don't approve. But don't be surprised if you end up changing your mind."

5

I was in the bar early the next morning, right after nine, partly because I'd woken up every couple of hours thinking about Mickey. Any encounter was disturbing, but I had a sense he wasn't as committed to the idea Burton had been murdered as he'd sounded, as if he were trying out a scenario where someone wanted Burton gone. It beggared belief that the entire apparatus of the Boston police, which would have focused hard on a cop being killed, hadn't turned up the possibility Burton's death was anything but random.

I carried out the step stool from the back room, a plastic spray bottle of window cleaner, and a roll of paper towels. Taking down the liquor bottles from the three-tiered rack in front of the mirror, I lined them up on the bar top. Brad Meldhau worked through a long composition from his Live Trio Album as I sipped from a cup of Dunkin' and wiped down the glass.

Mickey's insistence that I owed Burton still pissed me off. The gangster always ran to the paranoid side—he had to, to survive—but the idea Burton had died for some reason other than being in the wrong liquor store at the wrong time was magical thinking.

Meldhau shepherded the trio across the bridge of "The Very Thought of You" as the upstairs door squeaked open.

Syndi trudged down the stairs, a canvas bag from the WGBH pledge drive slung over her shoulder. She shuffled across the black and white linoleum as if her feet hurt. Not just her feet. Her entire body limped.

"Rough night?"

She headed into the kitchen.

"Leave me alone."

"O-oh-ka-ay."

If I didn't know she wasn't a drinker, I'd have thought she was hung over.

Some of the smears would not come off, but I dusted the bottles and replaced them on their shelves. She emerged from the back, carrying two mugs of fresh coffee.

"Sorry. The truth shouldn't piss me off so much."

She was pale as rice paper and her normal thinness was deeper, almost anorexic. Scabs decorated the inside of her elbow and the skin on her face was blotched. Her eyes were scraped and raw.

"And a good morning to you, too."

"I said I was sorry." She coughed.

"If you're sick, I don't want you in here."

Ever since the plague came to town, people noticed the slightest cough or sneeze in their general vicinity. Broadcast germs could now be fatal.

"I'm not sick. Not the way you mean, anyway." She pushed the mug in my direction. "You want this or not?"

I'd finished the Dunkin'. This would be stronger and taste better. And my curiosity was up.

"Thanks."

She walked around to the outside and took a bar stool. Whatever she had to say, it wasn't coming easily.

"What are you thinking about for lunch?"

She sighed like a tire giving up air.

"I made a gazpacho yesterday. Maybe BLTs? It's supposed to be over ninety again today."

She wasn't wearing her chef's coat, only a white apron over

a black Harley-Davidson tank top. I'd gotten the HVAC guy in finally, but the temperature in the kitchen still wouldn't drop below eighty.

"Sounds good. We're set for the weekend? Supplies?"

She nodded, clutching the mug as if its heat could tame her shiver. It wasn't that cold in here.

"You told me once there was only one reason you'd ever even think about firing me."

I picked up the coffee and breathed past a sudden constriction in my throat. A relapse to heroin would explain her ragged look. And it wouldn't have happened overnight. Where had I been, what had I been doing, that I hadn't noticed?

"You're back on the needle?"

She wasn't high right now, but miserable, and not only in a physical way. She raised the mug, lowered it without drinking.

"It was an accident." She winced at my frown. "Almost."

My heart hurt for her. Getting straight had helped to drag her out of a peck of other troubles before she came to work for me. Now it was day one all over again. And the hardest part was committing to another try in the aftermath of a slip.

"Not sure how that could be."

She twirled a pink metal coin on the bar top, watching it spin before she slapped it flat. It was the sobriety chip she'd earned from Narcotics Anonymous for being clean for a year.

"You never slipped?"

"I know addicts don't stop being addicts, even when they're not using."

She closed her eyes.

"Yeah," I said. "I know it sounds like a Hallmark card, but it's true."

Her face flushed.

"Well, you're a fucking addict, aren't you?"

"It isn't illegal and it isn't going to kill me. Which is more than you can say for what you're doing."

"What I did." She straightened up, trying for dignity. "It won't happen again. I think I broke a rib, puking in the shower this morning."

"Lovely image. Thank you."

I was as angry at myself as I was at her. I hadn't been paying attention. To the bar, to her, to anything. Grief over Burton had made me selfish.

"So that makes us both a couple of fuckups."

"Yeah." Her shoulders relaxed a fraction.

"I have been absent." I looked her in the eye. "You're not going down that rathole again?"

I knew the way she'd answer, how any addict would answer, but I had to allow her hope.

"I thought I was getting away with something. Chipping. I can't be that stupid again."

"I'd rather hear you say you won't be."

She rubbed her hands, chapped and raw, over her face.

"Look," I said. "I know I've let things slide a little. We need to get this place back on track."

She finished her coffee and clinked the mug on the bar.

"The kitchen's set up for today. I will say the floor out here could use a wash."

That wasn't her job. Was she doing penance?

"Give me that." I nodded at the pink coin.

She looked hurt, then flicked it across the bar. I laid it on the back bar and came out to help her stack the chairs on top of the tables.

"Probably should go up and lock the door," I said. "Takes a while for the linoleum to dry."

6

While Syndi washed the floor, I wiped down the bar top and mopped the sticky duckboards behind the bar. I felt guilty, as if my inattention had been the cause of Syndi's slip. I wasn't done mourning Burton, but I had to stop wallowing.

You wouldn't think a clean floor and a sparkling mirror would make that big a difference, but we had a dozen more customers in for the Friday afternoon happy hour than we'd seen in a while. Then, around seven-thirty, between a dinner rush and what looked like a reasonable drinking crowd, the landline I kept under the bar rang, startling me. I hadn't heard it in weeks.

"Esposito."

"Elder Darrow."

I knew the voice immediately and looked around to see if anyone had seen me flinch. At the far end of the bar, a single woman in a red silk top smiled at me over the rim of her glass of chardonnay.

"Who is this?"

"Susan, Elder. Susan Voisine?" She sounded amused.

"Yes. Susan."

"I just heard about Burton. I am so sorry."

I wanted to wisecrack about the Pony Express carrying the news out to Oregon, but I was so surprised to hear from her, I only mumbled.

"Thank you."

"It was an accident? I didn't hear the details. Something random?"

26

"He was shot. Walked in on a robbery at a liquor store."

"Oh, God." Her voice husked. "Such bad luck."

"Being shot to death? You could say so. Why are you calling?"

We'd ended badly. I was long past any lingering desire—fuck, call it love—for her, but hearing her stirred up the muck of the things I'd done wrong, she'd done wrong. All the ways we'd screwed something up that could have been spectacular.

She laughed, a dry snapping sound.

"Still smarting?" She adopted the explanatory tone she used to tell you things you ought to know already. I used to think it was cute. "I called you the way any friend would. To offer my condolences. I didn't think history would get in the way of basic politeness, but maybe I was wrong. I am sorry for your loss."

The *pro forma* sentiment irked me, too.

She'd been the one who decided to separate. My involvement in Burton's cases frightened her, she said, carried the possibility of violence to my doorstep too often. She decided couldn't live with that, to the point of heading for the other side of the country.

"How's life in the Beaver State? Did Patryc ever come back to your practice?"

"Things are fine. Life is fine. I didn't call to catch up on trivia. I wanted to know how you were doing with it. With Burton."

"I'm fine."

The silence stretched. I wondered if she believed me. And if I cared. I didn't owe Susan anything, but she wouldn't settle for monosyllables.

"It was difficult. Still is." Grief simmered up and I pushed it down. "Especially because it was random. But we're getting through it."

"We."

"His friends. His girlfriend, Francesca. We're adjusting."

"Grief's a sneaky bitch, Elder. You don't want to ever start thinking you're done with it."

Typical she would remind me of the obvious. I knew about grief—I thought about my mother and father every day—and in a lesser way, because of her.

"Thanks for the reminder."

"How's your drinking?"

I wanted her off the phone. She'd abdicated any rights she had in my life, my behavior.

"I drink. Not a lot. It's under control."

More silence. She didn't push. I got ready to hang up.

"Good," she said. "That's one bright spot."

"There isn't one."

"I'm sorry. I put it badly. I mean it makes me worry less. About you."

"I didn't know you still did that."

"Oh, stop being a dick for a minute. Can you?"

Not a question I could answer.

"I'm grateful you won't be dragged into those violent situations anymore. You'll be safer."

Instead of a benefit, that felt like a loss. Some of the things we'd done had energized me, given me more juice than I got from running a bar and drinking.

"If you say so."

"I'd like to see you."

She said it fast. I was too surprised to answer.

"I have to be in Boston next week. Vendors' conference for the school districts."

Anticipation rose, but it could have been dread.

"Bring tropical clothes—the weather has been brutal."

"We do get the Weather Channel out here." She paused. "Could we meet?"

"Things have been pretty busy at the bar."

"Elder." Her voice was sad and gentle. I hated her sympathy. "If you don't want to see me, all you have to do is say so."

But I couldn't say that, and I couldn't say yes.

"You know where I am." And carefully, quietly, I hung up the phone.

The woman in red waved her empty glass. I quick-stepped down the bar, eager to get myself back to work.

7

The heat wave that smothered New England made the populace cranky. Even after I announced last call, no one was inclined to leave the air-conditioned comfort of the Esposito. I resorted to my least favorite room-clearing trick, playing Blossom Dearie at volume. Syndi left at eleven as usual, and though I worried about her, I was mostly thinking about Susan Voisine and whether I had the capacity or the inclination to get involved again.

The prospect of her being in Boston next week did not lighten my step as I exited the bar through the fire door, into the paved parking area in back where I kept my Volvo. The wet smack of the July night brought out a greasy sweat on my forehead and I walked quickly to the car, eager to get its AC blowing. The stench of garbage, prevalent no matter how carefully Syndi secured the dumpster lid, penetrated the air and brought a tight dry feeling to my throat.

I blipped the doors open and reached for the door handle, hearing a scrabbling sound on the pavement behind me. There were always vermin back here, but the sound was too loud for a rat. A dark bulk rushed in from beyond the cone of the safety light and slammed me into the side of the car.

Breath burst out of me. The sharp pain in my side said I might have cracked a rib. I tried to turn to face my attacker, but his hefty body pressed me against the car door and pushed my face into the window so my voice came out strained.

"I don't do a night deposit. Wallet's in the left rear pocket."

The mugger shoved his groin against my rear end, grinding me into the car. I'd been mugged before, and while the usual object was to scare the victim into submission, this felt personal. I let myself go limp. A raspy voice whispered in my ear, intimately.

"If all I'd wanted was your money, *cher*, you'd be lying there on the ground."

He punctuated the threat with another push of his hips, then backed away.

"But if you're intelligent enough to stand still and listen, maybe we could have a small chat."

I couldn't identify the accent, a sibilance that stretched his vowels a little, though not enough to make him sound Southern. I turned around, the key fob dangling from my upraised hands.

He wore knee-length green nylon basketball shorts with the Celtics' leprechaun logo, a black sweatshirt with the sleeves chopped off, and a red and black Luchador mask.

"Huh," I said. "Isn't that cultural appropriation?"

"I'm a bigger fan of Mardi Gras than Mexican wrestling. It was all I could find."

"Guy as pale as you are should do purple. Or green. Match the shorts."

The fist to my gut told me we were done trading quips. I threw up all over the asphalt, making him dance backwards on his sneakers to avoid the splatter.

"Very brave of you to make jokes. But it makes me worry you might not be paying attention."

He grabbed my shoulders and straightened me up out of the protective crouch.

"We have all night to dance, my friend. But it's not what I'm getting paid to do. You ready to listen?"

I was frozen, the way a mouse under a cat's paw must feel, immobile and hoping for mercy.

"You are quite the talker," I said.

I wanted to hear more of the accent, try to pin it down.

"Indeed." His smirk raised the elaborate mask an inch, then lowered it. "Are we past the I'm-cuter-than-you-are part of the program?"

I massaged my stomach, where a massive bruise was heating up.

"I'm listening."

He leaned forward, put two fingers under my chin, and lifted it. That was more of a violation than his humping me.

"I hope so, Mr. Darrow. Because I'm only paid to say things once. If you don't hear me, consequences follow."

My fear and adrenaline abated to a tolerable level.

The mugger stepped back again. I straightened up off the car, hands held up in a gesture of peace.

"Say what you have to say and go home. It's too hot for games."

"Your boss."

"I'm self-employed. I don't have a boss."

He faked a punch at my chin and laughed when I flinched.

"I'm speaking of Mr. Barksdale."

"I don't work for Mickey. Never have." And, needless to say, never would.

"And yet you are on a first-name basis with the man." He reached up to adjust the mask. I saw a small fleur-de-lis tattoo on the back of his hand. "No matter. I'm here to tell you one small thing."

I nodded at him.

"Mr. Barksdale's notion that your policeman's death was anything but random happenstance? Is a figment of his no-doubt redoubtable imagination. And you yourself should accept that fact, as well."

"That's what you have to say? You couldn't have walked into the bar, had a nice cold drink, and told me the same thing?"

A chuckle sounded behind the mask.

"I would venture to guess this conversation reinforces the message a little better…"

I pressed the button for the Volvo's remote start and the engine turned over. The mugger whipped his head around as I stepped into the hardest push kick I'd managed since the soccer pitch at Exeter, landing my foot right between the man's legs.

He levitated. His subsequent keening scream almost drowned out the sound of the engine and made me smile.

I thought about booting him a few more times, but it seemed smarter to retreat.

Cushioned in the cool leather seat, I drove sedately out of the alley, my eyes on the rearview mirror. The Luchador mugger stayed heaped on the ground. The chilly air from the dashboard vents dried the sweat on my face but did nothing for the throb in my gut.

8

The garbage trucks on Comm. Ave. woke me early, and by the time I was shaved and showered, I felt reasonably together.

The mugging implied a second criminal faction in the city. The Acadian in the Luchador mask was not working the Barksdale side of the street, unless this was some twisted double bluff of Mickey's, trying to crowbar me into agreeing Burton's murder hadn't been a random act. Much as I hated the idea, I had to inform him what happened in the alley last night. If I didn't, he would take it out on me.

The outside air was drier this morning, which lightened my mood. As I unlocked the door to the bar, I smelled the faintest hint of autumn in the air and wondered how Burton had contacted Mickey when they needed to talk.

The upstairs door didn't squeak. Syndi must have lubed the hinges. She was in early, too.

"Morning."

No reply, which was normal, neither of us being a morning glory. She wore a long-sleeved olive T-shirt from a 10K race on Mt. Washington, her thin frame swimming in it. But her color was better and she walked with her shoulders back and her head up.

I fiddled around behind the bar, cutting up fruit, wiping down the taps, polishing glasses. The uptick in business had me hoping my temporary negligence hadn't ruined the bar. Any restaurant or bar owner will tell you how fickle and fragile a customer base is. If things continued to improve, maybe I could afford to bring in live music again.

I pulled up a playlist with some more current musicians—the Marsalis brothers, Christian McBride—but low, so Syndi couldn't hear. I'd given up trying to upgrade her musical tastes.

So how was I going to find Mickey to warn him?

For a second morning, Syndi brought me coffee. Was this a new routine? Or did she have some other secret she needed to confess? I hoped not—I couldn't afford to lose more trust in her.

"All right today?"

Her face clouded, then she shrugged as if trying to convince herself she didn't care what I thought.

"Day at a time. Isn't that how the saying goes?"

Throwing the A.A. mantra up in my face? I'd tried the program, once upon a time, but it didn't stick. Too much sharing.

"That's the way I always heard it."

She sipped her coffee, white as milk, and probably sweet.

"Your father. I need to talk to him."

Her shoulders locked up as if I'd swung at her.

"We don't talk. I'd think you'd prefer it that way."

"Why's that?"

"How long have you run a bar in this city, Elder? You know the crap that goes on in the background."

"So?"

"Do you really want people on the straight side thinking you're partnered with him? Or even associated?"

She was right about that. Though I liked that she was worried about my reputation, and the bar's.

"I appreciate your worrying. But I need to talk to him. Preferably today."

"You shouldn't. Nothing good ever comes out of it."

Her family history pinched at her. She was also remembering Alistair Dain in here the other day, threatening me.

"Don't have a choice. And I've run this place fine for quite a while. I'll be OK."

"I don't know anything about his business. But I do know this much. Your friend the cop?"

She knew Burton's name, but she'd never liked or trusted him.

"He worked like a buffer for you. Kept Mickey out of your business. Mostly."

Did she mean that literally? Because gangsters loved businesses like bars and restaurants, with umpteen ways to steal money, launder cash, and so on.

"I don't think Mickey would want my headaches."

She made a face and started for the kitchen.

"I have to get to work."

"Do you know how I can contact him?"

Her face was serious as winter. She recited an address.

"It's on the edge of Chinatown. But let him know you're coming. He hates a surprise."

"It will be fine. I need to warn him about something."

"Your funeral. Just keep your head up. I mean really up."

Lunch hour was busier than it had been in weeks, helped by Syndi's genius for hot-weather dishes. I would never have thought the Esposito would serve a half-dozen different salads.

When she emerged from the kitchen around two, her face was shiny, the T-shirt dark under the arms and around her waist. She was angry as a debarbed hornet, holding her phone as if it had burned her.

"Well, that was no fucking fun." She shoved the phone down into the pocket of her pants.

I'd been drinking club soda and thinking about calling my old contact at the Berklee School to see if she knew any students willing to play for the exposure. I hated asking anyone to perform for free, but the finances were going to need bolstering before I could afford to pay anybody.

"What?"

"Talking to my old man."

"You didn't have to do that." The last thing I wanted to do was complicate their relationship. "All I needed to know was how to find him."

She shook her head.

"He doesn't even keep an actual office anymore. It was last year he was in Chinatown. The year before, he was working out of a fruit stall in Haymarket."

"I could talk to him over the phone."

"Mickey doesn't do phone. Anything."

"I'm sorry if he put you through it. He can be intense."

"Intense. 'How's your health these days, Synthia? Are you staying clean? Have you taken up drinking instead, now that you work in a bar?' Jesus."

"I'm sorry. I wouldn't have asked if…"

"Oh yes, you would have. If you thought you needed to. You and him aren't all that different."

"Mmm. Thanks."

"He'll meet you at the library, the back side. Three PM."

"OK. Thank you."

"You won't tell him about it?"

Her slip.

"Hell, no. That's your business."

I took the pink sobriety coin off the back bar and pressed it into her palm.

"This belongs to you anyway. You have to be your own judge and jury."

She teared up.

"You know I'm the reason he won't do anything with drugs. So maybe I am doing the world some good?"

"We're all doing the best we can."

"Easy enough for the man with money to say." She slapped the coin down on the back bar. "Let's leave this right here for now. If you still want to talk to him? You know where he'll be."

She spun back into the kitchen. She still didn't think it was a good idea.

By mid-afternoon, the place was deserted. I stuck my head into the kitchen, where someone was whining through the transistor radio about losing their truck and their dog.

"Going out. I'll lock the upstairs door, unless you want to man the bar."

She shook her head. She sat at the little desk in the corner, leafing through invoices and matching them to the checkbook. She peered over the tops of green-framed reading glasses that made her look like a librarian.

"Watch your ass. He's my fucking father and I don't trust him. And you're not even family."

I took her seriously enough that I tucked the house gun, a Ruger LCP Burton had gifted me a couple years ago, into the back of my belt. I'd never shot a human, but I went to the range every so often, so I knew which end went where. I would tell Mickey what the mugger told me and let him worry about it from there.

I stepped out onto Mercy Street and flagged down a cab, already eager to be done with the chore.

9

Bragden Street runs behind the Boston Public Library, and I saw right away why Mickey had picked it for our meeting. It hooked in off Huntington Ave and ran straight to the junction with Essex Street. You could stand anywhere in the short block and keep an eye on whoever was coming or going.

The back side of the library was blank concrete-block walls with small inset windows like gun ports in a castle, an occasional corrugated steel door for vehicle access. I was halfway down the block when Mickey stepped out from behind a dark brown and cream El Camino.

Grabbing my elbow, he propelled me toward Copley Square.

"Nice ride," I said.

"Seventy-nine. The last real year. Come on."

We rounded the corner to the great granite façade and the main entrance, where an old man in a thin white nylon shirt sat on a bench with his back to the wall, reading a Ross Macdonald paperback. Beyond him, on the stairs, a clutch of middle school girls giggled and traded lip gloss. I looked up at the legend over the entrance: FREE TO ALL. Maybe the last thing that was.

Mickey pulled me over to the central staircase and we sat. For someone who'd wanted to keep our meetings quiet, sitting on the steps of the main library, exposed to Copley Square, was a fairly public pronouncement of his presence.

"Siddown. You're hovering."

"You're not worried someone might see us together?"

Because I was. I didn't want to reinforce anyone's idea that I was working for him.

"No one expects to see me this far downtown."

I sat down on the warm granite beside him.

"Got yourself mugged, I hear." He lit a cigarette with a red disposable lighter.

"That wasn't one of your guys?"

"No." As in, don't be an idiot.

"How did you hear about it?"

"Not because I had anything to do with it. News travels around. I know my name was mentioned."

"If you know that, you must know why."

"Even if I did, I need to hear it from you, the way you heard it. So tell me."

I described the encounter with all the detail I could recall. He grunted when I told him about the mugger's accent and drilled me hard on what he'd said until I was sure I'd recounted it verbatim.

"So what does all this tell you?" he said.

A body above us blocked out the sun and a deep voice spoke.

"You simply may not smoke here."

Mickey looked up, over his shoulder. All I saw was a pair of legs in flannel dress pants—in August, for chrissake—and a pair of polished cordovan loafers.

Mickey ground out the end of his half-smoked cigarette in the shiny leather of the speaker's left shoe.

"So sorry." His voice was a very not-sorry sorry. "I won't do it again."

The shoe's owner huffed but wisely retreated. The sunlight returned.

"Bean counters. So I'm asking you this, bartender. Was the mugger telling you the truth? Do you believe him that the death of my good friend and yours was the act of a random universe?"

I wanted to. It would hurt less if there hadn't been a reason. But I didn't see the logic in someone trying to convince me what mostly everyone believed. It was waving your hands in the air and proclaiming there was nothing to see over here.

"Shit." I was reluctant to admit it. "I don't know. I guess not."

"You don't know."

"Why would someone try so hard to push the story it was random?"

Mickey lit another smoke.

"Maybe someone wants you to be suspicious. Of me."

"Double blind? Too complicated. And why should I care what you do?"

"If I killed Burton? You'd care. They think you're working with me." He spoke as if he knew who was behind the message. "Which means you might as well do what I asked you to do. Ask some questions, see if anyone on the legal side thinks it could have been a hit."

I shook my head.

"Burton's gone. Nothing changes that. And this is your fantasy, not mine."

"You've been brought into it. Whether you like it or not."

"I'm telling you, I'm not getting involved."

"You might not have a choice."

Across the plaza, a tall, elegant man—blue blazer, charcoal slacks, green bow tie, and loafers—legged it in our direction, towing a uniformed cop. Mickey saw him but didn't react.

"If they think you're involved, bartender? It doesn't matter. That's why you shouldn't let this go."

There was that word again: should. I stood up.

"I brought you the message, which I thought I should do. But I'm out of this. Don't ask me again." I pointed across the Square. "And you better haul ass. That is one pissed-off librarian."

I was talking to the air. When I turned back, Mickey had

disappeared. I stepped off the stairs and started walking toward the corner of Boylston Street.

"You there." The man with the ruined loafer shouted, his voice high and aggrieved. "Halt."

* * *

"Never saw the man before in my life. He was trying to panhandle me."

The librarian didn't believe me, but the cop was happy enough with the explanation.

"You have to watch out for the homeless in the Square, sir. They can be very aggressive."

I didn't bother correcting his assumption all the panhandlers were homeless.

"Thank you, officer. I'll try to be more aware."

The librarian's stare stayed on me as I turned up Boylston and hailed a cab. Mickey was pushing on me again, though not so hard as he could. I would have expected more threats or promises, or maybe both.

The cab dropped me off on Mercy Street, right at the front door. A vanishing breed of driver, a middle-aged white guy, gestured at the small brass sign.

"Never been there," he said. "Good place?"

"The best. Come by anytime."

10

Syndi still sat at the little desk in the kitchen when I stuck my head in.

"I'm back."

She raised her hand without looking up from the papers she perused.

Out front, I cued up big band music. I'd fulfilled my duty to Mickey, informed him he might have enemies. But I couldn't shake my curiosity about the way the message had been delivered. And why they'd used me as the messenger.

Mickey still seemed convinced that Burton had been murdered for some reason other than wrong place, wrong time. He hadn't offered any more than intuition as evidence Burton had been murdered, and that could easily be paranoia.

My Acadian friend and his bosses had a stake in Burton's death remaining what it appeared. They knew Mickey wasn't convinced. But all the sleight of hand only increased the possibility Burton had been killed deliberately.

Syndi walked out of the office and stood at the bar beside me.

"Lotta deep thinking going on out here."

"Not deep enough."

"I've been going through the books. You know we're on the edge. The bar is, I mean."

I'd let her take over the checkbook a month ago, a gesture of trust. What she was saying wasn't unexpected. We'd had a very slow month since Burton died.

"Meaning?"

"You know as well as I do how a business works, Elder." She scooped ice into a glass and filled it with water. "Money comes in, money goes out. Whatever stays behind here isn't always that much."

"We need cash?"

I had plenty of money outside the business, inherited from my father. But I'd decided long ago the Esposito would live or die on its own.

"Not yet. But you need a string of good days and nights to make it to the end of the year."

I noticed the pronoun had changed from "we" to "you."

"I hear you. But this isn't such a predictable business. You can't tell what will bring people in."

"But you can take care of business." She sipped water. "Focus on the bar. Maybe bring back the music. Pay more attention to what's going on here."

I took a long breath.

"Look, losing Burton threw me off for a while. You never lost a friend?"

I felt terrible the second the question was out of my mouth. She and Marina, my first cook, had been close friends—they'd gone to culinary school together. Hurt made her eyes swim.

"Sorry," I said. "But I've worked through everything I need to work through. I'm back on track. You haven't seen me drinking as much as I was, have you?"

"I'm not so worried about the past," she said. "The bar will survive."

"Then what?"

She bit her lip, then turned for the kitchen. I grabbed her arm, thin as a broomstick.

"What?"

"My father drags people into his orbit. You should know that by now."

She knew I'd met with Mickey and extrapolated the worst possible outcome, that I was working for him. I was flattered she would worry that much.

"It's not the way you think. I'm not going over to his side. Someone gave me a message for him and I delivered it."

"That's not what worries me. You and Burton used to get tangled up in situations. Which is exactly what you're doing now."

"Absolutely not." My curiosity wasn't dragging me anywhere. "There's nothing for me to get tangled up in."

She stared me down.

"You need this place, Elder. And I need this place. You do not need to be running around playing private eye, no matter how much Mickey pushes on you."

"Then we're in agreement. I'm not involved in running anything but this bar. So can we get on with our day?"

A group of young women in shorts and plaid bowling shirts clattered in through the upstairs door and down the stairs. I reached for a clean beer pitcher.

She wasn't convinced.

"That's all I want to do, too. Now and going forward. And that's all you need to do. Get on with the day."

11

Usually, I treated myself to breakfast on Saturday mornings. Saturday was my busiest time and I liked to go into it well-fortified. On a good Saturday night, I might have time to choke down half a sandwich between customers. But this morning, I needed the time to sit and think. Syndi's money worries were my worries, too. There were places we could tighten the belt if we had to.

It was nearly impossible to find an old-style lunch counter in Boston anymore. Most of the places I'd frequented over the years had dolled themselves and their menus up in pursuit of the tourist gold. I hoped this little hole in the wall on the back side of Park Square would maintain a little longer. All I ever needed was a couple of eggs over easy, wheat toast, and a decent cup of coffee. No chatty wait people with nose rings and tattoos, no cream cheese stuffed French toast. No café lattes.

I was sitting at the counter with my back to the street door, so it wasn't surprising I didn't see her come in. I did clock the double-take the guy in the Bruins jersey gave, which made me turn my head.

And there was Susan Voisine, all four and a half feet of her, dressed in black-striped linen pants and a loose turquoise top, perfectly suited for a day already climbing toward ninety degrees. She'd grown out her ash-blond hair and dyed it black, cinched it in a short ponytail. Her mouth showed the amused smile I remembered so well, the satisfaction she'd put one over on me.

I inhaled toast crumbs and coughed, reached for my water glass. Her smile broadened as she sat beside me.

"Nice to know I can still have that effect on someone, at my advanced age." She snagged a piece of bacon off my plate. "You need a slap on the back?"

I drank some water to clear my throat. Even though I was glad to see her, I was still angry. Angry at the feeble reasons she'd given for breaking it off, angry for the time we'd lost.

"You psychic?" I said. "How did you know where to find me?"

"Elder? I do have a memory. Saturday morning breakfasts at Tootie's on the Square? The only thing I didn't know is if they'd knocked it down to build condos."

She smiled at the waitress on the other side of the counter, a hard-faced redhead with a half-sneer and a pot of coffee.

"Do you have any herbal tea? Maybe chamomile?"

The waitress gave me a pitying look. Yeah, I was in trouble.

"How Oregonian of you." I mopped up the last of the egg yolk with a crust. Maybe chewing would keep me from saying anything more stupid.

"I didn't want to come to the Esposito. You know why?"

I had an idea but shut up and listened.

"Out here in the world, you're more like a normal human being."

I tipped my head in a question.

"No. That's not right. What I mean is, in the bar, it's like you are the bar. It's you, but it's your costume, too. Something you wrap yourself in."

I sipped my coffee carefully. Tootie kept the pot hot.

"A year and a half apart, and you start out psychoanalyzing me? I don't remember that working out well the first time around."

She leaned in, smelling of limes and black tea.

"Well, what I really want to do is fuck you silly. But I don't think Tootie would appreciate it."

"I know, I know. 'I'm already silly.'" I had to recite my line, even if I was irked. "Why are you here, Susan? Besides all those warm and fragrant memories?"

The lightness in her manner faded. The hot water arrived in a tiny lidded pitcher. She poured it over the tea bag.

"I know you a little bit, Elder. And I knew Burton, too. It had to be a shock."

Like a hit from a stun gun, but yeah.

"I'm getting through it. But you never liked him."

"I didn't like what he did to you." She pinched the tea bag dry and laid it on the saucer. "Dragging you into his cases. Those were his job to do. Not yours."

That tired old, same old, argument.

"That implies I didn't have a choice."

"Oh, Elder. Male friendship? Someone ought to write a book. You couldn't say no to him. For all kinds of reasons."

"Sounds like an old tune to me."

She leaned into me, her small weight solid against my upper arm. It gave me a physical charge.

"Things have changed. I mourn the man on your behalf. Your good friend. But I'm happy to know he can't pull you into danger anymore. Bring any more violence into your life."

Which was the reason she'd given up on us in the first place, her fear my being around Burton would splash violence on both of us. I'd thought that was a convenient excuse—a middle-aged alcoholic was no woman's idea of a prize.

"So you came back to pick up the thread again? Make amends?"

The surge of hope made me angry, at myself. But my mourning was over and I was getting the bar back on track. It might be the right time.

"To the extent amends need to be made?" She stared into the untouched tea. "On both sides? Yes. If you agree, of course."

The thickness in my throat meant I could only nod.

"We had something worthwhile," she said. "I think it's worth circling back."

"I never rented Henri's apartment."

We'd met when she came to Boston to care for her father, one of my tenants at the time.

"You gave up a year and a half's rent? That's a lot of money."

"After Mrs. Rinaldi died? I felt like living alone. And since I own the building, all the rents are negotiable."

She laid a hand on my arm.

"I do have to attend this conference. I'm staying at the Park Plaza."

"Fancy."

"But I'm done with Oregon. There's nothing left for me there."

I felt the thrill again, layered with fear.

"Then welcome to Boston."

"Check?"

The redheaded waitress hovered, her expression warning me. Of what? I laid a twenty on the counter.

"Keep it," I said. "I don't need the change."

12

Did I still love Susan enough? Did she love me? As I unlocked the door to the bar that morning, anxious to get out of the heat, I wondered what the hell love was supposed to look like, anyway. We had been more than compatible physically—my memory kept serving up steamy scenes—but when she'd run away to Oregon, I'd had to work hard to forget, so her absence would not become a constant presence in my mind. We'd probably still react to each other physically, but had the emotional possibilities run their course? Could we go back?

The inside air was colder than it should have been. I wondered if I'd forgotten to adjust the thermostat before I left last night. As I walked across the floor to turn the lights on, a figure standing in the shadows by the bar startled me. He cleared his throat with a short bark and turned up the lights.

"Good morning, sir." Alistair Dain sat down on a stool at the corner of the bar. "I wondered if I could join you for a cup of coffee."

The cardboard tray from Dunkin' held one cup, uncapped and steaming. Anger made me breathless.

"How the hell did you get in here?"

Dain waved a hand.

"Your security is not everything it should be, my friend. I came to the neighborhood because I realized we needed to have another chat."

He sported a different seersucker suit today, a mint-green stripe. He crossed his thin legs, ankles bare above leather huaraches.

I tried to breathe myself calm.

"I had a long discussion with your boss the other day. Where I reiterated my position. Maybe the story hasn't filtered down to your level yet."

His lips pinched tight. He didn't like the reminder he was low on the food chain.

"So, for your benefit. Again. I am not now, nor have I ever been, working for Mickey Barksdale. And he's all right with that."

"May I ask you to sit and discuss with me a moment? Please. I'm not here on Mr. Barksdale's behalf, except perhaps peripherally."

That was a surprise. Mickey didn't encourage independent thinking or action by his troops.

"Are you running a rogue operation? A rump parliament, maybe?"

Mickey had spoken about negotiations, upheavals in his world. Was this my first glimpse of it?

Dain frowned.

"There's nothing of the derrière in this. Will you sit? My neck hurts from looking up at you."

"I have a bar to get ready, Dain. I don't have time for a kaffeeklatsch."

"Save your vocabulary tests for someone who's impressed by words. Sit down and listen to me. Five minutes will save you some pain."

The snap in his voice reminded me I was not only pushing back against Mickey but an entire organization loyal to him. I pulled out a stool and sat.

"Five minutes."

Dain picked up the open cup and sipped from it. He made a face, as if it was cold.

"First of all. Let me apologize for my brusqueness the first time we met. I was unaware of your lengthy history with Mr. Barksdale."

Dain intrigued me. He was young enough that he'd barely cleared high school, yet had the diction and manner of a small-town New England banker. He hadn't picked that up from Mickey.

"I have no relationship with Mr. Barksdale."

"Understood. May I console myself by thinking you'll allow for the zeal of a loyal subordinate? In other words, could you forgive me?"

I pinched off a nod.

"Do you use your voice, Mr. Darrow? Or am I not worth your words?" His tone took an edge.

"You're here. I didn't invite you. State your business."

I'd been hoping the encounter at the library meant I wouldn't be having any more of these conversations.

Dain sighed the sigh of the perpetually disappointed. I would have laughed at his theatrics if I didn't suspect he was dangerous.

"I have concerns about my employer's state of mind." He spread his hands, thick-knuckled and scarred, on the bar. "Mr. Barksdale is utterly convinced your police detective friend's murder was not random."

"Without any evidence to back him up. I don't understand it, either."

"Good. Then there is little chance you're going to be tempted to take up his request for you to investigate."

I felt like I was walking on ice that crackled underfoot. Did Dain represent an element in Mickey's organization that was challenging him? Even if they thought they were protecting him, he wouldn't like it. Aligning myself with them wasn't any smarter than aligning myself with Mickey.

"I've been clear from the beginning. Burton's death was a shock. To all of us. But I'm not going to spend any time chasing down a chimera."

I threw in the extra vocabulary word just to be an asshole.

"Excellent." He picked up the cardboard cup and tidied up the tray and napkins as if about to leave. "You understand my concern is—was, until now—that Mr. Barksdale's attention not be diverted. By anything. These are complicated times."

He was alluding to the negotiations Mickey had mentioned, which I also wanted to know nothing about.

"You have nothing to worry about, Alistair. My message has been consistent, from the first time he asked. This is not my circus."

I left out the part about monkeys.

"Excellent," he repeated.

Gathering the trash, he walked behind the bar, poured cold coffee down the sink, and discarded everything else. I didn't like the familiar way he walked back there.

"So we're clear, then?" I said. "No more after-hours sneak entries? No more overwrought conversations? And no more of your semi-threatening bullshit."

Dain wiped his hands on a bar rag, then buttoned his suit coat.

"Assuming you're faithful to your side of the agreement? Of course. No more contact at all, if you choose." He surveyed the room. "Though I would enjoy running this establishment."

Dain climbed the stairs. The street door opened. A sharp exchange of words burst into the air. The door closed and Syndi ran down the stairs.

"The fuck is he doing back here, Elder? What are you up to now?"

* * *

It took me until midafternoon to calm her down. To be fair, despite his promises, Dain worried me, too.

"I don't know how to say it more clearly than this."

We were sharing a late lunch, a chicken salad sandwich and a mug of cold soup.

"I am not involved with Mickey in any way, shape, or manner. Nor am I planning to be involved. Dain doesn't want me to be, and even if Mickey keeps looking into what he thinks happened, he's getting pushback from his own people. Which I do not want to be in the middle of."

"You don't know him. Them." She wiped her fingers on a napkin. "Nothing is as simple as anyone pretends it is."

"I know. I don't care—and I don't understand the man's motive. It's not that he's all that broken up over Burton's death. But I've got nothing to do with it."

"Of course, he's not broken up," she said. "With Mickey, it's about power, his place in the world. If somebody killed your friend without his permission, it was a challenge to him, his being in charge. It means there's a rogue element."

I heard "rogue elephant" and almost smiled. It was the kind of malapropism Burton and I would have shared a lifted eyebrow over. One of those sly blades of grief cut into me.

"Mickey should have the message by now. Not only from me but from his own people, assuming they're not afraid to tell him. I have no connections and no access. Anything I ever had came from being Burton's friend, through his authority. If he hadn't been a cop, he and I would probably have been the stars of a middle-aged buddy movie."

She carved me with a look that said she still didn't believe me and carried our dirty dishes out to the kitchen. I didn't see how else to convince her, other than by my actions. Though, in this case, that meant my lack of action.

13

I spent part of Sunday worrying about Susan and what Syndi thought, but finally let it all go, took a long nap, ordered in a pizza, and watched an ESPN 30 on 30 rerun.

Monday night at the Esposito, against all odds, was one of the best we'd ever had, certainly the best since Burton died. Which was an odd way to define it, but that was how the grief moved in me, setting random landmarks in my life. Philosophy aside, the joint jumped.

I found a musical groove early, a two-hour playlist I could repeat without offending anyone, a mélange of ballads, bebop, and Dixieland that shouldn't have worked but rose and fell in a strange warm arc. It brought structure to the time, part background, part foreground, and the music propelled me through doing what I loved, serving the bar.

These were the people I'd wanted to build the Esposito for, people who loved the music, who loved that vibe. They were a diverse collection, but all of them hip enough to appreciate a Charlie Parker solo or hum under their breath along with Chet Baker. Age made no difference—there were gray beards and brown beards and no beards at all.

In a pause, I stopped across the bar from Pedey Thomas, who'd written for the *Globe* for decades and had just taken a buyout to stay home and write a novel.

"Remind you of anything?" I said.

He shoved his empty glass across the bar.

"Only how hard it is to get a beer in here when you're busy. You still too cheap to hire any help?"

I recalled the help I'd had over the years as I drew him a Narragansett, my one legacy tap. They were mostly good people: Jacqui, Marina, her mother Carmen, Isaac. The place had outlived them all, except for Isaac, who was studying neural networks at Stanford. The bar had seen some rough times, but we were on the other side of that now. The Esposito would endure.

I carried the draft back to Pedey.

"The writing thing doesn't work out, you could always come back here and work the taps."

He grimaced.

"I don't know where I got the balls to think I could write an actual book. I'd almost rather be a Walmart greeter."

I left him staring into his beer, my mood impervious to his disgruntlement. Every table was full, only one empty stool at the bar, and unlike in the early days, people weren't drinking to obliterate themselves. The alcohol was adjacent to the music and the conversation. It was as if I'd managed to conjure up a Platonic ideal of the Esposito.

I stretched my back and drank some club soda. Platonic fucking ideal—right. I was a bartender, a purveyor of ease and pleasure. Simple as that. No one here was worrying about their mortgage, their car payments, their children's drug habits, the state of the world.

When Wes Montgomery swung into "Bumping on Sunset," an all-time favorite, I even felt teary. This night was one of the half-dozen small perfections I'd known since the place opened. I wanted to wrap it and store it in memory for whatever came after, grateful for the peace and the reminder of how hard I'd worked for it.

And if I'd known everything else that was coming, I would have tried harder to preserve the memory, knowing I would never feel this way again.

14

When the Uber dropped Susan off, minutes after I got out of the shower Tuesday morning, I offered to take her out for breakfast. She said she'd rather cook. I offered her a Bloody Mary and was surprised to learn she did not drink anymore, not even the Cape Codders she used to like, that concoction that looks like windshield washer fluid and tastes like fruity kerosene.

"Not even a nice Pinot Noir?" I knew nothing about wines except the varietal most widely grown in Oregon.

"I kept waking up with little headaches, not really hangovers, but never clear-headed. Besides, alcohol does a number on your DNA."

She looked lovely, in a long oatmeal shift over black tights. I tipped my glass of Scotch in her direction.

"This doesn't bother you now? My drinking?"

She looked out the bay window.

"I'm all done worrying about that, Elder. One of the things my therapist has me working on is the idea that wanting a particular outcome doesn't mean I have to make it happen."

That constituted an improvement over our previous relationship, though I was adjusting to the idea she wanted back into my life. It felt uncomfortable, like when I was a kid and my mother bought me new clothes that ran big, knowing I'd grow into them.

"Your culinary skills have improved."

She'd taken a sad chunk of cheddar, some limp scallions, and some past-date eggs, and pulled together a creditable quiche.

"I had a second job for a while, cooking at a restaurant out on the coast. The Otis Café. Marionberry muffins the size of a baby's head."

"Sounds like a good time."

"More fun than the consulting work, for sure." She crossed her legs underneath her in the Morris chair. "I don't do regret, you know? But leaving here, leaving you? As close as I came."

I fought back the urge to down my Scotch and pour another.

"I don't know how to answer that."

"You don't have to say anything. Let me get this off my chest."

I started to joke, then curbed myself.

She gazed at the cool gray walls, the paintings I inherited from my father, the Edward Hopper of the lighthouse at Cape Elizabeth, Georgia O'Keefe's *Black Iris*.

"You and I never talked about my upbringing. But you must have guessed it was hard. The thing you and I had, that I'd never had before? Unconditional love."

Her size and her looks would have caused her havoc growing up. I shut up, let her talk.

"The reason I ran from you? You know it. It was the violence Burton brought. I always need to feel safe, Elder. When you weren't with Burton, I had that."

Why would she ever believe a man like me—middle-aged, no special skills—could keep her safe? I sat back, listening for the rest.

Except she looked at me expectantly, as if I should say something.

"I'm flattered. But I'm not any kind of…"

"Every time that safety was threatened, I bailed on you. I admit it. I bolted as far as I could go and still be in the country."

"Susan. We don't need the past to have a present. If that's what you want? I can forgive you if that's what you need."

"No. Nobody does that but me. I wanted you to understand why I kept leaving. And how I could come back."

My heart and my brain were confused. I couldn't keep anyone safe in this world. The obligation to do that felt weighty.

"I'm still the person I was," I said.

She looked at the glass of Scotch, which I'd barely sipped.

"I know that. And I know that's who I love."

The word hovered in the air between us like an exotic bird. I believed it was the first time either of us had said it out loud. I shifted in my chair, distracted by the soft notes of Miles Davis playing "I Fall in Love Too Easily." Couldn't have scripted that.

"I'm sorry Burton's gone. I know he was a friend to you. But to me, he was the reason you kept getting in danger. And bringing me. You're not going there anymore."

I hoped she was right, that I'd convinced both Mickey and Alistair Dain to leave me alone. But was it a certainty?

"True enough, I guess. That was the whole reason? Really?"

"I'm a cautious woman, Elder. Physically. And in other ways. I've had to be. I can only protect myself up to a point."

I'd never thought of working with Burton as risky. Had he been protecting me?

"It wasn't ever about me loving danger. Or daring things."

"I know, I know. Male bonding, friendship, all that. Not wanting your friend to think less of you. Whatever that means…"

She had it wrong, but I didn't think I could explain it. It wasn't so much about gender as about doing the right thing, acting like the person you thought you were.

"Where does this put us, then? What is it you want?"

She turned her pale blue-green eyes on me.

"You, Elder. I want you. I want us. I want us to take this as far as it will go."

A warmth spread through me, nothing to do with the whiskey.

"Well?" Her uncertainty made me feel better. "What do you think?"

I set the Scotch glass down on the coffee table, stood up, and held out my hands. Miles slipped into another ballad.

"I think we could dance to this," I said. "Shouldn't we?"

15

The poet's month of April notwithstanding, Wednesday is often the cruelest day of the week. But as I drove the Volvo down the narrow alley alongside the brick building that housed the Esposito and tucked it in close to the loading dock, I felt loose and happy. Susan and I had christened the dawn together, and my feelings for her were as full as they had ever been. It was good to feel desired, to know that someone was thinking good thoughts about you.

Even the humidity had abated. The air was still, but the temperature was ten or fifteen degrees lower than last week. I could tell because I didn't start sweating immediately when I climbed out of the car.

The first item on my to-do list was to call my friend Regina at Berklee and see about finding some musicians. The remainder of last week and then the weekend had been as busy as Monday night, reminding me that, as long as I stayed focused on serving drinks and minding my own business, things would be fine.

I parked in the back and walked up the alley to Mercy Street, feeling light and strong and ready for anything. Syndi would want to argue about paying the musicians, but it wasn't fair to ask them to play for nothing. If they were good enough to play in public, they were good enough to be paid.

Syndi, sober, was a boon to my bar. Maybe I ought to offer her a small stake in the business, get her a set of keys.

I kicked the rubber doorstop into place to let the outside air filter in. The Esposito was a basement bar, and even with the air exchanger, cleared out slowly. Early in the morning, the atmosphere carried the aromas of spilled beer, cooked food, and urinal cakes, a general stuffiness that took a couple hours to clear away.

I flicked on half of the house lights at the bottom of the stairs. The floor was clean, the chairs up on the table, the glasses all racked and stacked.

Behind the bar, I turned on the rest of the lights, found a playlist of instrumentals to keep me company, then walked into the kitchen to turn on the grill and the fryer for Syndi. Both of them took an hour to get up to temperature. The exhaust fan was already running. I frowned. I was careful to turn everything off at night. The electric bills seemed to grow every month.

When I first saw Syndi, I wondered why she was sitting on the floor. Her knees were bent, her back propped against the front of the big refrigerator. Her head hung between her thighs, the hair on top of her head thin, black roots showing.

I smelled the metallic pong of vomit and reached for her arm, limp in the long sleeve of her chef's coat. An object clattered to the floor on the far side of her body. Her fingernails were purplish, her face a dusky blue—cyanotic, a word I'd learned the last time she'd overdosed when I'd been able to rescue her with Naloxone. Too late for that this morning. She was long gone, the engine of her death the plastic syringe on the floor beside her.

I pushed the loose fabric of the sleeve up and exposed a length of rubber tubing knotted around her arm, the dot of dried blood where the needle with its gift of poison had entered her body. I had to grab the counter as I straightened up, faint.

"Ah, hell, Synthia. Why?"

Her utter stillness, the fragility of her bones, her arms and legs splayed as she fell sideways onto the floor, ruined me. The war she'd been waging was lost, maybe had been for a while, and I was bereft.

I looked around the kitchen for something to cover her, then stopped. The EMTs wouldn't be able to revive her, but I'd been around Burton long enough to know Homicide would send someone to the scene. I needed to leave things alone, heartbreaking as seeing her like that was.

I sleepwalked to the front of the bar, dialed 911 on the landline, and sat down on a stool to wait.

16

While the medical examiner examined Syndi's body, a detective from Homicide did show up, walking down the stairs into the bar with a phone at his ear as if preoccupied with something more important than a drug overdose.

I recognized Liam Macdonald, from a raid he and Burton had conducted several years ago on the culinary school Mickey Barksdale laundered money through. That was the time I'd been injected with heroin and almost died. Burton never had much use for Macdonald, who today showed not a flicker of recognition for the bar or for me.

As he poked incuriously about in the kitchen, I realized the Esposito had been locked up tight when I left on Saturday night. How had Syndi gotten inside? And why had she picked here to shoot up? Doing it where she lived would have been more likely. Was she making some kind of statement? To me?

Macdonald asked me a few perfunctory and obvious questions. I didn't mention the connection between Syndi and Mickey. If he didn't know it already, he'd find out soon enough.

"Do I need to close down? So the forensics people can work?"

He shrugged, his mind clearly elsewhere.

"I'd wash the floor where she was sitting. But otherwise? You're good to go."

I turned off the grill, the fryer, and the fan, and walked out front to take the chairs down off the tables, moving like an old man.

The pink sobriety coin on the back of the bar almost broke me. I slipped it into my pocket. She and heroin had been a better match than I'd thought.

I didn't get the place open for business until after one, cleaning up the mess the EMTs left. My day drinkers must have had an intuition about the tragedy, because no one showed up until midafternoon.

I was listening to an album Eric Clapton made with B. B. King when the upstairs door opened. I groaned under my breath. Probably should have just shut down for the day. I had no desire to serve drinks or talk to anyone about anything. But when the deadbolt snicked shut, my stomach froze. Only one man did that.

I shut the music down.

Mickey stepped off the bottom step and staggered. I would have thought he was drunk, if his stomach hadn't been so bad he couldn't drink White Russians. His face was blotched an angry pink and white, and he steadied himself on the chair backs as he made his way to the bar.

"I ought to have you killed." The raw-rimmed eyes glowed as he levered himself up onto a stool.

I did not feel the fear his pronouncement should have caused. The man in front of me was a wreck, composed entirely of grief.

I shrugged, as useless a response as anything I could say.

"I couldn't possibly feel as bad about this as you do, Michael. But she wasn't just my employee. We were friends."

He supported himself on the bar with his forearms as if his body was too heavy to hold up. Tears dripped on the wood surface. I looked away. It felt dangerous to witness Mickey in the deep clutch of misery.

"And she was my daughter, bartender. My only one. Even if we didn't always get along."

'Didn't ever get along' would have been more accurate, but who would argue with a suffering father? Why was he here? Were he and I supposed to mourn together? With Mickey, there was always more than one reason. For everything.

"You're not drinking today?" He sounded accusing, as if I weren't taking his tragedy seriously enough.

"Didn't feel right."

He lifted his head to look at me, his face slack and gray.

"Let us have one. You and me."

I was in the presence of a wild animal. I couldn't predict what he'd do. I hadn't killed Syndi, but could I trust him not to turn on me?

"What will it be?"

He scanned the tiers of bottles.

"That Macallan. That's your drink, isn't it?"

"The eighteen. It isn't cheap, but the first one's on me."

Grieving or not, he wasn't going to drown his sorrows on my dime.

"Nice of you." He grumbled.

"You had stomach trouble, the last time you drank here."

He waved that away and slid a fifty onto the bar.

"Set it up. At least until that's gone."

Someone yanked at the upstairs door. We ignored it. I poured two shots and left the bottle on the bar.

"To children." He lifted his glass. "Can't live with them, can't live without them."

He sank the shot and shuddered as if his stomach had rebelled. I followed suit, though I heard his toast in a darker way than he might have meant it. Could he feel responsible for the overdose?

I picked up the bottle to pour one more. I was not getting drunk with him in solidarity. He stopped me with an upraised palm.

"Hey. I'm not the one who's a fucking drunk here."

He never did deviate from his basic nature for long. I racked the bottle as he passed his empty glass back and forth between his hands.

"They're still trying to get at me."

I managed not to roll my eyes. He'd sense it, even if he didn't see.

"Michael."

"The timing can't be a coincidence, can it? All my challenges? Burton, my good friend, murdered outright. My daughter has to die, too?"

I blew out a sigh.

"Michael. It's hard to hear. But she was an addict. How many times did you put her through rehab? This was inevitable."

"I'm telling you. This is different. They killed Burton as a message to me. And then they killed Syndi when I didn't accept the message. They're coming for me next."

I hammered my stake in the sand once again.

"I told you before. Even if I believed your paranoia, I'm not getting involved."

His chest inflated, rage drowning the grief he'd brought in the door.

"What the hell does it take to get you to care, bartender? I need your help. I would owe you. I know people who would kill for that privilege."

Which was exactly the reason I wanted nothing to do with him.

"All I'm asking is you handle the straight side. Ask a few questions." He banged his shot glass on the bar, reminding me of how Burton used to call for another drink.

"Michael. Mickey. Burton died, and I'm done with it. You keep calling me a bartender and that's what I am. I am not getting involved."

He had reverted to the thug I knew best: self-important, paranoid, his rage barely contained. It was as if he'd visited the bar to dump his torment on my floor.

"You say so now." He bared his teeth. "But there's a way to make you help me."

He climbed off the stool, a block of dense and incandescent fury, and pointed a stubby finger.

"And I will find it, my friend. You can make fucking book on that."

He jogged up the stairs as if rage replenished his energy.

I poured myself one more shot of Scotch and turned on the music, wondering why I wasn't as afraid of him as I always had been.

17

Which is not to say the threats didn't worry me. The bar came to life late in the afternoon, and though I hated to disappoint the parties who came in for dinner, business was lively enough to take my mind off Mickey temporarily. The weight of losing Syndi was more difficult to forget.

He wouldn't be pushing me so hard if he didn't feel vulnerable. I had the sense his dominance in the city was being challenged. By outsiders? From within?

Susan surprised me by dropping in around nine. The remaining crowd was small—it was still early in the week—but the conversation was generally calm and the drinking stayed civilized. I remembered how much I liked to watch her walk down the stairs. Hip-hopping, because of her height.

She wore a short emerald jacket over a shorter white skirt that boasted about her legs. Her smile was tentative as she crossed the floor, attracting more than a little attention from a couple of my ever-hopeful male patrons. I scowled them off.

They returned to their drinks, but not until she stepped behind the bar and offered me her cheek for a kiss.

"Nice surprise. Nothing going on at the conference tonight?"

She smirked.

"The after-dinner panels are the worst. People drinking in the bar, sleeping off dinner. I'm done for the day. And night."

"You staying?"

I mixed a bourbon sour for a brunette who'd been casting an acquisitive eye in my direction until Susan walked in.

"I hope so." She set a black leather purse on the bar. "I checked out of my hotel. My suitcase is in the rental."

"Not in the loading zone, I hope. The meter maids are brutal."

She checked her delicate gold watch.

"At ten on a weeknight? You forget I used to live in this city? No public servant's working an overnight shift unless they're getting triple time."

"On your head."

I delivered the bourbon. The brunette pushed a twenty at me.

"Keep it," she said, trying to tell herself she hadn't been thinking what she'd been thinking.

"Something for you?" I asked Susan. "Cape Codder?"

"Just the juice, maybe."

Shit. I'd already forgotten she didn't drink.

"I thought and thought," she said. "About what we were talking about this morning?"

I set the glass down. Here was her answer to how we were going to try it this time. The fact, she was spending tonight with me could be a last hurrah or the first in a long string of nights together. My chest felt tight.

"If you rent me that apartment, at least I'd have a place to live." She sipped the cranberry juice, eyeing me over the rim of the glass. "Oregon never did feel like home."

My heart opened and flooded me with warmth I'd forgotten I could feel. I reached over the bar and squeezed her hand.

"Done and done. I can't tell you how good that makes me feel."

When she frowned, though, my happiness wobbled. What?

"It's still furnished?"

"Henri's stuff. Whatever you didn't sell."

"I sold my condo in Portland. As is. I don't own a thing except my clothes, which I'm having shipped."

It clicked. She meant this to be permanent.

"You're staying for good."

"You know me, Elder. I make a choice, I'm all in."

Only one of the things I loved about her.

"You're something. And I'm a happy barkeeper."

I argued myself out of closing up early, taking her home, restarting our calendar. But I felt so full it made me realize how empty I'd been, since before Burton had died, even. Her return was a gift I hadn't expected.

"You were looking a little morose when I first came in. Anything wrong?"

It was past last call. I'd locked the doors and was cleaning up. I was glad she couldn't see my face—I debated not telling her, but I didn't want to start off with a lie, even one of omission.

"You wouldn't have met the cook who replaced Marina?"

She shook her head.

"Syndi. She died this morning. Of an overdose."

Susan closed her eyes.

"Oh, Elder. I'm so sorry. What a terrible run you've had. Did you know she was an addict?"

I wrung out the bar rag and draped it over the faucet.

"I did." I didn't tell her the story of Syndi OD'ing before and my reviving her. "I thought she was coping, but I guess she wasn't."

"It's a terrible thing. My brother? The man you thought was my lover when you called last year? It took him seven years to get clean, and that was only pills."

I owed her the rest of the story, even if it frightened her.

"It happened here. In the kitchen. Which I can't figure out. Whether she was sending me a message."

"This day needs to be over for you. Can we go?"

Some of my leaden feeling dropped back in. I did need to get out of here.

"Why don't you go get your car? You can follow me home."

18

Home. An idea, an ideal, one that made more sense to me if Susan were going to be there. I felt light as fog as I let myself out the back door and got into the Volvo. Even the garbage in the dumpster seemed to stink less.

She was standing beside her rental car, a nondescript gray Camry, as I eased my car over the broken pavement seam at the mouth of the alley.

"The seat won't go all the way forward. Can we switch?"

I got out and let her sit in the Volvo's driver's seat, showed her how to adjust the controls. Then I climbed into the Camry. It was a little cramped but doable.

She took off down the street, running a little faster than I would have, even at two in the morning. She knew the way.

I followed her to the end of Mercy Street, made the right onto Tremont, and the quick left onto Berkeley, which gave us a straight shot over to Comm Ave. I wished she would slow down—the Volvo's tailpipe threw sparks when she hit a high spot in the street—but I knew how she'd react if I told her that. Which, happy soul that I was, made me wonder about all the arguments we might have to come.

She'd turned onto Comm Ave and passed the First Baptist Church when the rear end of the Volvo flared red. At first, it looked like more sparks from the muffler, but when the reddish light stayed steady, I thought the brake lights might have stuck.

Then a lick of flame seeped out through a seam at the base of the Volvo's hatchback.

"Shit."

I rammed the Camry's gas pedal to the floor, honking my horn, trying to catch up to her. As I closed, the fire spread up out of the trunk toward the rear windshield. She couldn't have seen what was happening behind her. She sped up, thinking I was playing.

I accelerated up beside her on the narrow boulevard. As I came even with her window, she looked over and wagged a finger at me. I waved for her to pull over and, finally, she read my panic, wrestled the wheel to the right, and stood on the brakes.

The Camry shot past before I could slow. I screeched to a stop twenty yards down the road, in front of the old Ames-Webster Museum, now the sometimes home of a Saudi sheik. As I opened my door, the back of the Volvo erupted in a ball of flame.

I popped the Camry's trunk, hoping for a fire extinguisher, but the fire was already too big for that. I ran toward the Volvo. Twenty feet away from it, a thick wall of heat and acrid black smoke stopped me. I couldn't see past it into the interior of the car.

There was no explosion, only flames rising and rising until the smoke cloud obliterated all sight of the burning vehicle. There was no way she could have escaped.

"Ahhhh."

My anguish flew into the night. I staggered back and the granite curb bruised my tailbone as I fell. In the distance, sirens rent the quiet of the hot August night. I closed my eyes, stunned into desolation.

* * *

Hours later, I sat in an interrogation room at the precinct on Harrison Avenue, a small square space soaked in the smells of fear, cold coffee, uncirculated air. I was dazed, my hammering headache warring with a sense of unreality. I felt nothing, though I did not doubt that grief would return later. And the rage—this was no accident.

Someone brought me a dubious gift, a cup of rancid coffee, then left. I wished Burton were here.

When the door to the room opened, I was surprised to see Liam Macdonald, the detective who'd attended Syndi's overdose. He looked at me flatly, as if he still didn't recognize me. Could he be that stupid?

"Terrible thing to witness." As if we were continuing a conversation.

Why was he here? He couldn't be the only Homicide cop in this part of the city.

"You were in my bar this morning. My cook, with the overdose."

"So I was." He didn't look surprised. Maybe the affect was part of his shtick. "Two violent instances involving one person. In one day. Makes a fellow curious."

Burton's voice echoed in the back of my brain, telling me to shut up, not trust Macdonald, insist on a lawyer.

"Keep talking like that and we can sit here for a few hours while I find an attorney."

Macdonald looked startled, as if a dog had snapped at his pants leg.

"My apologies. Making assumptions is a professional failing. Why don't you tell me what you saw."

"Again."

I'd been through it once with the original detective. The reason Macdonald wanted me to repeat the story was, of course, to look for inconsistencies, judge whether I was lying. The fire was no accident, and I could have been the one to engineer it. Or that would be a possible hypothesis.

"The tailpipe of the car was dragging on the ground. Sparks came up off of it. It was just in for service—the mechanic would have noticed that."

"Then?" He nodded encouragingly.

"Then, as she made the turn onto Comm. Ave.…."

"Wait. You could tell it was a woman? How?"

"It was my car, Macdonald. She was a… friend."

"OK. Go on."

"Flames started to creep up out of the back. Around the seams."

My heart sped up. Cold sweat greased my forehead, reactions I hadn't had time for before.

"I tried to pull up beside her and warn her. She got the car over to the curb before it went up."

"Exploded?"

"The fire expanded, very fast. I couldn't see the car for all the smoke and flame."

Macdonald peered at me, listening for anything false in my story.

"Car fires usually start in the engine. Not in the trunk."

"It had to be arson. Deliberate." My throat seized on the words, on the idea Susan had been in peril because of me. Again.

"Not for me to say." Macdonald closed his notebook. "That it?"

I nodded.

"You're free to go, then."

I was still dazed by the idea someone had sabotaged my car. And murdered Susan.

"OK." My knees shook as I tried to stand. "Can someone give me a ride?"

19

The next day, I realized that no one's grief is interesting to anyone but himself. And so I bottled it. Or, more accurately, unbottled it. I got the Esposito open and operating, but only by dint of steady doses of strong Scotch. I went to the cask-strength Macallan—130 proof—because it took fewer drinks to maintain the numbness. A vestige of pride kept me from drinking in front of my customers, but anyone who came in the day after I lost Susan knew I wasn't myself.

The alcohol didn't banish the pain so much as push it away, making it more like a cloud bank on the horizon than a present storm. And the weight of a third death multiplied all my low thoughts into a full-on depression. When I wasn't mourning Susan, I was thinking about Syndi's overdose, remembering Burton's stupid violent death.

No one from the cops, Macdonald or otherwise, followed up with me, either for further questioning or an update on the fire. No one even called to confirm it was arson, which was obvious enough that I wondered why Macdonald would be coy. The fire was a message to me, but I could not read it yet.

The *Globe* printed a small piece in the Metro section about the fire, without details of casualties or its source. When I was sober enough to consider it, it gave me the terrible feeling I'd caused Susan's death, but my brain kept avoiding that idea. The abyss of grief wanted to claim me, and the best I could do was put on a clean shirt and open the bar.

I barely mustered an iota of give-a-shit when, late Friday afternoon, Mickey showed up, accompanied by his personal assistant. I was so deep in the funk, their presence barely registered. Slumped on a stool behind the bar, I watched Mickey march across the linoleum.

"Didn't have to lock the door to talk to you this time, did I? This place is deader than Kelsey's nuts."

"Michael."

Dain raised a plucked eyebrow at the familiarity.

"You are a fucking mess, bartender. And so is your place."

"If you say so, Mickey. You of all people know the last couple months have been a long strange trip."

"Never liked the Dead. I'm more of a Black Sabbath guy."

I tipped my head and picked up a glass from under the bar. Drinking in front of Mickey didn't count as drinking in front of a customer. Dain posted himself at the bottom of the stairs, in the event a customer interrupted whatever Mickey had come to say. Dain sported the blue pinstripe seersucker today.

Mickey hauled up a stool.

"I've been looking around. Asking some questions."

I toasted him.

"You do you, Mickey."

"Put that shit down and pay attention." The snap in his voice penetrated my haze.

Dain looked over.

I returned the glass to its home under the counter and sat up straight, ready to be schooled. Or beaten up. Even killed. None of those outcomes seemed much worse than where I was.

"You've been asking questions." I proved I was listening. "Pertinent ones, I hope."

"Ali," Mickey said.

Dain crossed the floor.

"Go make this mook some coffee. I want him to understand what I'm trying to say."

Dain disappeared into the kitchen, flicking on the light. I could have told them, from long experience, that coffee didn't sober you up. It made you into a wide-awake drunk. But Mickey was serious, and this was no place to play the fool.

I pulled my attention together, along with the dregs of my pride.

"I'm here, Michael. I'm listening."

Then you can get the fuck out, so I can continue the wake.

Mickey pulled at the collar of his T-shirt—Harley-Davidson Dubai. Only Mickey would travel that far and buy a souvenir tee. A smile moved my lips.

"Something's funny."

"Nothing. You want something to drink?"

He leaned across the bar.

"So do I have your full attention now?"

I'd lost my desire to smart-ass him. All I wanted was to be left alone.

"As I said, I've been asking questions." He pulled out a pack of Lucky Strikes. "You might be surprised how wide my network stretches."

"I doubt it."

"This tragedy of yours."

"Which one." I winced at my self-pity.

"The most recent one. Your girlfriend. No one from the cops has called you?"

"No. What about?"

"About the fact it was no accident. It was a hit."

"What? How?"

"A silicon bag full of gasoline and some electronics." He waved his hand at the details.

I reached for my glass.

"Are you sure?"

"I'm positive. Besides, who else would drive your car?"

"Why in hell? I've got nothing to do with any of this. Why would someone go after me?"

Dain came out of the kitchen with a carafe and a mug.

"Someone who thinks you're working for me. Do you believe me now? That someone's out to get me?"

"By killing my friends?" I was sobering up, which sucked.

He glowered.

"My daughter. My friend Burton."

"I don't see it."

"No offense, Darrow. But are you stupid? You don't have any trouble with your deliveries? Your linens and produce? Your meats?"

"Syndi took care of all that."

I knew what he was implying. Everything he mentioned was a traditional mob enterprise.

"And who was Synthia's father?"

So Mickey had been looking out for the Esposito on his daughter's behalf, making sure no one cheated me?

"And you and Burton were friends." He hadn't lit the cigarette yet. "If you can't see what's going on, I don't know how to convince you. Try and keep up."

He ticked on his fingers.

"First of all. Burton gets killed in a liquor store robbery. You know how unlikely that is?"

"He wouldn't have stayed out of it. If he saw what was going on, he would have jumped right in. That's not unlikely."

"Agreed. But the kid who shot him? Stone junkie, high as a dirigible, and packing a revolver. Notoriously inaccurate weapon."

"Circumstantial."

I didn't know why I was fighting the idea so hard.

"And there was something about the shooting angles being wrong. Where the bullets came from?"

"How would you know something like that? You've seen the police reports?"

Of course he had.

"My network."

He had contacts on the cops. Not surprising.

"You're jamming the evidence to fit your theory."

"Bullshit. This thing with Burton kicks up at the exact time I'm trying to hold off pressure from external constituencies?"

Whatever that meant. The fancier his words got, the less I trusted him.

"So naturally you conflated it all."

He rolled on.

"Then you get mugged, except it's not really a mugging because you don't get your ass kicked. And it turns out to be a message to me."

Getting slammed around by the guy in the Luchador mask sure felt like an ass-kicking.

"This is the mugging where someone was trying to convince me what I already believed, that Burton's death was accidental?"

"Which tells us two things." Mickey ticked more fingers. "Someone is heavily invested in the idea that Burton's death was a random event. And that someone thinks you and I are working together."

"Which, I don't have to remind you, we are not." I set the mug down on the back bar. Dain was never going to make a good assistant if he didn't learn to make better coffee.

"It doesn't matter what reality says." Mickey lit the cigarette. "It's what people believe. And these people clearly don't like the idea of us working together."

"Why would anyone think I could do anything?"

"Maybe someone who knows your history with Burton, thinks you have contacts you're tapping on your own. And there's Synthia." He sounded sad, the sort of sadness you hear when someone loses a pet. Or the favorite aunt who used to slip five dollars into your birthday card.

"You saying the OD wasn't an accident?"

It was either paranoia or something going on in his world I wasn't privy to.

"More pressure on Mr. Barksdale." Dain chimed in, supporting Mickey's fantasies now where he hadn't before. "A lot of people didn't know he had a daughter until last year."

Meaning the first time she'd overdosed.

"And my car? That was part of this." I was waiting for the police to tell me when I could claim Susan's body. I didn't think there was anyone else to bury her.

"Reinforce the message," Mickey said. "You were the target. Someone's afraid of you being involved. Probably relates to my problems."

"Which you won't tell me about? What's the big prize, Mickey? It must be major, to cause all this ruckus."

"I can't talk about that right now. But the car fire was a direct message, to keep your distance from Mickey Barksdale. I don't think anyone was supposed to die."

He hadn't seen the amount of flame and smoke consuming the Volvo. Someone had expected me to die.

"And you still think I should pitch in with you?"

Mickey spread his hands.

"You have skin in the game now, bartender. Whether you like it or not. Someone thinks you're playing."

I owned barely enough sober brain to know there was truth, if not whole truth, in what he was talking about. But I also knew I was drunk and that no decision I'd ever made in that state had come out well. I needed to be sober to inspect his line of reasoning, see if I still thought Mickey was wrong then.

"What is it you want from me? If I help."

Mickey and Dain both relaxed as if I'd agreed to something.

"If I'm right," Mickey said. "This started with Burton. It's what I've been asking you to do all along. You have the contacts in law enforcement, from before. You were his best friend. You have questions. People will talk to you who won't look at me."

"And tell me what?"

Mickey was off the stool. He reached across and patted my hand, a weird avuncular gesture.

"You'll know it when you hear it, boyo. You'll know."

20

The next day, sober as a minister on Sunday morning, I had to admit Mickey was right about some of it. But I hadn't made a single move on Mickey's behalf, even though we'd seen more of each other in the last couple of months than I had in years before. Someone was making assumptions based on that, but the conversations didn't mean we shared any goals.

Even though it was Saturday, I could not bring myself to open up the bar. Susan's death, especially since it was accidental, anchored me to depression. What had happened was exactly what she feared, that the violence I attracted would spill over onto her. I could not see myself smiling at people today, dispensing drinks, playing music, making conversation. Losing her numbed me in the way Burton's loss had, one more in a chain of events I wasn't sure how to survive.

After everything I'd lost in the last month, what was there to go forward for? A struggling bar business and an addiction I tried to fool myself into thinking I controlled? All that was left was to sit in my armchair and drink.

* * *

By mid-afternoon, I achieved the alcoholic equilibrium I sought, the state halfway between sobriety and knee-walking drunk that lets you believe you could function, even drive a car. Except that I had no car anymore. And the drunkenness did nothing to eradicate my deep sense of guilt over Susan, all those accumulated sorrows, only shove them into the background. The most obvious sign I was stuck was that I had no desire to hear any music.

I was thinking about eating something when the street door buzzer bleated. I winced and walked to the bay window and looked down at the street. No Sixties muscle car was parked down on Comm Ave, which was a relief. It wasn't Mickey calling.

I buzzed whoever it was in without asking—who was left I hadn't lost?—and cracked the apartment door, sat back down in the recliner with the side table, the glass, and the half-empty bottle.

Francesca pressed the apartment door wider with the backs of her knuckles, which I'd seen Burton do scores of times. Was that a cop habit, to make sure you didn't leave your fingerprints at a crime scene? Was this a crime scene?

Even in my stupor, I appreciated her beauty. Her chestnut hair was braided and piled up on her head, exposing a long graceful neck. The wide brown eyes glowed with a life that reproached my own state of mind. The navy jacket and trousers over a white shirt were more utilitarian than usual but tailored to fit like custom.

She sniffed the air and made a face.

"Bad time?"

"Never a good one." The whining disgusted me. I picked up the bottle. "Buy you a drink?"

She sat in the Windsor chair across from me, crossed her long legs, adjusting the holster on her belt.

"No, thank you. And I'm guessing you don't need another one, either."

"And I'm guessing I'll be the judge of that."

"I came to pay my condolences. Maybe another time would be better."

"Meaning what?"

"Relax. I know you're walking a hard road."

"It's funny how we talk about *paying* condolences, as if they had some actual value." Her official appearance ticked a thought. "You're not dressed like an art cop this morning."

Her normal assignment with the FBI as part of the Fraud section dealt with things like museum thefts for insurance swindles and other scams. She tended not to dress like a police detective.

"Temporary assignment. Seconded to BPD Homicide over a possible connection to one of our cases."

"They can move you around like that?"

"I guess you always worked for yourself. Boss can do what boss wants."

"You're looking into it for a mob link?"

"If by it, you mean your car fire, the answer is yes. I'm on that team."

"What gangster connection?"

Mickey wouldn't benefit from killing me. What other gangsters were there?

"Theoretical, at this point. But it's the kind of splashy message they favor."

"So no one's arguing it wasn't murder."

She frowned. "No one's talked to you."

"Not since Macdonald interviewed me, that night. Why?"

"There was no one in the car."

"What?"

"No human remains were found in the wreckage."

"She got out? Where did she go?"

"I was hoping you knew."

"I haven't heard a word from her. Or anyone else. Wait. Is Liam Macdonald assigned to this? Or are you?"

"He's investigating the attempted homicide part of it, whether it connects to anything else. I've got the OC connection. If any."

Why hadn't Macdonald called and told me Susan wasn't in the car? Was this a gratuitous bit of cruelty? And how had Francesca gotten assigned to it? The way I understood the BPD, they would kick and scream over inserting an FBI agent into a police investigation.

"Burton ever tell you his opinion of Macdonald?" I said.

"Lazy, too sure of himself, loves his desk chair more than knocking on doors. That about cover it?"

As long as she knew who she was working with.

"You're in an unusual situation."

"Confidentially?" she said. "There are also questions about commitment inside the department. To building cases against certain gangsters."

She was talking about Mickey. He'd implied he had an inside connection on the cops.

"Oh. So the FBI is innocent of anything like that?"

"Let's not rake over history. I was happy to take this on, get out of the fraud world for a while and do some actual police work. So tell me why someone wanted to scare the shit out of you? Were they warning you off something? And what can you tell me about your girlfriend?"

"You mean why didn't they just kill me outright?"

"You must have some idea."

I couldn't explain Mickey's delusion and have it sound sensible.

"Francesca. Was Burton's death really random? Were there questions about anything?"

The swerve made her alert.

"What do you mean?"

"I heard something was wrong with the firing angles, the paths of the various bullets."

"You heard a bunch of fucking gossip. Who told you that?"

"Look," I said. "We can talk about Susan all day long, but she wasn't the target. And I don't have any idea why someone would want to do that to me, for god's sake. I'm a fucking bartender."

"You're lying about something."

Why was I holding back? I didn't need to protect Mickey and I no longer cared if he was angry with me.

"You're a cop, Francesca. You see conspiracies everywhere—it's in the job description. I'm telling you it's a mystery."

She stood up, readjusted her weapon.

"Elder. I feel the same way you do about losing Burton. You can drink yourself into oblivion if you want. Or you can help me do something about it."

She wouldn't be talking about "doing something" if she didn't believe Burton's murder wasn't random. I poured myself more whiskey.

"Don't see what I could do. Nothing to offer here."

"I do not fucking believe you." She stood up and shook her head. "When you get ready to do something for your friend besides wallow? You know where I'll be. You're not the only one who lost someone here."

And she stalked out of the apartment, the soles of her shoes squeaking on the hardwood floor.

Off to do something, no doubt. But what the hell would that even look like?

21

After Francesca, there was nothing to do but finish the bottle. Then crack open another one. When I woke up, it was dusk and my pants were wet, and not from spilling my drinks. I sat there in the chair for a few seconds, disgusted with myself and worried. No matter how drunk I used to get, that never happened. Fortunately, I'd moved from the leather recliner into a wooden armchair I'd bought at a yard sale, one with the Harvard seal. The university would not have been pleased with the defilement.

Half of the second bottle of Macallan remained, but my stomach turned at the thought of another drink. That felt like a positive step. I carried the bottle into the kitchen and poured the remains down the sink, the fumes making me gag. It wasn't as grand a gesture as it might have been. Six more bottles sat in the cupboard below the sink.

Wincing, I shed the wet underpants and trousers, emptying the pockets automatically: wallet, handkerchief, a fold of soggy bills. My fingers closed around a hard metal circlet, Syndi's sobriety coin.

"Ah, fuck." And I threw it across the room.

A hot shower dissipated the fog, leaving the familiar throbbing thunder of a hangover headache. I scrubbed myself dry and donned fresh clothes. "Wallow" was the word Francesca used, and I did feel swinish.

Around eight, I realized I was starving. The only food in the refrigerator was a chunk of Manchego, green along one edge, and a half bottle of champagne I'd bought before finding out that Susan didn't drink anymore.

Susan. Where was she? How had she escaped that conflagration? And why hadn't I heard anything from her?

I slammed the refrigerator shut. My head pulsed, punishing me, the alcohol residue and all my failures combining to drip poison into my brain.

I grabbed my keys. I would go down to the bar, make myself a sandwich, and get ready for Monday morning. I could not be alone here in this frame of mind.

With the locks unlocked and the apartment door open, I stopped, walked back into the bedroom, and got down on my hands and knees. Fumbling under the radiator, I fingered out the pink coin Syndi had been so proud of. It didn't mean to me what it had to her, but I slipped it into my pocket anyway, a memory and a talisman. Maybe a reminder I ought to be grateful to be alive.

22

As I approached the turn off Mercy Street, into the alley that led to the parking area in back, I saw the Esposito's front door propped open with a brick. I'd replaced Susan's car with a rented Volvo until my insurance company quit screwing around. Parallel-parked in the loading zone, I walked back down the sidewalk. The bulb over the door was lit yellow, though it wasn't yet full dark, and music played, down in the bar. It was the wrong music, a repetitive and rubbery-sounding classic rock.

I tiptoed down the stairs, not wanting to announce my presence, but you couldn't have heard a dozen Irish dancers over the whiny guitar and the voices. Maybe fifteen customers spread across the room, a half dozen at the bar, a table of seven or eight men in their twenties with pitchers of beer. Most of the conversational noise came from them.

Behind the bar, Alistair Dain presided at the taps, an apron tied around his waist to protect his striped suit pants. He was chatting with a tall pale redheaded woman who seemed to be hanging on his every word.

Some sugar syrup-voiced singer started nattering about sailing. The beer drinkers cheered as if they'd requested the song.

"The fuck." I stalked behind the bar and pushed my chest into Dain. "What are you doing here?"

Dain tried to ice me down with a look. The redhead slipped away. He tipped his head back toward the kitchen. I steamed.

"See the boss."

"I am the boss. So get your ass out from behind my bar right now."

He sneered his laughter and held up his hands, untied the apron, and tossed it on the back bar.

"Can't run a bar if it never opens." He stepped around me to join the table of beer-drinking bros.

I cut the music, killing sailor-boy in mid-jibe. The boys' table groaned. I stepped back into the kitchen.

The cook was not one of Mickey's minions, but the great man himself, a red bandanna wrapped around his head, a long striped apron over T-shirt and jeans. The apron looked custom-made, striped canvas with brass buckles and a double long string. It covered him down to the tops of his yellow clogs.

He waved a serrated knife at me, cut a sandwich in half, piled fries from the metal basket onto the plate, and pushed it through the pass-through.

"Take that out before it gets cold. Guy in a Hawaiian shirt, name of Bill. At the far end of the bar."

"Michael."

"Before the fries get cold. All right?" He wiped the knife on a towel and slotted it onto the holder.

I delivered the plate and walked right back in, still steaming. Most of the customers appeared to be Mickey's boys.

"Hell of a nerve, Mickey. Taking over my bar." Irritation made me careless of pissing him off. "I don't come over to Charlestown and try and run your business, do I?"

He lit a cigarette, as if he knew smoking in the kitchen would piss me off further.

"You have the stones, you're welcome to try." He stared at me, hard-cold. "My guys wanted some beers. This place is a business. Any business, you want to succeed, you have to be consistent. You can't be all, like—oh, I'll open for a couple hours on Monday, close on Tuesday. Open up all day Wednesday. People get confused, they don't come around. I would think you'd know that."

As if I hadn't run the place for decades.

"You have no right." My head pounded harder.

"No right to what? Help out a grieving friend? Help him meet his responsibilities."

"My responsibilities."

"You open a bar, you're part of the neighborhood, the community. You owe people."

A stone gangster lecturing me on community?

"How did you get in here?"

"Didn't Alistair warn you your security's for shit? We've got to get you some better locks. A real alarm system."

I saw where he was going.

"No, Michael. I am not signing up to be part of the Barksdale empire. I've run this place straight for as long as I've had it. Not going to change."

He peered at me through the smoke.

"Maybe you have and maybe you haven't. Maybe you only stayed independent this long because of the company you keep. Kept, I should say."

"You're saying Burton protected me from you?"

He'd suggested that before. That would put a spin on their relationship I hadn't suspected.

"Not in so many words. But it was understood that you, and the bar, were off-limits. Which gives me something of a responsibility to help you out here, doesn't it?"

I wouldn't have thought Burton gave a shit about the Esposito except as a place where he drank for free. We hadn't had that close a relationship. Or had we, and I hadn't known it? Of course, Mickey could be lying through his veneers.

"Look, bartender. This isn't a hostile takeover. For a lot of reasons, I need a neutral zone, somewhere I can bring my associates, have a cocktail, discuss business matters without having to watch my back. Nothing criminal will take place here, I assure you."

The lies in his speech were too numerous to count. And when Mickey started talking like he was in the House of Lords, it was a warning.

"Absolutely not."

"It is a bar. A public place. You can't keep out everybody you don't like."

Before I said anything else, a glass broke on the floor out front. I pointed at Mickey.

"You'd be surprised. This isn't over."

The tableau at the bro table was my worst memory of the Esposito's olden days: Alistair Dain standing up, his hands in the air. Middle-aged thug, haircut like an Italian soccer player, in tight black jeans and a tank top from Riley's Roast Beef, knife out in front of him. Redheaded woman, eyes avid as a fox, stood behind Dain's shoulder.

"You best come here and get it, *cher*. Because I'm going to give it to you one way or another." He poked the switchblade toward Dain's midsection.

It was the man who'd mugged me, without his Luchador mask. Mickey shoved past me.

"That's it, Armand. Put the toad sticker away. You have any sense at all? This is a public place."

The three or four customers who weren't here with Mickey's clan broke for the stairs. Armand pressed a button on the knife and the blade withdrew. He smiled at me, cementing my recognition.

"All right, you clowns." Mickey clapped his hands like a kindergarten teacher ending recess. "Let's go and let the rest of these nice people finish their drinks. Mr. Darrow is back behind the taps."

The table broke up, its occupants heading for the stairs. Mickey threw me one more cold look.

"For the moment, anyway." And he followed his posse up the stairs and out.

The last person in the place, Bill of the Hawaiian shirt, dragged a French fry through the ketchup on his plate.

"Shifty little fucker, isn't he?" he said.

I took his beer glass for a refill.

"You have no idea."

23

The remainder of the night was calmer. I poured myself a glass of Macallan after Bill left, hoping to chase the hangover, but at closing time, I realized I hadn't touched it. The redhead Alistair and Armand had been fighting over left with the rest of them, and I wondered what her role in Mickey's gang might be.

I locked the upstairs door—for all the good it would do, apparently—and shut down the music. Mickey's attempted takeover meant something, but it may only have been him reminding me of his dominance, especially in front of a group of his minions. I doubted he would want the hassle of owning and running the place.

But the power move made me realize I could no longer be passive about what was going on around me. I was immersed in this kettle of fish without knowing everyone and everything that was in it with me. But if I gave in to the despair I'd been cultivating so diligently, the universe was going to roll right over me, indifferent as a death.

A night or two ago, when I'd thought Susan was dead, I might have welcomed that. But the mystery that was Mickey had awakened a nasty elf in my brain, my curiosity. It stood up, stretched, and looked around at the world, hungry for answers. Suddenly, I needed to know what was going on, why people I cared about had died, and anything else I might have missed along the way. What I could do about it wasn't clear, but something had shifted in me.

My dreams that night were drenched in comic book colors, beasts and demons, no sense of place or story, only long battering waves of frightening images, long-toothed, slobbering, foreign skeletons and architectures. I slept most of Sunday, too, too exhausted to worry about drinking or eating.

And when I woke on Monday morning, I was as rested as if I'd been away on a Florida vacation, my head so clear it felt like a mistake. If one night without whiskey could do that, what would a year do? Or more plausibly, a week?

Francesca was not at her cubicle at the precinct, but a fresh-faced male cadet at the front desk told me she liked to eat at the Trampled Shamrock, a lunch counter around the corner on East Dedham Street.

"Who told you I was here?" she said when I sat down opposite her.

She was chewing on a piece of caramelized grapefruit. The *New York Times* Style section was spread across the table, and though she occupied an entire four-top, no one seemed to want to say anything about it, though there was a line waiting at the door. Either she was a regular, or people had noticed she was armed.

I didn't want to sink the cadet's career before it got started.

"Everybody knows the cops eat here. I wanted to apologize."

She eyed me unhappily, thinking no doubt of our conversation last night, refolded the newspaper, and set it to one side.

"You decide to clean up your act?"

"What's that supposed to mean?"

"Just what I said…"

"Never mind. You implied there was something off about Burton's murder."

She shook her head.

"No. You implied that. I don't know where you heard that story about the forensics, but you don't want to be running around spouting conspiracy theories. And you still haven't told me who your source was."

If I wasn't going to stay passive, if I wanted things to move forward, I had to give her something.

"If I heard it from Mickey Barksdale, would that surprise you?"

"I suspected as much. Something funky is going on in the land of the munchkin gangster."

I would have loved to hear her call Mickey that to his face.

"And how does a fraud-squad type know so much about gangsters in Boston?"

She managed to look offended.

"We're not all specialists, Elder. And when I got invited to help BPD, I was briefed. Captain Martines is kind of a dick, but he's a data-digging fool. Your pal Mickey is under some kind of pressure."

"As in?"

"Undefined, as yet. We don't have enough ears on the street. Budget cuts mean less money for CIs."

I couldn't help thinking Burton could have found out. She nodded.

"You're right. But he's not here, is he?"

"For sure. So there's nothing to the story the bullet angles were off?"

She shifted in the chair.

"I'm walled off from that part of the investigation, if it's still ongoing. The personal angle, I was told. Because I knew Burton. Feels more like the local cops weenie-wagging at the FBI. I should hear rumors though. You know how cops love to gossip."

I tucked that away. If she was limited to looking into gangster connections to my car fire, she wasn't going to know whether Burton's case stayed closed. Even though she'd been sleeping with him.

She wiped her mouth with a napkin, smearing her bruise-colored lipstick.

"I am glad you came looking for me."

The waiter dropped a paper check on the table. He hadn't asked if I wanted anything. Maybe he wanted his table back.

"Why's that?"

She laid a twenty and a ten on the bill.

"I don't know if anyone talked to you. The car fire was definitely arson."

Pretty old news—I'd known that just by watching it.

"OK. And intended for me. Unless you think someone had a motive to kill Susan. Any idea who torched it?"

She shook her head and waved off change from the waiter.

"I'm still wondering if you have any idea where she is?"

I was stunned. Did she think I'd disappeared Susan? Or was hiding her?

Francesca noticed the crowded doorway and picked up her *Times*.

"Let's walk. It's stuffy in here."

Outside the Shamrock, we turned right, back toward the precinct.

"There's really no chance the fire was intended for Ms. Voisine?" she said.

"No one could have known we'd switch cars. And she has no connections in Boston anymore. She'd been living out in Oregon." My voice caught. "She was moving back to live with me."

Francesca stopped on the sidewalk.

"Shit. I am sorry. I didn't know that." We started walking again. "But no ex-lovers, violent or otherwise, in the picture? A spurned spouse?"

"It's starting to sound like you're investigating all the homicides, real or attempted. Burton's too?"

She kept her eyes on the sidewalk as we turned the corner onto Harrison Avenue.

"I can only say this because you've met the man."

"Macdonald."

"I'm feeling like he's short-arming things. You and I know his reputation."

"He's taking it too easy?"

"This feels different. Like he's avoiding reasonable possibilities. Not trying to build the strongest case."

That fired my anger. A homicide investigator calling it in?

We stopped on the sidewalk in front of the precinct doors.

"Look," she said. "I'm running mainly on intuition. I could be wrong. I never worked with him before."

"Trust your gut. And if you can't do that, trust Burton's take on the guy. Though god knows why someone would want to be a homicide cop if he wasn't going to do it the right way."

She put a hand on my arm.

"Burton had a lot of respect for you, you know. He told me it took a lot to get you pissed off, but once you did, you were all in."

"He really wasn't that great a friend."

She hitched her bag up on her shoulder and looked surprised.

"How's that?"

"I don't know. Call him focused, self-involved. Whatever. Nothing ever claimed his full attention but the work."

"I know what you mean. Part of him was always elsewhere. Plus he acted like he didn't deserve anything better."

"He never let himself off the hook."

"Meaning?"

"He was always on a case. Did he ever relax around you?"

"Rarely. I'd call the man extremely mission-driven."

The corporate-speak made me want to roll my eyes, but she was right. His mission was to speak for the murdered, and he approached it with the seriousness of a priest.

"He did tell me that if you took something on, you were in it to the end," she said. "We don't want to lose anyone else to whatever's going on. But if you're in, I'm in."

That made me feel better.

"You're not going to tell me to keep my nose out of it? Macdonald would."

"I'm telling you to be careful. Keep clear in your mind who we're dealing with here."

"Mickey Barksdale."

"And whatever other unsavory types he might be messing about with."

We were getting looks from the other cops coming and going through the precinct entrance.

"Have you or anyone else heard what Mickey might be going through? Some kind of upheaval out there in gangster land?"

"If I knew, I'd tell you. But no. I will stick my nose into anything they let me, the arson, murder, whatever shows up. But let me do the investigating. No matter what you and Burton used to get up to."

"Understood."

And I'd ignore the warning if I saw a reason.

"However. If you can find out what's going on with Mickey?" she said. "That'd help a lot."

So I was exactly where Mickey wanted me, with access to the investigation into Burton's death.

"Don't shut me out of it."

"No one's going to do that. Unless something in the official investigation needs to stay hidden to build a court case."

Now it sounded as if she were investigating and not Liam Macdonald. She turned to start up the stairs.

"If you can ingratiate yourself with Mickey? What would help do that?"

"If you can track down the thing with the firing angles, the forensics? Whether it's bullshit or not. And who might have told him."

She made a face like she'd bitten a lemon.

"I'll try," she said. "But don't count on it."

24

Whenever the topic of a murderer's motive came up in our conversations, Burton used to snort.

"Most of what I deal with is a lack of motive. At least anything rational. The cause of a killing is usually overreaction, loss of control, anger. For a lot of these idiots, killing is a reflex act for an insult, like swatting at a mosquito. We don't get a lot of whodunnits. Or geniuses."

This didn't feel like a whodunnit, though the reasons people had done what they had done were still obscure.

I Ubered back to the Esposito, thinking about what Francesca had and hadn't said. My gut was telling me what I'd been trying to deny, that Burton's death was a deliberate killing, and assuming that, there had to be logic behind it. No evidence supported the gut feeling, though.

Knowing that Susan was alive didn't make me feel less guilty. I'd never wanted her to be dragged into any of this. She had to have been frightened out of her wits. Had she disappeared on her own? Where was she? And would she contact me to let me know she was alive? She'd had her worst fears realized. Maybe she'd left town again.

I unlocked the bar door and started on my morning routine, trying not to think about her. She was peripheral to Burton's murder, only involved by accident. If I got to talk to her again, I would try to remind her of that. Maybe that would make her feel safer.

I left the kitchen lights dark, though business demanded I find a cook soon if the Esposito were going to survive. I turned on music, found Syndi's sobriety coin in my pants pocket, and laid it on the back bar, to remind me of her.

My taste in jazz was traditional enough, players everyone knew like Miles and Bird and Dizzy; I was also trying to educate myself about the new generation, expand my repertoire. Trying out new playlists was a welcome distraction. I selected one with a dozen names I'd barely heard of and queued it up.

The prep work done, I poured my morning glass of Scotch and set it under the bar. My first order of business, if I was going to help Francesca out, was to contact Mickey again, as little as that appealed.

Business was brisk enough through the lunch hour that I stopped thinking for a couple hours. The few people who asked about food resigned themselves to drinking their meal, and it wasn't until around twelve-thirty I had time to recognize the ache in my stomach as excitement and anticipation, spun with a small amount of dread. I was not ready to rest, to shelve my grief over Burton, until I understood how and why he died. I'd become a believer.

"Light dawns on fucking Marblehead," I heard Burton saying.

My stomach relaxed, though I reminded myself I knew fuck all about investigating anything. When Burton and I got involved in something, his case was already moving forward. He had a suspect or a piece of information. Francesca might be available for official questions. What I had to offer was more ambiguous, vague bits and thoughts to work with.

First, the car fire. Clearly, it was a message for me to back away from whatever I'd been doing. Or whatever the arsonist thought I'd been doing, since I hadn't collaborated with Mickey at all.

So the escalation to arson connected back to the mugging by the man in the Luchador mask. The way he'd used the endearment *cher*, which I'd heard before, poked at my memory. Burton had once known a New Orleans cop named Antoinette Bordaine, who punctuated her sentences that way. Except that she'd died at the hands of Frank Vinson, the Big Easy's counterpart to Mickey Barksdale.

There was also the counter-fact that Alistair Dain had tried to convince me to discourage Mickey's belief Burton had been murdered. Was he disloyal to his boss? Or so loyal he thought he knew better than Mickey? Could he have been behind the mugging, a ploy to discourage me?

If so, did that mean two different factions wanted the same thing? For Mickey to stop paying attention to how Burton had died?

Questions, questions, questions, and no answers at all. The brutal escalation of the car fire was an anomaly, a message that could have been delivered in a simpler way.

I worked my way toward closing time, smiling without meaning, keeping the music fresh, building the cocktails. What I needed was more than a hint of what was happening in Mickey's world, a clearer window into what had him off-balance. I didn't know yet how to find that, but at least I had a clear sense of what I needed to do. And maybe in the process, I could resolve for myself why I'd fought so hard against the notion Burton's death was not random.

25

The next morning, I realized from the unfamiliar clarity of my head that I had once again not drunk last night. I didn't know whether to congratulate myself or worry. After so many years of heavy drinking, a sudden drying out might have unexpected physical effects.

Burton once likened the process of investigating a murder as lurching from one detail to another until you found a connection that made sense. That was nothing more than him denigrating his own experience and expertise, but since I had no detecting skills of my own to draw on, I needed a starting point.

I considered the possibilities as I finished a bowl of granola. I didn't want to engage with Mickey again unless I had to. It was too dangerous, and he would continue to try and manage me, tell me what to do, who to talk to. I needed to be discreet about being seen with him anyway, if my meetings with him had been a provocation. More serious acts of violence could be heading my way.

Alistair Dain might be a good entry point, if I could find him without involving Mickey. He'd opposed Mickey's enlisting my help, but why? Those mysterious "negotiations" Mickey had alluded to? Were they the source of all this trouble?

Three or four hours until opening time was long enough to get a line on Dain. I took a chance on calling someone who should know enough about the gangster world to give me a hint about how to find Alistair Dain.

Ten minutes on hold had me gagging over a slurring string-sappy version of "Blackbird." No one asked who I was, and finally, they located Liam Macdonald. The cop's voice was wary.

"Macdonald."

"Elder Darrow."

"Mr. Darrow. I'm sorry. There's nothing I can share with you at this time."

He thought I was calling for an update on the fire.

"I know that."

"Then what can I do for you?"

"I'm trying to locate someone. An old friend of Burton's."

Macdonald vented his suspicions.

"I hope you're not gearing up one of your amateur investigations."

"Nothing like that. The two of them were in the bar a couple weeks before, and the friend left something behind. I think he might be known to the authorities. I'd just like to return his item."

"Someone involved in the car fire?"

Amazing how Susan's near-death had turned into a simple car fire. Distancing, I supposed, the way an oncologist talks about a pancreas instead of a patient.

"I don't think so. But he has connections to the criminal side of the world and I thought you might know him."

"You're not asking for help finding Mickey Barksdale, I'm sure."

"Alistair Dain."

"What's the item?" That was a swerve, but I was surprised he hadn't hung up already.

"Not your concern. But it's nothing illegal. All I need is a way to locate the man. Or contact him."

"I'm not Burton, Darrow. I don't want you thinking you can call me up for help every time you want to know something."

"It's a small favor. And then I'll let you get back to your work."

Which, at this point, was what? As far as Macdonald was concerned, Burton's case was closed. No one had died in the car fire.

What else did he have to occupy his time?

"Hold on. Let me see if anyone's heard of this guy."

I smiled. Either he wanted to pretend he didn't know who Dain was, or he wanted me to think he was working hard.

The line clicked as he cut off a syrupy version of "I Will Always Love You." Celine Dion had a lot to answer for.

"No address on file," he said when he returned. "One of the people here thinks he hangs out at a place called Noog's. On Stoley Street."

I nodded. There was a thread I could pull on. I questioned Macdonald's motive in telling me, but that could wait.

"Thank you, Detective. I'm sure Mr. Dain will be happy to get his copy of *War and Peace* back."

Macdonald disconnected, no doubt struck mute by the image of a gangster reading a Russian novel.

26

S toley Street in Charlestown is mostly residential, and like
many of the formerly marginal neighborhoods in the city
where the incomers had money and aspirations, was dragging
itself upscale. Out of the corner of my eye, I caught the upthrust
digit of the Bunker Hill Monument as I drove up and down the
adjoining streets, looking for a parking place. Mrs. Ward taught
us in the fourth grade that the Battle of Bunker Hill was fought
on Breed's Hill—more evidence you couldn't trust the history
books.

The pace at which Charlestown had gentrified amazed me.
Like most people who live in a city, I tended to stay in my own
neighborhood, shop at the same stores, walk the same streets every
day. My vision of Charlestown was mostly aging three-deckers
and scruffy bungalows, but the section I was in today was as clean
and prosperous-looking as the new South End.

I found a parking space a block over and squeezed my rented
Volvo into a space between a black Tesla and a Mini Cooper.

The map on my phone did not have an address for anything
called Noog's, but Stoley Street was a short block. I started walking
and in the middle of the stretch of sandblasted brick façades,
found a bay window that displayed tables and chairs. Plain gold
capital letters in the lower right corner of the window spelled out
NOOGIES. No apostrophe.

I mounted the brick stairs, which had been repointed recently, and stood before a blank steel door painted red, formidable enough for a bank vault. I twisted the old-fashioned doorbell knob warted in the middle and felt vibration in my fingers.

The door swung outward, forcing me to step to the side. A whippet of a man in a tight white T-shirt, khaki trousers, and black ballet flats glowered at me. He sported a red heart tattoo the size of a silver dollar on his left forearm and weighed about thirty pounds less than he should have for his six foot four. It might have been the shoes, but he made me think of Gene Kelly.

"This is a private club."

He pointed to a small brass sign screwed to the brick, to the right of the door.

"So it says. I'm trying to locate Alistair Dain. I was told I might find him here."

Gene Kelly's face looked bemused, as if I'd stumbled on a password I had no right knowing. I had to assume that if Dain did hang out here, NOOGIES was an establishment with a criminal clientele.

A hand reached over his shoulder and pulled him gently away from the door.

"I'll handle this, Donald."

Donald-not-Gene stepped back. Alistair Dain took his place in the doorway. His smile did not engage his eyes.

"Mr. Darrow. To what do we owe the pleasure?"

* * *

"What a terrible story. I heard about the fire, of course, but I'd thought it was an accident. How fortunate your lady friend escaped."

My bullshit detector was pegged in the red, and I did not like the casual reference to Susan. I still had no idea where she was.

"You came to my bar a couple of weeks ago and suggested I not encourage Mickey in thinking that Burton's death was anything but a random occurrence. I'd like to know why."

He nodded as if he'd anticipated the topic. Donald had served us coffee, after asking if I wanted a drink. I had refused.

NOOGIES was a combination bar and restaurant, though too small for more than ten or fifteen patrons at a time. The bar was the size of one you'd put in your man cave, but incredibly well stocked. I saw a bottle of Ley 925 Diamante tequila, the most expensive in the world, something I definitely couldn't afford to stock. The tables were laid with stiff white cloths and heavy cutlery.

"At the time, I hadn't realized Mr. Barksdale had sought you out." He fiddled with a bread knife, his lying smooth as butter. "I thought you might be soliciting his help for a project of your own, and I was concerned he was putting energy into a situation peripheral to a major ongoing effort of ours. Advice is part of my portfolio."

Something more important to Mickey than Burton's death? It had to do with the "negotiations."

"But you know now what Mickey was asking me to do. And that I turned him down flat?"

"I do."

"Someone else apparently doesn't."

He raised an eyebrow, a trick I always wished I could learn. My mother used to stop me in my tracks with it.

"Is that so."

"Couple of weeks back? I was mugged. Informed in words of one syllable I should stay away from Mickey and not encourage him in the idea that Burton's death was anything but random. Sounds exactly like what you wanted from me."

"No one from our side of the fence mugged you." His face darkened. "I would know."

"You can see why I wanted to ask you directly."

"Your hypothesis being the car fire was an escalation."

"Mickey and I talked right after the mugging. It might have looked like we were working together, that I hadn't taken the hint."

"Convoluted." Dain lay the bread knife down precisely where it had been. "Though I can see how you would arrive at the conclusion."

I wondered if I was imagining too complicated a solution, misinterpreting correlation for causation. But the fire had not been accidental, and I had no other hypothesis to try.

"You're telling me there's no connection, then? Between your request to me and the fire?"

I was, in effect, accusing him of lying. Dain crossed his arms and glared.

"Normally, Mr. Darrow, I would ask Donald to drop you on your head out in the street for insulting me in that fashion. I am only accommodating you because of your relationship with Mr. Barksdale. Please listen carefully.

"The reason I did not want Mr. Barksdale encouraged in his belief about Detective Burton's demise is that his power in the city is under challenge. We—his organization and me—are dealing with pressure from outside forces trying to infiltrate and steal the fruits of our long labor. It was imperative then, and still is, that Mr. Barksdale's attention not be diverted by minor issues. This is an existential situation."

His fervor made the story believable, at least to the extent he believed what he was saying.

"Understood. So who else might have the same goal? To obscure the fact that Burton was murdered? Or does someone want me to stay away from Mickey for some other reason, and that's just an excuse?"

Dain flipped a hand.

"Possibly someone killed the detective for their own reasons. I wouldn't know. All I do know is that neither I nor Mr. Barksdale is the source of your troubles."

"Oh, no. This has everything to do with Mickey. Just not in the way that's most obvious. Who are these competitors who are trying to muscle in?"

Dain spoke to the long lean shadow in the kitchen doorway.

"Mr. Spengler. Would you please escort Mr. Darrow to the street?"

Dain leaned in, close enough Donald wouldn't hear.

"A friendly warning. It would be neither intelligent nor healthy for you to return here. Good afternoon."

Not that friendly a warning, as NOOGIES' door lock snapped shut behind me. The day had warmed up, the humidity ten percent past the tolerable. As I walked around the block to my car, I turned over the little I'd learned, mainly that a power struggle was consuming Mickey's attention. The rest of it repeated what I knew, if in slightly more detail. I did believe Dain's denial of a connection to the fire—neither he nor Mickey had a good reason to target me.

I stopped on the sidewalk when I saw someone had graffitied my windshield—*Yuppies Go Home*. What, we were back in the Eighties?

The back window said *Eat the Rich*. I rubbed it with my finger: soap. I laughed and opened the tailgate, took out a rag and a bottle of washer fluid. Looked as if Charlestown was only halfway gentrified, which as a Boston native, I approved.

Sitting in the driver's seat with the AC blowing, I contemplated whether I had time for another move before opening the Esposito. The Gene Kelly lookalike—Donald Spengler?—prodded something in my memory, and the connection would irritate me until I figured it out.

Something dropped from the sky and exploded on my windshield, spraying red fluid all over the glass. I shied, thinking it was blood, then realized it was only food coloring and water. The remains of a balloon caught in my windshield wipers. I cut my wheels out of the parking space and escaped the neighborhood. Gentrification, indeed.

27

My belief Burton's death was deliberate was more satisfying than believing it had been random. And that seemed perverse. But as I unlocked the front door to the bar, I could hear him in my head, reminding me about everything I didn't have.

"Facts, Elder. Evidence. Guesses and intuition are bullshit without backup."

What I didn't understand was who wanted me not to talk to Mickey, and why. The assumption built into that was that, eventually, we would discover Burton had been murdered for a reason. I supposed it could be a head fake, someone trying to confuse the situation. I shook my head at my mental gyrations.

I flipped on the lights and set up some Grant Green to listen to, cut up the lemons and limes, and thought about what to do next. I was committed now to finding out what had happened, and the most surprising thing was that neither Dain nor Mickey scared me much anymore. It wasn't bravado so much as knowing we more or less wanted the same thing. Mickey wanted to know what happened to Burton, and Dain would accede to Mickey's wishes.

Dusting the liquor bottles, I found Syndi's sobriety coin on the back bar and realized I hadn't had a drink in several days. On impulse, I slipped it into my pocket, a way to honor her more than any commitment I was making.

The afternoon and evening were busy enough, but, I kept

seeing mental images of the car fire, Susan at the wheel, terrified. I imagined things I could not have seen, hair on fire, the rubber gasket on the windshield melting. At one point, I thought I smelled gasoline and the char of burning flesh and had to run to the toilet to vomit. Where had she gone? And why hadn't she let me know she was all right?

By around eleven, both my stomach and the business had settled down. I needed the truth of what happened to Burton, but I also wanted to find the person with a black enough heart to drag an innocent like Susan into this.

I was staring at the darkened stage where, in happier times, live musicians had played, and barely noticed when someone walked down the stairs until I heard Pedey Thomas, sitting at the bar, moan under his breath.

"Holy shit."

I looked up as Francesca stepped up to the bar.

"You look like someone ate your dog," she said.

She was a million-dollar vision in lemon-colored linen, a loose sleeveless shift that dropped only halfway down her long tanned legs. The material grazed her everywhere it needed to be to highlight the shape of her body. The glint of diamonds at her ear lobes reinforced my sense she was well-off, probably not living on her FBI salary.

"Side-boob," Pedey coughed into his hand.

I glared at him.

"Francesca."

She realized I didn't have the cop's thick skin, the layer that transmutes pain and horror into black humor.

"Sorry," she said. "I forget."

"Forget what?"

"Compartmentalizing—first thing a street cop learns. Never forget, never regret."

"Any news? On anything?"

"Believe it or not, I came by to see how you were holding up."

"I'm open." Or the bar was. "Has anyone heard from Susan?"

She shook her head.

"I'd worry more if you weren't open. If you were sitting back in your apartment marinating in Macallan."

My anger was unreasonable, but that didn't stop it from bubbling up. Susan had worried about me and look what that had gotten her.

"I'm fine."

"Uh-huh."

"Is the name Spengler familiar? Donald Spengler?" The Gene Kelly clone was still stuck in my brain.

"Can a girl get a drink in this place? A Sombrero, maybe?"

I caught her eying the glass of Scotch I'd poured myself the other day, sitting on the back bar. Which I hadn't touched. I moved down the bar to mix her drink.

The diamonds in her ears were matched by a good-sized stone on a chain that dipped down toward her cleavage. I couldn't remember seeing her flashing jewels before.

When I set the Sombrero in front of her, she was writing in a tiny blue Moleskine notebook.

"Ess, pee, ee?"

I nodded.

"In what context?"

If I got in too deep, it would help if she knew where I'd been. I recounted my visit to NOOGIES, the conversation with Dain, my recognition of the doorman.

"Jesus Christ." She took a sip to calm herself. "Don't do that."

"Do what?"

"Run around playing detective. It never got you into anything but trouble when you did it with Burton, did it?"

Not entirely true. She disappointed me. Maybe I'd been hoping for the same kind of connection with her I'd had with Burton.

"I'm already in the middle. Maybe I could act as a bridge between the gangsters and the cops. It can't hurt."

"No, no, no. It absolutely can hurt. Just because Mickey Barksdale hasn't snapped your neck yet? Don't be naïve."

Her resistance stiffened mine. I owed Burton this much.

"It's fine, Francesca. I'm not going to be stupid about it. And I will bring you anything I find out."

She sucked the rest of her drink in through the straw, making a clattering noise with the ice cubes. I'd never seen her so angry, which perplexed me. What was I missing?

"If something doesn't drag you down before that." She banged her glass on the bar top.

"Donald Spengler," I said. "When you find him, I'll be shocked if he doesn't have a record. And that he isn't connected to all this somehow."

28

Having made my decision, I slept deeply and dreamlessly. My body hadn't felt tired, but my brain must have needed a temporary shutdown. I was up and out of the apartment early Wednesday morning, and by the time I made it to the bar, the liquor distributor's truck was idling by the back door, blocking my space. I parked in the street out front.

A figure leaned on the wall by the front door, deep enough in the building's shadow that I could only make out dark jeans and a loose white shirt. I locked the Volvo and walked toward the door.

"Sorry. We don't open until eleven."

When I saw who it was, I stopped short and held up my hands. I hadn't seen the face behind the Luchador mask, but the bulk was familiar, and as soon as I heard his voice, I knew this was my mugger.

"No, no, *cher*. Don't you worry yourself. I have come to apologize to you."

The pain and embarrassment he'd caused rippled through me.

"Not wearing your mask today? You're brave enough to show your face now?"

He was taller than I remembered, but blocky. And older. He must have been sixty, his employer an equal opportunity type. His face was a set of starved angles under close-shorn hair.

"Shouldn't you be home collecting Social Security? You're blocking my door and I need to get to work."

His smile passed into a dark stare.

"I'm trying to apologize here, *cher*. It would be the Christian thing to do to let me say my piece. Then I can get out of your hair."

I slid the key into the lock and turned it.

"Inside. You have a name?" I pulled the door wide. "Something I can call you besides asshole?"

"Antoine. Everybody calls me Twan."

The name connected to something in the past, but I was damned if I knew what. I wondered if not drinking was bleeding away my brain power.

"House rule. No one drinks before eleven."

He chuckled, following me inside. Having him behind me made me jog down the stairs.

"You have a lot of rules for such a shithole bar."

I started to flare, but he was only trying to provoke me. I doubted an apology was the actual point of the visit, but the sooner I heard him out, the quicker he'd be gone.

"You have something to tell me? Besides you're sorry?" I pointed at a stool. "Have a seat."

I hustled to the back door and opened up for the delivery. The broad-shouldered young woman in a jumpsuit and a plaid flat cap tapped her clipboard impatiently.

"You know, you're not such a good customer I can afford to wait around," she said. "And Dutch wants a check in hand the next time before I deliver anything."

I nodded, still concentrated on Twan, and showed her where to pile the cartons of booze.

Out front, he'd had helped himself to a pour of Barbancourt.

"Don't see this in the bars too much." He held up the glass and admired the color. "You've been to Haiti?"

"Friends."

"It's good to have friends." He sipped and regarded me.

"You work for Mickey, then?"

He snickered, though he had been at the table of bros the day Dain and Mickey took over the Esposito.

"Not exactly. I see you remember our second meeting."

"You mentioned an apology. Was that it?"

"I did. Which also has to do with the fact I don't work for Mickey Barksdale. As you implied. It's more like an exchange program." He smirked. "Junior year abroad."

"You're from New Orleans."

"Born, bred, battered, and baptized." He seemed pleased I'd noticed.

"Which means you work for Frankie Vinson."

"Please. Those of us so honored as to work for him refer to the man as Mr. Vinson. Maybe Frank. But never Frankie."

I absorbed this wrinkle. The last time I'd heard about Mickey and Vinson in the same sentence, they were feuding. In fact, Mickey had almost killed him.

"So. The apology?"

He was here under orders, and they weren't Mickey's. He swallowed the rest of the rum and exhaled, reciting an apology a committee of politicians could have written.

"I would like to say I'm sorry if you felt threatened or were hurt by anything that transpired the other evening. It was nothing personal. I was operating under a set of instructions."

The non-apology apology, beloved of our time.

"Now why would Frank Vinson care what I think about anything?"

"Not my place to ask that kind of question. I do what I'm told."

"Like the Nazis, am I right?"

Quick as a snake, he reached across the bar to grab my shirt. The fact he was an old man made him scarier. It would be remarkable if the apology for a beating turned into another beating.

"Mind your mouth, Mr. Man. I'm not always under orders from someone else."

The liquor truck driver came out of the kitchen and pushed the clipboard at me, gazing at Twan hungrily.

"You want to check this in so I can get out of here? And remember, cash on delivery the next time."

I turned my back on Twan and walked out back to count the bottles. Once I signed the delivery slip, closed the back door, and walked out front again, Twan was gone. As was the rest of the bottle of Barbancourt.

29

If Frank Vinson were back in Boston, Mickey's troubles now had a logic. Several years back, Vinson tried to move in on Mickey, though more because of Vinson's infatuation with a Boston jazz singer named Evangeline than with any desire to expand his business. I hadn't had anything to do with that, though I had known Evangeline, paid her to perform at the Esposito, and, once, even slept with her.

My main memory of the whole thing was Burton's tale of one night in Maine, when Mickey bound and gagged Frank Vinson and handed Burton a pistol to kill him. Mickey was trying to convince Burton that Vinson was responsible for the death of Marina, Burton's lover at the time, and my cook.

The bar business petered off into nothingness by midnight. I had the place all cleaned up, the bar wiped down, the perishables stored, but even though no one was in the place, I withstood the urge to close early. I poured myself a drink. Two or three days without it made the Scotch taste spectacularly good.

The apology from Twan was an unlikely ploy, but I couldn't see what was driving it. Vinson wouldn't care about my feelings being hurt. Was it a sign that Vinson and Mickey's negotiations were progressing satisfactorily? And if so, that it wasn't productive to annoy someone Vinson thought was working with Mickey?

One AM shuffled in on very slow feet. I shut everything down, checked that the back door was locked, and shut off the lights. As

I climbed the stairs, without the distraction of work, I returned to thinking about Susan's mysterious absence, the future we might have had. I hoped, wherever she was, she was all right.

Tears burned my eyes as I locked the front door. Was that loss permanent? Could I do anything to make it right?

Two AM now. Boston was never a late-night town, the way New York was, and I was surprised, as I made the turn off Mercy Street, when a single headlight came on behind me.

I rolled down the window. The engine noise sounded like a motorcycle with a breathing problem. My heart started knocking and my hands froze on the wheel. Moving toward sobriety had slowed down my reflexes, clouded my thinking. My sense of self-preservation was duller than it had been.

The headlight jumped into my rearview, thirty yards back. The side street had no streetlights, but the vehicle used its signals to signify the right-hand turn as I made it, as if to mock me. I thought about jumping on the Expressway, but the Volvo wouldn't outrun what sounded like a big-engined bike.

Feeling like a mouse being chased through a maze, I followed my normal route to Comm Ave, lucking into a parking space two doors down from my building. I stayed in the car for a few extra seconds, the metal shell feeling protective. I grabbed the Ruger from under the seat. Twan had implied that the gangster crowd was not interested in me anymore, but that didn't mean everyone had gotten the message.

I rolled down the window. A dark sedan, one headlight dark, chugged up beside me, its windows wide open to the night. The engine needed a tune-up so badly its tappets clattered. I raised the pistol. Was this going to be a drive-by?

"Easy, chum. Got a couple questions for you." Liam Macdonald called across his front seat. "Got time for a chat?"

* * *

"I suppose you think that was funny, chasing me across town. If you wanted to talk, you could have come into the bar."

Macdonald ignored the Ruger I set on the counter, went straight for the recliner and sat down, pushing the button on the side that sent the seat back and elevated his feet. He looked like he was preparing to take a nap and he knew it was pissing me off.

"I would have. Except you were holding a meet with one of your gangster buddies."

"He's not my buddy." I let my irritation show. "Are you surveilling me?"

I wondered how much he knew about Frank Vinson and whatever negotiations were going on between him and Mickey. Macdonald was Homicide, not Organized Crime, and I doubted he'd shift his ass out of his own lane for anything less than a street war.

He didn't reply.

"You have questions for me?" I said. "That's why you're here?"

"Is it too much to expect a drink? You're not very hospitable." He shook his head. "Nah. I guess an alkie wouldn't keep it in the house."

There was Macallan under the sink, not that I was offering this asshole any.

"Not so much a question as a request," he said. "I need you to call the lovely Ms. Gatoberri off."

I couldn't have been more surprised if he propositioned me.

"Call her off what?"

He lowered the footrest and glowered at me.

"My ass. You know exactly what I'm talking about. The car fire thing? You went around me to get her involved. It's my case—I don't need anyone stirring the pot."

"No one got killed, did they? I thought you were Homicide."

"There may be a link to something else I'm working on."

"Sounds like an internal matter for the police department. I can't tell an FBI agent what she can and can't do."

"She's not a real murder cop. She works fraud cases, not murders. I'm trying to build a Homicide case the DA can try, not chase down truth, justice, and the American way."

"Liam. You're talking to the wrong man. I have no input into how Francesca spends her time."

Macdonald bolted to his feet, the first urgency he'd shown.

"You'd better be wrong about that, chum. Because there's only so many ways this can go. And none of them ends up with you looking good."

30

I knew if I went to bed now, I wouldn't get to sleep. And drinking another glass of Scotch wouldn't help. It was so long since I'd strung three or four sober days together I'd forgotten the pleasure of a clear head. On the other hand, withdrawal made my body achy and twisted, and that wouldn't help me sleep, either.

It was a positive development that Francesca challenged Macdonald. Burton had pegged the man as a lazy cop, especially when Macdonald tried to blame Marina's murder on Burton. The motive was supposedly that Burton was Marina's heir. Macdonald hadn't known Burton well enough to understand he was as likely to give away an inheritance as keep it. He cared little about money, unless it was who was paying for the drinks.

Money. I couldn't forget the pile my father had left me, grown to four and a half million dollars by now. I hadn't touched it since his death, a decade ago. If the Esposito hadn't survived on its own, I wasn't going to drop my inheritance in the pot to save it.

What I disliked was the sense things were acting on me, that I didn't understand all the forces grinding together. I wanted to take action, but I couldn't see yet what that meant.

I sat in the Queen Anne chair by the bay window and stared into the deserted darkness of Comm Ave. No answers there.

I woke up in the chair with a minor headache, which did not survive two cups of strong coffee and a hot-then-icy shower. As I walked down the stairs of my apartment building into the warm morning, I thought I might make it through the day. As long as the caffeine kept coming.

A green and cream Checker taxi, the black and white checkerboard stripe running the length of its flank, sat double-parked in front of my building, choking off this side of the avenue. It shone like the moon, its blocky frame hunched over spit-shined tires. Mickey must have branched out from restoring muscle cars. This would have taken a prime spot in a vintage car museum.

As I admired it, the rear door swung open. Mickey slid out of the black leather seats and onto the sidewalk, carrying an enormous arrangement of lilies and carnations and baby's breath. He pushed the bouquet into my hands.

"It's only right. I'm sorry for your loss."

It was a little late for these to be for Burton. Was he telling me something I didn't know, about Susan? Or were they for Syndi? The cheap cliché about being sorry uncoiled my rage. I was tempted to shove the flowers back in his face. Even if he hadn't driven all this death and destruction, his presence on earth was what made it possible.

The vase was slippery with water. I accepted it. Mickey looked subdued. Contrite? Guilty, even?

"OK, Mickey. Thank you. Very nice."

I didn't think I'd ever seen him wordless. I wondered what had impelled the gift of flowers. Was it supposed to be an apology?

We stood and looked at each other until a black BMW behind the cab laid on its horn. Mickey turned and leveled a look at the driver that would have shriveled his balls if he'd known who he was beeping at.

Or maybe he did know. The Bimmer cranked a U-turn and screeched off in the opposite direction.

Mickey's ice-blue eyes seemed to ask me for absolution. But for what offense? I was the wrong guy to exculpate him anyway—we didn't even live in the same parish.

"Very nice," I said. "Let me take them down to the bar."

He spun on a toe and climbed back into the cab. The massive vehicle glided off up the avenue into the morning. I was considerably more perplexed than I'd been when I started the day. What did the gesture mean?

31

Back when I first opened the Esposito, Mr. Giaccobi's Firenze Café was on Prince Street in the North End. Neighborhood politics forced him out about ten years ago, and now the coffee shop and bakery were at the corner of Mercy Street and Holbrook, a couple short blocks north of the bar.

The walls were papered with black-and-white photos of Sicily and Sardinia and travel posters from other parts of Europe, but the papers and drawings from his granddaughter's first-grade class had been taken down.

"Mr. Darrow."

Despite my asking, he never called me by my first name, but the old man's voice radiated pleasure at seeing me. I felt guilty I hadn't been in to see him sooner.

"Where have you been keeping yourself?"

He must have been deep into his eighties, his face brown and wrinkled as a walnut. He wore a short-sleeved plaid shirt in muted greens and grays, and a pair of black cotton pants belted high around his middle.

I set Mickey's flowers on the counter. I couldn't have them in the bar without being reminded of their significance; I'd decided they meant that Mickey was still expecting something out of me.

"For you."

"These were for your friend? Detective Burton? I read about that in the newspaper. Very sad. For you, especially. Yes? And for the city.

He was a defender."

That was the perfect word for Burton, defending the boundary between civilization and chaos, the demarcation that could make the city more livable for everyone. I shook away the deep thoughts.

"I thought you'd like them."

The bouquet added brighter color to the café. Giaccobi set them beside the ancient cash register, the bobbing Hello Kitty doll, and the crucifix. He liked to cover all the bases.

"They do smell fine, don't they? You can stay for a coffee?"

I sat at one of the small round metal tables, the stool padded with a circle of thick leather riveted to the seat. Instrumental music, mostly strings, flowed from dusty speakers up in the corners. It was music I would have hated in any other context.

"Of course."

Being in the presence of someone who didn't want anything from me, who was outside the complicated world I was paddling around in, made me feel calmer. My occasional coffee with Mr. Giaccobi did not constitute an intimate relationship, but it was familiar and helped me feel normal.

"Triple shot, please. And do you have the pignoli cookies?"

"Do I not? Or I have cannoli."

"Not before breakfast."

He grinned, dispensed ground coffee into the espresso machine's handle, and tamped it down. The coffee shop was deserted for a weekday morning, except for a middle-aged woman in a flowing black dress who nursed a cup of coffee in the corner. I nodded at her.

"She comes in every morning after the eight o'clock Mass. A widow." The old man set the cup and a small plate of nut-studded cookies in front of me. "May I sit with you?"

"Please." I was surprised and honored. "What happened to the children's corner?"

For a long time, Giaccobi dedicated considerable wall space to the first-grade class his granddaughter taught in East Boston.

Now that wall showed only sun-bleached squares.

Giaccobi made a spitting sound.

"Layoffs. This beautiful girl finds the thing in the world she loves to do, and then the school district decides to fire teachers. So they can hire more administrators. To heck with what the kids need."

"Ah, shoot. I am sorry. What's she going to do now?"

"She's doing a little baking for me. But we got along a lot better when we weren't together all the time."

I smiled. Giaccobi would be an exacting boss.

"But this is not your problem. How is that beautiful woman I saw you with the last time? You know it would do you good to marry someone like that."

And sadness crashed over me. Wherever Susan had run to after the car fire, she and I were clearly done. All over again. The old man saw my pain and laid a work-hardened hand over mine.

"She left you? Then she doesn't know what she's lost."

I swallowed a bitterness that had nothing to do with the espresso and changed the subject.

"Your granddaughter. Is she only a baker? Can she cook?"

Giaccobi frowned.

"You're looking for a cook again?"

I hadn't been, actively. But as crusty as Syndi could be, I missed having someone in the kitchen to talk to. And I needed to serve food if the bar was going to survive.

"I am."

"I will ask her if you want. I don't know what she wants right now. Or if she knows what she wants." He stood up as a young couple came in the front door. "Thank you for the flowers. I hope to see you more."

I picked up a pine nut with the tip of my finger and ate it, feeling I'd done one positive thing today.

"Always a pleasure to visit."

The old man bussed the table and limped back behind the counter. His frail walk made me wonder what would happen when he couldn't do this anymore. Or didn't want to.

32

I laid out a light supper for myself on the bar while the Esposito was still empty—Cabot cheddar, crackers, bread and butter pickles—and poured myself a couple ounces of Scotch, mostly to prove I wasn't trying too hard to quit. The landline rang.

"Esposito."

"You sound almost upbeat," Francesca said. "I wondered which Elder I was going to get today."

"I didn't know you had this number."

"It's not unlisted. Just hard to find. Are you decent?"

That was a stupid question. Especially since I was at work, not at home.

"Which I suppose means you're standing outside my bar."

"On the sidewalk. Good guess."

A garbage truck roared by. I heard it through the phone and my open door. Why were we playing games?

"Come in. There's no one here."

Francesca's looks made people like Liam Macdonald underestimate her, the common assumption someone that attractive couldn't also be smart. This afternoon, she dressed like one of the rich ladies at a Boston Polo Club tournament. She wore a lavender sundress that looked expensive, her hair was up, and she carried a broad-brimmed straw hat with a ribbon that matched the dress. Those gaudy diamond earrings glittered in the bar lights. I had to concentrate so as not to think lustful thoughts about my dead friend's woman.

She side-eyed my dinner.

"Big eater, huh?"

She picked a square of cheese off the plate. A large sapphire ring glinted.

"You have anything nonalcoholic to drink? I'm as dry as Arizona."

The chitchat was supposed to soften me up.

"Club soda?"

"You're not mixing that with your good whiskey, are you?"

"Or orange juice."

"Club soda it is." She sat sideways on a stool and crossed her long tanned legs.

"Is this about Susan? Did you locate her?"

"Is what about Susan?"

"Can we not play twenty questions? You're not here because I have the best club soda in Boston."

"No. It's not about Susan. No leads on that at all. Either me or Macdonald. Do you know where she is?"

"I don't."

"Well, I haven't given up on her. Not yet."

Though eventually, she would. And the BPD would. Or slough it off onto a cold case squad, updated once a year, or if a new bit of evidence surfaced. I would have been satisfied to know Susan was alive and safe.

"Then what?"

"Does the name Ricky Maldonado mean anything to you? Gangster type?"

"Never heard of him."

"Maybe you knew him as Icky Ricky?"

"Now there's a terrifying name for a gangster."

"Yeah, well. Did you know Burton kept notebooks? I couldn't believe it when I found them."

"Really."

I wouldn't have thought of him as that cerebral about his work. She picked at the ribbon on her hat.

"This guy Spengler you asked me to look into? Used to be a dog's body for Icky Ricky. Years ago now."

"So?"

"So Ricky was a low-level drug guy Mickey pushed out of town about ten years ago, when Mickey was consolidating the criminal classes. You were around for it then, according to Burton's notes. How much of it do you remember?"

"Not much. Native American guy involved. Tommy something? And Burton's case had to do with counterfeit pharmaceuticals."

I remembered more than I wanted to say to her. That was the year Alison Somers committed suicide, because of those same pharmaceuticals.

"If Spengler is back in town," she said. "Maldonado must be, too."

"He and Mickey would have to make up."

"Unknown. But this could be some of the pressure Mickey's feeling."

"Is any of this on Macdonald's radar?"

"He's checked out. Rumor is he's quitting the department."

A rage wave flushed through me. Burton had been an asshole at times, and a fickle friend. But he'd always done his job.

"So if Ricky's back in town, why? To sell drugs? Because you know Mickey doesn't."

"You said Mickey was complaining about some negotiations. Could Ricky be a threat to him?"

"No idea," I said. "He made it sound like all his businesses were in a fluid state."

I was about to tell her about Vinson and the New Orleans connection when she said something that froze me.

"I do have something new on Burton. And you may not like it."

I picked up the glass of Scotch.

"If you're about to tell me Burton was on the take, I'm going to throw you right out the back door."

"Nothing that sleazy. And not about his character."

"What?"

"I need to know you're not going to fly off the handle when I tell you."

"You came to tell me." I sank the whiskey in one warm lovely swallow. "Quit dancing."

"We've got a little more evidence Burton's death wasn't everything it looked like at the outset."

"Now there's evidence?"

"It's not cut and dried. To the point, people higher up the ladder are trying to ignore it."

"One of those people being Liam Macdonald." Who we knew loved keeping his desk clear, not complicating his life.

"I think it's worth looking into. But I've been told to stay in my own lane. Which is supposed to be the fire."

"And the gang connection to it? But that could mean Mickey." She rocked a hand back and forth.

"Maybe, maybe not."

"Evidence of what?"

"It's technical. Which is why people are trying to wave it off. But you already heard about it."

"What. Is. It."

"Bullet trajectory analysis. You know what that is?"

Another cop who thought everyone else was stupid.

"No. But I can infer from the big words."

"The shots that struck Burton…"

"Multiple?"

"Four shots. Three came from a different angle than the other one."

"What other one?"

"One shot went straight past his shoulder, grazing him. While he was standing up. But the shots that killed him were fired from an acute downward angle."

"As if he were on the ground?" The whiskey soured in my stomach. "From the same gun?"

"The same gun."

My chest felt choked.

"And Liam Macdonald doesn't think this is worth following up."

"The forensics weren't definitive until yesterday. But yeah. For him, this is a closed case: dead perpetrator, easy solution. Done and dusted."

"Even though it was a cop."

"Even though. Macdonald wasn't Burton's biggest fan. As you know."

"Still. His bosses are letting him half-ass it?"

"I can only press so much, Elder. To them, I'm the outsider who got dumped in their middle."

"What if I go in and talk to Macdonald's boss? What's his name? Martines?"

"Fuck no. Not unless you want to screw me over. They'll know it was me who told you about the forensics."

Which was how Mickey had known, his inside source. Could that be Macdonald?

"Can the car fire be connected to Burton's murder?"

"I don't see how."

"But if you could link the fire to Burton, they might let you investigate?"

Time for a fuller disclosure.

"Right after Burton died," I said. "Mickey Barksdale came to me with the idea Burton had been murdered. I blew it off as him being paranoid."

"Why in the world would he come to you?"

"Because he knew I was Burton's friend. Mickey wanted me to look into it for him."

"Why?"

"He thought I knew some of Burton's connections on the cops. That I might be able to find out things he couldn't."

"Why would Barksdale care whether Burton was murdered?"

"Mickey thought it was a message to him. A threat." Here's where I was wading in the muck. "He thought Burton was his friend. Plus his power in the city is under some kind of pressure. Someone encroaching on his turf."

"Mickey and Burton were friends?" She frowned.

"Only in Mickey's tiny little mind."

She stared into the bar mirror, parsing it.

"So someone challenging Mickey took Burton out as a warning, thinking they were friends? It was a hit? And set up the car fire, because they thought you were working with him?"

"You just said the forensics support that."

"I have to think about this. Maybe take it to Macdonald."

"Keep me out of it. For the same reason you didn't want me going to Martines."

"What?"

"Exposure. I don't want Mickey knowing I'm talking to the cops. I'm pretty sure he has someone on the inside."

"Except that was what he wanted you to do. Talk to the cops."

"Not about his business."

She adjusted the hat on her head.

"It's germane. I'll have to pass it along."

"And the connection to the fire?"

"A weak one. I don't see it yet. But I'll keep it in mind."

I watched her hips sway up the stairs, not confident any of this would change the official findings on Burton. I was still going to poke around, make sure the evidence didn't get buried. And unlike in the past, Burton wasn't around to help me.

135

33

The next morning brought me no new revelations, no certainty, no hint of how to proceed. Mickey had tolerated Ricky Maldonado, an obese and foul-mouthed gangster with a small piece of the pill business, mainly because Mickey didn't sell drugs himself. Ricky had owned a luncheonette on Brookline Ave until his operation fell apart and he had to flee to Miami Beach.

He'd left because Burton and I were investigating the death of Alison Somers, a young jazz singer who'd been on the verge of a spectacular career in New York when she committed suicide. I hadn't thought of her in a long time, but her name still caused me a pang.

I made coffee and sat at the bar with the *Globe* for a while, distracted by that and by what Francesca had said yesterday and what I could reasonably do about it.

Because I needed to act. No one on the Boston Police was listening to her, maybe because she was a woman, but certainly because she was FBI. And Liam Macdonald had apparently quit on Burton's case weeks ago. Macdonald would need his face rubbed in new evidence before he'd accept it.

Mindful of Alistair Dain's caution not to come back to NOOGIES, I scrabbled through the receipts in the register drawer and found the card he'd left two weeks ago. It bore a 617 number, imprinted in black. If you couldn't remember whose it was, I guessed, you didn't need it.

Voice mail demanded I say my piece. I left a message saying I needed to talk to Mickey. I didn't care anymore if I was causing trouble. Things needed unsticking.

I climbed the steel stairs at eleven to unlock the street door and saw a young woman walking down Mercy Street in the direction of the bar. She raised a hand when she saw me and I waited in the doorway. Long gone, fortunately, were the days when I had half a dozen derelict day drinkers waiting for me to open.

She was thirty or thirty-five, with frizzy red hair barely contained in a ponytail. Five-six, maybe one-thirty, she had the tapered torso of a swimmer, wide shoulders, slim waist, and a confident way of moving, as if she were comfortable in her body. She wore new chef's whites and orange clogs. Her eyes were a startling gray-blue, the hue of wet granite.

"Mr. Darrow?"

She stuck her hand out with the certainty of someone who believed in the proprieties.

"I'm Alicia. Renzi?"

I frowned. She was dressed to work in a kitchen. I hadn't called the staffing company.

She smiled.

"I'm betting Grampy never mentioned my actual name. I'm Tony Giaccobi's granddaughter."

"Of course. Come on in."

She chattered as we descended the stairs.

"I took a chance on coming by. I didn't know if you needed someone right away, but I'm going out of my gourd working with Grampy. I love him to death, but he is a very particular old man. He does everything the way he's done it forever."

She ran out of words as we reached the bottom and she looked around.

"Oh, what a neat place! Is that Miles Davis?"

She walked over to my gallery of black and white photos, all the jazz greats. My cynical side wondered how much research she'd done beforehand, but her enthusiasm didn't seem faked.

"You're a jazz fan?"

She held her thumb and forefinger an inch apart.

"My parents used to listen to it all the time."

Her parents. Jesus.

"Used to?"

"They moved to Florida. My dad got tired of shoveling snow. It's all country music for them now. Grampy said you were looking for a cook."

Right to business, though I would have a hard time thinking of Mr. Giaccobi as anyone but Grampy from now on.

"Have you worked in a kitchen before?"

"If I can wrangle thirty-five first graders through their milk and graham crackers, I'm pretty sure I can handle it."

"Do you know how to cook? And have you ever cooked in a restaurant? Or a bar?"

"Try me out. You don't have to pay me."

Her jaw firmed. If she'd played a sport in college, it was probably soccer, favoring endurance and persistence as much as speed and skills. It was hard to argue with her offer.

I counted two hundred dollars out of the till and handed it to her.

"I don't believe in unpaid internships. The ones where you're supposed to be grateful for the experience? This pays you for today and tonight."

"It's too much."

I liked her already.

"The kitchen is through there. Get familiar with what we have. We won't do anything more complicated than sandwiches and fries today. Salads, if there are any greens. Make me a list of what needs restocking."

Her eyes teared up. I wondered if I was making a mistake. This bar didn't need more emotional wrecks. But it read as gratitude.

She tucked the bills into the pocket of her chef's pants.

"Thank you, Mr. Darrow. I'll show you what I can do."

"Elder." I thought about her parents as jazz fans, that older generation. "Call me Elder."

* * *

I was pleased to be able to say that, yes, lunch was available, even if the selection was only two kinds of sandwiches and French fries. Supply chain issues, I offered people with a wink. It was an all-purpose excuse these days.

I didn't have time to check up on Alicia, but the plates kept showing up on the pass-through in a reasonable time, so I figured she was managing.

The rush—minor, but steady—ended around one-thirty, and I walked into the back to ask her to make me a sandwich. Tendrils of the wiry red hair had escaped the ponytail—I'd forgotten to tell her to wear a hairnet—and three fingers on her left hand were decorated with bandages. The formerly pristine chef's jacket was smeared with colors where she'd wiped her hands.

She caught me staring at her fingers.

"Your knives are really sharp."

That had been a point of pride for Syndi.

"They have to be. You OK otherwise?"

She blew hair off her face.

"Kind of fun, actually. Don't know how long that lasts."

"Come out front and take a breather once you clean up. It'll be quiet until dinner time."

"Does that mean I'm hired?"

"For now."

Fifteen minutes later, she appeared, carrying two plates, each with a chicken salad sandwich on whole wheat, chips, and a pickle.

"Was it OK I made one for myself?"

"Of course." Who knew how well she would manage a bigger menu, but she'd done all right with lunch. I took a bite of the sandwich. My appetite was stronger these days, now that I took in fewer of my calories from Scotch.

We ate in silence, listening to a compilation of guitar music: Bill Frisell, Grant Green, Wes Montgomery. Without the all-day drinkers, whose presence I didn't miss, the bar tended to clear out around two and stay deserted until five after five, when the first homeward-bound commuters popped in to fortify themselves.

So when the upstairs door opened, I was surprised. And when the man walking down the stairs appeared, I stiffened.

"In the back." I pushed my plate over to Alicia. "Please."

"What? I'm not done eating."

"Take it in the kitchen."

I did not want Mickey to see Alicia, to know I had already replaced his daughter in my kitchen.

34

I'd instigated the meeting, but despite the fact I feared him less, I wasn't all that comfortable around Mickey, especially in his current state. He looked as if he'd been up all night.

"This had better be important, bartender. I didn't think we were going to be talking every day. You're lucky I happened to be over this way—I can't drop everything and come by when you call."

And yet here he was. I had a knot in my stomach. The people who didn't want me talking to Mickey were going to get much more aggravated if they were watching.

"You need to hear what I found out."

He groaned as he mounted a stool.

"You keep any uppers back there? No-Doz? Any wakey pills?"

I was shocked. His hatred of drugs was well-known, at least somewhat because of Syndi's addiction. Burton used to joke that Mickey wouldn't take an aspirin if he thought he was having a heart attack.

"No. Sorry."

"Give me one of those White Russians, then. Or something else with milk in it."

I skipped the joke about the Dude abiding and made the drink.

He sipped it and grimaced, as if his stomach was fighting him.

"So. The fuck is on your tiny mind?"

"You were right all along, Mickey. Burton wasn't an accident, some random robbery."

He sipped his drink, without making the face this time.

"You found something new?"

I repeated the story Francesca told me, that the forensics report conflicted with the idea Burton's killing was random, that the rumor he'd heard about the angle of the bullets was true.

"So Burton was on the floor when he was shot?"

"Three bullets to the chest, after the thief was dead, and down on the floor himself."

Mickey frowned, as if he couldn't see it.

"In the sequence, Michael. Burton wouldn't have been shooting if the robber hadn't shot first. The robber died with one shot. Someone else shot the second set of bullets."

"Pretty wild. Where did you find this out?"

I wasn't going to give him Francesca.

"Doing what you asked me to do. Asking questions. Talking to people."

"Sounds like bullshit. Those reports can be faked, you know."

"What? All of a sudden you don't believe he was murdered?"

"I didn't say that. But I've been looking into it myself." He pinned me with an ugly sneer. "Since you told me you couldn't be bothered. And I don't think there's anything to it."

"To Burton being killed for a reason? That there was a contract on him?"

The change of attitude whiplashed me.

"No one in Boston had a contract out on Burton. I would have known. The whole thing had to be an accident. He was in the wrong place at the wrong time."

"That's not the song you were singing a couple of weeks ago."

Mickey drained the glass.

"Well, I know more now than I did then. My advice is to drop this. Now. Accept it was a terrible accident and move on. No one was out to get him. Or me."

The turnaround astonished me. He pointed a stubby finger.

"And I don't want to hear about you trying to float this anywhere else. Leave well enough alone."

He turned and started for the stairs.

Alicia had come out of the kitchen at the sound of our raised voices, carrying a wooden potato masher. I flashed back to the day Syndi emerged from the same kitchen, ready to defend me with a knife.

She watched Mickey climb the stairs.

"Do you know who that asshole is? 'Cause I do." She smacked the head of the masher into her palm, as if ready to take someone on. "What the hell kind of bar are you running here, Elder?"

The upstairs door clicked shut. She set her weapon on the bar.

"Question stands," she said. "I know him. So what kind of bar is this? Are you a criminal?"

"How do you know who that was?"

"Mr. Darrow. My grandfather has run a coffee shop in the city of Boston for sixty-some years. And most of it in the North End. He's met a gangster or two, and he knows pretty much everything and everyone. If he doesn't, he knows someone who does."

I fumbled for an explanation that wouldn't scare her off.

"Mickey Barksdale was connected to—a source of information for—a friend of mine who was a Boston cop."

Her eyes narrowed.

"Burton. I know."

"How?"

"Grampy."

Mr. Giaccobi had educated his granddaughter about more than the coffee shop business.

"Then you know Burton was killed not long ago. Walked in on a robbery at a liquor store."

"Grampy said the two of you were close," she said. "I'm sorry for your loss."

143

The cliché sounded more heartfelt than when it came from Mickey's mouth.

"Mickey was convinced Burton was killed on purpose, as a message to him."

"And he was coming to you for answers?"

I didn't blame her for being skeptical. There was no simple way to summarize the relationship Mickey had with Burton, and now with me.

"But that's the last you'll see of him in here. This is not his regular hangout."

In fact, if Mickey truly had changed his mind about Burton's death, I didn't expect to see him in here again.

She squinted at me.

"If you're running some kind of illegal operation out of the back room, better tell me now, before I get to like my job too much. I plan to go back to teaching, and a felony conviction isn't going to look good on my permanent record card."

"Mickey and I are done with each other. All I want to do is run this bar. I'm as innocent as your grandfather."

She smirked.

"That's not as high a bar as you think it is. How well do you think you know him?"

She picked up the masher and walked back into the kitchen to prep for the dinner rush.

I stuck my head into the pass-through.

"Let's be sure the kitchen's stocked. Weekend's coming up."

She held up a spiral-bound notebook she'd been writing in. Her face was serious, as if she were still evaluating my honesty.

"Right here."

I poured myself a short Scotch and drank it without thinking, wincing as it met the chicken sandwich.

Mickey's turnaround perplexed me, especially in the face of Francesca confirming the forensics issue. I doubted anyone would fake something like that—too many people would have to collude. Maybe Alistair Dain had finally convinced Mickey of Dain's view of the murder.

Or was Frank Vinson pulling Mickey's strings? Twan had come to see me on Vinson's behalf. The negotiations Mickey was talking about—did they have something to do with Vinson? Were they working together? Or not?

I dismissed Ricky Maldonado as a player. He'd been a minor hood the last time he was in Boston, and long gone when Vinson made his first attempt to unseat Mickey. He'd self-exiled to Miami after his pill-dealing operation blew up, literally. But one of his old cohorts, Spengler, was working with Dain now, which implied Ricky had thrown in with Mickey.

The possibilities made my head hurt. What was clear was that I couldn't count on Mickey for any help finding out what happened. In fact, I could end up confronting him. But that bothered me less than the fact Burton's murder might go unpunished.

A pair of thirty-something males, expensive suits and handmade shoes, clattered down the stairs. I checked the clock: 4:55. They'd ducked out of the office a little early. I put on my ready-to-serve face and hoped I'd stay busy enough for the next few hours to let the back of my brain chew over what to do next.

As Grant Green's *Iron City* rambled along in the background, slick as silk, one of my new customers raised his hand and ordered a very dry gin martini. I rolled my eyes at the new cocktail generation, who apparently didn't know what a martini comprised.

35

The next morning, I wondered if what I planned to do was a good idea. I hadn't been to the scene where Burton lost his life, and though I'd never been with him at the beginning of a case, wasn't the first step always to visit the scene of the crime?

Leon's Liquor Barn was a one-story square concrete block structure in the exact center of a parking lot in Revere, just off 1A. It looked like a military blockhouse, the surrounding brush and trees all scraped away as if to give its occupants a clear field of fire. The whitewashed exterior walls were grimy from car exhaust and other forms of pollution. The front windows were obscured by lottery signs and advertising posters for various tipples and cigarettes. The left-hand window also boasted a neon sign flashing **Bu we ser** in acid green letters. The vertical steel bars only added to the welcoming feeling.

A Nineties Nissan Altima, faded red with a New Hampshire-shaped patch of Bondo on the left rear fender, nestled up next to the windowless side entrance. The glass door at the front opened with a rheumatic wheeze when I stepped on the rubber pad. My stomach felt like I'd swallowed a brick.

The man on the raised dais with the cash register, a Black man in his fifties with a shaved head and a thin chinstrap beard, barely looked up from the newspaper he was annotating in ballpoint pen. The typeface looked like the Daily Racing Form, though I was surprised it was still in print. The clerk's stool gave him the highest vantage in the store.

I walked deeper into the store. The hard liquor was on the farthest aisle in, opposite a wall of coolers holding scores of beer brands, hard seltzer, and a selection of the kind of wines that had to be very cold if you were going to drink them.

I followed the dark green and white linoleum squares to the whiskey section, looking for a good reason to be frequenting a liquor store at nine o'clock on a Saturday morning. But the fanciest Scotch on the shelves was Haig and Haig Pinch, a blend known more for its distinctive bottle shape than the taste or bouquet of the whiskey within.

I turned back to the register and waited until the clerk deigned to look down at me. He was a blobby character, in a Hawaiian shirt with Boston sports logos all over it, straining at the buttons. His arms bore dark purplish bruises as if he bumped into things a lot.

"Yeah."

His face was puffy, custom-matched to his body. I tried not to look at his teeth.

"You carry any single malts?"

I was standing close to the exact spot where Burton died, and I felt an irrational certainty that lightning could strike twice, that a robber would come in through the glass door and shoot me.

"Single what?" He frowned, as if I were speaking Urdu.

"Single malt. Whiskey. As in Scotch."

He was yanking my chain, but either for the exercise or because he knew who I was.

"You Leon?" I said.

"Who the fuck wants to know?"

"Your customer service attitude is so pleasant, I thought I would compliment your boss."

The wisecrack irked him.

"This is my store. Which means I don't have to serve assholes."

He pointed to a small metal sign that read "Persecutors Will

Be Violated." Either he had a subtle sense of humor or he hadn't read the sign carefully before hanging it up. I would have bet on the latter.

"What I'm trying to do here, Leon? Is buy a decent bottle of Scotch."

He sighed.

"Wooden cabinet at the far end of the row. Next to the peppermint schnapps. Give me your credit card."

I handed him the black AMEX I never used and accepted in return a key on a coiled lanyard. Leon was developing a sheen of sweat on his naked scalp, though it was cold enough in the store to pop your nipples.

Which might not mean I was making him nervous. Maybe he was a junkie. Or a pill head. Or even a drunk.

I turned the key in the lock of the coffin-sized cabinet and opened the door to see shelves of bottles, high-end brands like Johnny Walker Blue and Don Julio tequila. I saw a Benriach malt I'd never heard of and pulled it out. Something to add to my collection.

I carried the key and the bottle back to Leon, who'd watched me the entire time in the big round shoplifting mirror. I tossed him the key, set the bottle on the counter more carefully. He frowned like he couldn't believe someone would buy it.

"Where the hell did you get all that Pappy Van Winkle?" I said. "Stuff is like gold."

Leon ran my credit card and pushed it back over the counter without replying. I decided to push.

"Heard you had a robbery last month. I own a bar over in the South End. I know what a pain in the ass that kind of thing can be."

The flickering look told me he did know who I was. Which begged the question—why?

"Then you know people try not to think about it afterward. Or talk about it."

His graying teeth showed in a smile and he reached under the counter, exactly where I would have kept a gun or a billy.

"You need anything else?"

I locked eyes with him. Yeah, he knew who I was. And a sense of guilt was making him sweat like a horse.

"How about a paper bag, Leon? Would that be too much to ask?"

36

I couldn't decide if the trip to Leon's told me more than I already knew, except that he knew I was a friend of Burton's and that my presence made him nervous. It did help me visualize how things would have happened. The other three shots could have come from the dais behind the cash register or from someone standing over Burton lying on the floor. I didn't like Leon's attitude. Could he have been the triggerman? I'd learned from Burton that dangerous people didn't always look tough.

The USPS truck was parked next to a hydrant, several car lengths from the entrance to the Esposito. I didn't remember ever seeing mail delivery down here—the little I received, I picked up at the U-Pack-It place around the corner where I rented a box. It was unusual to have a delivery to my door.

As I unlocked the bar, the mail carrier, a sixty-ish woman with short gray hair tipped in purple, bounded from the front seat of the truck. She wore the regulation shirt and shorts and a bone fishhook pendant on a cord around her neck.

"Elder Darrow?"

I nodded. She handed me a sheaf of thin white windowed envelopes banded together with a grimy elastic, then extended the electronic tablet.

"Signature, please."

I fumbled with my keys and the envelopes, set the bottle down on the sidewalk, and scrawled my name with my fingertip. She disappeared so fast she must have been on a time clock. I picked everything up and walked inside.

Dropping the mail and the whiskey on the bar, I turned on some Yellowjackets for background music and headed for the kitchen to fire up the grill and fryer. Coming back to the routines made me feel as if there might be such a thing as normal for the Esposito. Last night's dinner, even with the limited menu, had cleaned out our supplies, and Alicia had only added one more bandage to her fingers' collection. It eased my mind to be operating at full strength again. Now all I had to do was worry about the city recalling laid-off teachers.

I tucked the bottle of Benriach under the bar. At that price, it wasn't an everyday drink. I'd save it on the long odds I ever had anything to celebrate.

As I set up the bar, I wondered again about Leon. Liquor stores were popular targets for robbery, and no doubt he had been armed. But all the shots into Burton's body had come from the robber's gun. Who, being a junkie, would have been far less cool-headed than your average gunman. So I could buy the first half of the story, Burton walking in and trying to stop the robbery, the one shot that wounded Burton, Burton's kill shot to the thief.

But in the only other gunfight I'd been in, chaos prevailed. And chaos mitigated against the chances of the junkie, assuming he hadn't died immediately, putting three more shots into Burton's chest. From above. Could Leon have come around and shot Burton, using the dead junkie's gun? Sure, but why? No reason, unless there was a contract.

And why hadn't Macdonald looked at that more closely? Could he be Mickey's source inside the department? And loyal enough to Mickey to soft-pedal a cop murder?

Alicia showed up around ten-thirty, carrying two bulging tote bags. Celery tops stuck out of one of them, onions, tomatoes, a half dozen baguettes.

"The cupboard was bare. I made a gazpacho last night out of what was left. And I went to the farmer's market this morning and got stuff for Caprese."

"I don't even know what that is."

"And some salad greens. We're going to do this, let's do it with real food."

More evidence hiring her was a smart move.

"How much did you spend? I'll write you a check."

She looked relieved, reminding me she probably didn't have a lot of money. When she told me, I whistled.

"Farmer's market, huh?"

"It's good quality."

"Thanks for thinking ahead. There's a delivery this afternoon that'll fill in the staples."

As she unpacked the bags in the kitchen, I was about as near to contentment as I got. The Esposito was back on track and running smoothly, which was critical if I was going to put energy into the rest of my worries.

Morning prep finished, I walked back into the kitchen and found Alicia halving cherry tomatoes and arranging them on a sheet pan. She splashed them with olive oil and slid the pan into the oven, then pulled a plastic container of bocconcini out of the fridge and started to cut them in two. A big bunch of basil sat next to the cutting board.

"Nice idea, the caprese. A definite upgrade."

She nodded at the compliment, intent on what she was doing. Her knife work was more competent and the bandages from yesterday had been replaced with bright-colored strips with cartoon characters.

I handed her a hairnet.

"Forgot about this. In case the health inspector comes in."

"As soon as I finish. And wash my hands. And Elder?" She said my first name as if trying it out. "Could you write me that check today? I need to pay my rent tomorrow."

"Sure. No problem."

I stepped back down to the office and sat, pulling the big blue checkbook out of the desk drawer. I was down to the last two checks and went to unlock the filing cabinet where I kept the spares. Then I realized what I'd seen.

The last nine stubs in the checkbook were blank. I never wrote a check without recording what it was for and how much. If you didn't keep up with the recordkeeping, it overwhelmed you. Someone had ripped three pages of blank checks out of the book.

"Shit." I sat back in the chair. Now I had a better idea of what those official-looking envelopes were.

I slit them open with a paring knife and piled the paper on the bar. Each of the nine flimsy tissues announced a check drawn against the Esposito's working account that had bounced.

I used the calculator on my phone to total up the loss, just under twenty thousand dollars. I kept a thousand-dollar balance in the account and had the bank sweep anything more out at the end of each day. The first phony check had cleaned out the account and each one after that bounced like a Superball.

I pinched the bridge of my nose against an oncoming headache. Who? How? And why?

"Goddamn it."

Access to my office was easy enough, if you were behind the bar. And I didn't lock the desk. Had this been Syndi? Stealing from me to finance her heroin habit?

I shook my head. Unless she was dealing, which her father would have known about and stopped, the amounts were too high. That much cash would have kept a houseful of dopers high for a month. And unless my sense of her was way off, she'd liked me, and the job, too much to screw us over. Still... she had been a junkie.

The notices included photocopies of the checks, all of which were dated the same day and made out to innocuous names: Adam Jones, Peter Christian. They'd been cashed at different branches, all out in the suburbs: Sudbury, Lincoln, Concord, branches I'd never been in person. This was a far more sophisticated grift than someone kiting a couple of checks to feed her drug habit.

Alicia stuck her head out front. She'd heard me curse.

"You OK?" She tucked an errant coil of ginger hair under the hairnet, then took in the flimsies on the bar top. "Uh-oh. Are those what they look like?"

"Indeed."

It couldn't have been her—the date on the checks was a week or more before she'd come to work.

"You know, you don't have to write me that check today. I can get by for a while."

I shook my head.

"We are not going under. I'll take care of this right now."

"No, really. It's OK."

"I said it's taken care of."

She held up her hands and retreated into the kitchen. I could apologize later. Then I did the thing I swore I'd never do and called my investment company to transfer money into the business checking account and cover the shortfall. It was a tiny percentage of my inheritance, but violating the principle annoyed me. I closed the old account, opened a new one, and convinced the nearest branch to have someone drop off a new checkbook. A fifty thousand dollar deposit bought respect from your banker.

No one had touched the petty cash box at least. I took out bills to repay Alicia.

"This makes us square on the produce. And don't worry. Your paycheck's not going to bounce."

"You're sure? I don't want to be the reason you have to shut the doors."

She was only half-joking.

"We're good. Now all I have to do is figure out who pulled this off."

Because I suspected when it had happened: the day after my monumental drunk, when I came in to find Alistair Dain behind the taps and Mickey making sandwiches. Mickey wouldn't have bothered with such a small-time move, but Dain might have. And there had been a table of assorted thugs yukking it up. It could have been any one of them.

I pushed at the memory. Besides Twan, who had been there? Was Donald Spengler among them? And were there others of Vinson's minions than Twan?

My relationship with Mickey was too volatile for me to ask, but I couldn't say why someone from Vinson's crew or Mickey's would want to bankrupt me. Maybe one of his underlings thought it would pressure me to stay away from Mickey. But if they thought they'd deterred me, they'd miscalculated.

I scrolled through my phone for Francesca's number.

She didn't answer. I left a message: call me please, here at the bar. Maybe she could help make sense of it.

I gathered up the paper evidence of the embezzlement and paper-clipped the pages together. I was tempted to burn them in the sink, but instead, locked them in the office with the worthless old checks. Who knew if I might need them later?

37

Early Saturday afternoons were never busy, especially in late summer. Sometimes a softball team dropped in before or after a game, but today not a soul showed, even for lunch. Which of course made me worry. The high point of the day was the bank courier dropping off my new checks in a glossy black leather cover, which I assumed was a gift from a banker who wished to see more of my money.

I wished I had a book. When I was drinking hard, I didn't have the attention span for even a long magazine article, but I'd taken literature courses in my first year at Harvard, before they tossed me out. Today I had an odd old urge to browse a bookstore and see what people were reading.

My attitude toward the music was fiddly, too. I tried four different playlists without finding one that didn't make my teeth hurt. So I stood inert behind the bar in silence, listening to the hum of the air conditioning and the sounds of Alicia working in the kitchen.

I was restless enough to consider how much longer I wanted to run the Esposito. I'd bought the place as an act of self-preservation, thinking the work of turning a dive bar into a nightclub, as well as being around alcohol, might mitigate the heavy drinking that threatened to kill me. Some days it worked and some days it didn't, but the bar was starting to feel like a burden. Was there a better life? For someone with enough money who didn't have to work, I wasn't living very large.

Even a fresh pour of Macallan didn't settle me. And what made me think I could do anything about Burton's murder, even if I learned who was responsible? I was a drunk and a bartender, and that was what I had to give to the world.

Alicia interrupted my self-examination with a cup of cold soup.

"Tell me what you think. I didn't want to put too much garlic in it."

I dipped the spoon and tasted. It was delicious.

"Don't change a thing."

"Grampy told me everything that's been going on. After your friend got shot. Then the fire. Your girlfriend?"

"She's missing, not dead." The last thing I wanted to discuss.

"He said your last cook died, too. That's a lot of people dying around you."

"Unless you're shooting heroin, you won't have to worry."

"Just… if you need someone to talk to? To bounce ideas off of? Because you're looking into what happened, right? Grampy said it's what you and Burton used to do."

"Hardly." I needed to keep her insulated. "He pulled me into one or two of his cases, usually because I knew someone who was involved. You know what a small city this is."

"I'm not trying to stick my nose in." She picked up the empty cup and spoon. "But I was very good at counseling first graders."

I whipped my head up. She grinned.

"Joke, Elder. Joke."

And she sashayed back into the kitchen.

38

It hadn't occurred to me that people out in the community like Mr. Giaccobi had any sense of what Burton and I had been doing. None of those cases generated any publicity, and if they had, Burton's bosses would have hogged it. I appreciated Alicia's offer, but I did not need to worry about her, too.

When the upstairs door opened, I was torn between being glad for a customer and missing the silence. Harder to think in the presence of other people.

An entourage of three clomped down the stairs in a single line. The man in the middle was obviously the important one. He stood around five seven, and though he wasn't naturally slim, he looked like someone who'd recently lost a lot of weight. The skin around his jowls was loose and his eyes were piggy, deep set over his cheeks. He wore a big gold signet ring and a tight black polo shirt, as if to highlight his torso. The white trousers were cinched tight at the waist and hugged his legs all the way down.

The trio stopped in a line about eight feet from the bar, out of my reach. The Bossman looked around at the walls.

"I like it. I can't believe I was never in here before, but I've heard good things."

The two bodyguards were standard issue: young, bulky, and glowering. The one to my left had intricate art-house sleeve tattoos, up and down both arms. The other one slumped his shoulders, regarding me with the indifference of a cat. He worried me more.

"You may have noticed this is a bar. What can I offer you? Something to drink? Some lunch?"

The boss stepped forward from between his bookends.

"I used to have a lunch spot in town. Over on Brookline Ave? Maybe you heard of it. Ricky's, it was called?"

I shook my head, though now I knew who I was talking to.

"Name is Richard." He stepped closer and extended a hand. "Richard Maldonado."

I guessed it wouldn't be prudent to call him Icky Ricky. I had to wonder why he was here.

"What can I get you gentlemen?"

Perpetuating the fiction they were here to sample the Esposito's hospitality.

Ricky hoisted himself onto a stool, but when the bodyguards started to do the same, he waved them away. They backed off, the tattooed one frowning, and took up identical cross-armed stances.

"I could murder a nice cold beer," Ricky said. "You have anything light?"

"Light as in color? Or in calories?"

His eyes deadened as if he thought I was jerking him around.

"Light as in Miller Lite."

"How about Amstel? From a bottle?"

"Fine. Open it in front of me." The foreplay was making him impatient.

I popped the cap and half-filled a pilsner glass.

"I don't get the sense you're here for the conviviality."

He sipped the beer, a pinkie extended daintily.

"You would be correct. I didn't want to come down on you, all dark and scary."

Dark, maybe.

"I appreciate that. I'm here. You're here. What do you have to say?"

The signet on his right hand showed the beaver of the MIT

class ring, what graduates called the brass rat. I wondered who he'd stolen it from.

"I also knew a friend of yours a little. Dan Burton?"

I was ready for that, but not what he said next.

"You need to understand that what happened to him was in no way accidental."

"And you know this how?"

He looked at me as if I were mentally challenged. He would have called it retarded.

"There'd been a contract out on him for a solid month before someone picked it up. But the requirement was for it to look accidental."

"Liquor store robbery's not really an accident."

"People have been disciplined."

"Why tell me this?"

He peered at me over the top of the glass.

"Because you seem like the kind of person who sticks up for your friends."

Someone was giving me approval to stay involved? But who? I thought Ricky was on Mickey's team, but Mickey himself had warned me off investigating.

"I appreciate your saying so. I'm sure his brothers and sisters on the force will figure it out."

Ricky snorted.

"Eventually, maybe. All I'm saying is, if you decide to do anything about it, you can count on a certain degree of support."

The approval was now explicit—I shut up.

Ricky nodded and dismounted the stool.

"I know it's a lot to take in. We wanted to make sure you heard some encouraging words."

He lifted his chin to the twin bruisers, and they turned for the stairs. As he passed the photo of Miles Davis, Ricky backhanded it, shattering the glass with his ring.

"I do hate that National Geographic music, though."
He looked back over his shoulder to see my reaction.
"We will talk again, Mr. Darrow. Soon."

39

Francesca called me back as I was thinking I might have to close up and go find her. She needed to hear what Icky Ricky had told me.

"What's the big noise?" She sounded harried, as if she had more important things to do. Until I told her about Ricky verifying there'd been a contract out on Burton.

"I'll be there in ten." She cut the line dead.

As she settled on the other side of the bar, she looked exhausted.

"You doing double shifts? You look beat." But still gorgeous.

"Don't ever say that to a woman, Elder. Especially this one."

Frustration pulled lines at the corner of her mouth.

"You're not getting anywhere?"

"Not on the fire. The arson guys are drowning me in techno-crap: char patterns, branch freezing, fuel residue in all the wrong places. I know the fucking car burned. I need to know why and who, not how."

Her lack of progress didn't lighten my mood, but it wasn't why I'd called her.

"This Maldonado character," I said. "Is he a real gangster? Or a wannabe?"

"Icky Ricky. You have to wonder how he earned that moniker."

"You want a drink?"

"You have any decent coffee? Not the swill you serve the rubes?"

"Wait one."

Alicia was chopping onions, a pair of ski goggles over her eyes. I started to smile. She pointed the knife at me.

"Don't laugh. It works."

I set up the one-cup coffeemaker, ran a K-cup through it, and carried the mug out. Francesca grabbed it as if her hands were cold.

"Cream and sugar?"

"As it comes." She inhaled the steam. "So the question is, why take out a hit on Burton at this particular moment in time? He's been here all along."

"Maldonado didn't give me any more than that. Could he be lying? Trying to muck things up?"

"The two of them crossed paths, in the past. You remember the Alison Somers thing Burton wrote about in his notebooks?"

I dragged the ball and chain of that memory out of the attic. A crooked psychiatrist schemed to pass off low-dosage pharmaceuticals manufactured offshore for full-strength ones. Alison and I had been lovers, but her antidepressants were too weak to keep her from suicide.

"Long time ago. I knew Alison, but I only got involved when Burton arrested the doctor."

"Well, here's the rest of the story. And you wouldn't believe the horny old-timers I had to interview to get it. At that time, Mickey was trying to pull all the criminal elements in the city together. Fragments of different businesses floating around, which was why a little fish like Ricky could push his pills."

"I remember that much. My cook at the time was dating one of his dealers."

"Ricky never had much of an organization. A couple of street pushers, and two guys who provided protection. A meth-head named Tesar and a low-IQ thug named Donald Spengler."

"Spengler's with Mickey now." I told her about running into him at NOOGIES.

"Which means Ricky is probably partnered with Mickey."

"Junior partner, if anything. Didn't he tuck his tail and run for Miami after the pill thing blew up?"

"He came back about six weeks ago. And when he left Boston, Ricky was a fat little man with a greasy spoon on Brookline Ave. Nowhere near enough juice to partner up with someone like Mickey."

"So something changed. I was surprised Mickey didn't kill him back then. He's always hated drugs. Maybe Mickey wasn't that strong. So what changed?"

"Not sure. But it sounds like he's involved."

"Except his story is the exact opposite of the one Mickey's tried to tell me. Ricky said it was definitely a hit."

"He didn't say who funded it?" she said.

"Nope. And he didn't seem to know he was contradicting Mickey. Or maybe he didn't care. By the way, if he was fat before, he's lost a ton of weight. And he looks like he works out."

She slid a black and white photograph across the bar. The man with his hand on the doorknob of the Rexall drug store was the shape of an egg, his head a smaller egg on top.

"He does not look like that now."

She shook her head. "Hard to believe Mickey has a weight requirement. Or a dress code."

"Here's a bigger question. Will Macdonald do anything if you bring him what Ricky told me?"

"With no more evidence than that? I doubt it. No one's going to put any stock in hearsay from a gangster. Especially a minor player like Icky Ricky."

It must have been tiring trying to push Liam Macdonald into working.

"He'd have to look into it, though. Right?"

She rubbed her face, the tiredness evident. Maybe she was mourning Burton still—grief came in waves, unexpectedly, neither predictable nor measurable.

"This is starting to feel a little bit over my head. I came from the fraud squad, remember? Art theft, stock scams. Very little violence, money motives exclusively. I'm not sure how well I'm handling this."

"What do we do with this, Francesca? We need to get this information into the Burton investigation."

"Maybe…"

"What?"

"Macdonald is useless. If I bring this to him, he waves his hands at me and tells me the case is closed. But maybe we could take it to his boss."

"Martines? And what's this 'we'?"

"You come in as a concerned citizen, he has to listen to what you have to say. Liam could blow you off."

I didn't love it, but if it kicked things forward…

"OK. I'll do it. Can you set it up?"

"I will. Thanks. Maybe this will get them moving."

I reached across the bar and took her hand.

"We will figure this out."

She wiped at her eyes with the back of her other hand.

"I know."

Alicia picked that moment to walk out of the kitchen.

"Elder. This beef that just came in is…"

Whatever was wrong with the beef, she stopped short at the sight of me holding Francesca's hand, spun on her toe, and returned to the kitchen.

"What the hell was that?" Francesca said.

"No idea." I shook my head. "Martines, right? Let me know where and when."

She nodded.

"Thanks for taking this on. I needed to feel like I wasn't the only one working."

I watched her walk up the stairs, wondering idly what ants had spoiled Alicia's picnic.

40

Out in the kitchen, Alicia pounded chicken breasts flat with vicious strokes of an aluminum mallet. If we'd known each other better, I might have read it as jealousy. That was ridiculous, if only because of the age difference.

"Everything all right? What was it about the beef?"

She whacked the chicken one last time, splitting the plastic wrap she'd laid over it and splattering the cutting board.

"Nothing critical. They're selling it as Choice, but it's only Select."

"You seem aggravated."

"Awful lot of crooks and cops hanging around this place, Elder. I guess I thought working here would be more like…"

"Like what? *Cheers*? I can't afford to curate my customers, Alicia. I like the way you're working out, but if my clientele is a problem for you…"

She donned an unconvincing smile and dredged the chicken pieces through a pan of seasoned flour.

"It's fine," she said, in a tone that meant anything but. "I'll get used to it. Or I won't."

* * *

Her worries about my clientele didn't get better that day. Alistair Dain walked down into the bar around four-thirty, in advance of the cocktail hour. He'd replaced the seersucker suit with a pale green—call it mint—linen, though this was a miracle linen that did not show wrinkles. His bow tie was a royal purple that shouldn't have worked with the suit but did. The man himself was still pale as milk. He crooked a finger from the bottom of the stairs.

"Mr. Barksdale would like a word."

The bar was empty, but that didn't compel me to obey a gangster's whim.

"Then Mr. Barksdale is going to have to haul his ass down the stairs. I'm trying to run a business here."

Unexpectedly, Dain tried to soft-sell me.

"Understood. But he would be grateful if you'd come outside to speak with him. I know you can appreciate what a positive thing it is to have Mr. Barksdale's gratitude. And you will understand why he can't come in."

Dain's beseeching manner was unusual, not the king proposing and the subjects disposing. It could be a setup. Maybe Mickey heard I was still looking into things and decided to take me off the board. Though that would only attract police attention and not help his cause.

"He can't do the stairs?"

"He'd rather not."

"Wait one."

Dain's face showed gratitude, in itself remarkable. I ducked into the back.

"Going to step out for a minute. But I'll be right outside the front door."

Still irked, she waved a butcher's knife at me.

Out front, I untied my apron.

"What's it about, Ali?"

"Not my place to say." He sounded bitter, as if he'd been left out.

The loading zone in front of the bar held the green and cream Checker cab Mickey had been driving the last time we met. I opened the front passenger's door and realized he wasn't behind the wheel today.

"Climb in," he growled from the back seat.

I slid onto the black leather seat and closed the door.

"Sandy. Screw." The driver, a feral-looking Indian man in a ball cap, slid out onto the street and shut his door.

Alistair Dain took up a sentinel position outside, at the right front flank of the cab. I had the sense he was waiting for something. But what?

I turned and laid my arm across the top of the front seat. The cab's interior smelled like leather polish and cigarette smoke.

"What happened to you?"

Mickey sat sideways on the broad rear seat, almost small in the expanse of pristine leather. A bright white cast enveloped his right foot to halfway up the shin.

"Not important. I need your help."

My neck hairs rose. Here we were again, him telling me what I was going to do. And any help he wanted was likely to be illegal, immoral, or both.

"What in the world could I do for you you can't do for yourself?"

He shifted his hips and winced. The crutches propped against the door clattered. He looked less scary than normal, but wounded animals bite that much harder.

"Your bar."

"My bar? The Esposito? You want me to give you my bar?"

He shook his head, pulled a pack of cigarettes out of the pocket of his denim shirt. I cranked down the window.

"Sell me, not give. I'm not trying to steal it from you."

With the implication he could, if he wanted to.

"It's not for sale, Michael." I already knew what he wanted a cash business for. It wasn't that long ago he'd tried to turn a culinary arts school into a money laundry, with a violent lack of success.

"It would be temporary." He was pleading, or as close as a

sociopath could manage. "Month or two at the outside. And you'd still be running it."

If Alicia was worried about my clientele now, I could imagine how she'd feel about working for the city's biggest gangster.

"Not going to happen, Michael. Sorry about that."

I wondered what the stick that came with this rotten carrot would be. Mickey had to know he was asking the impossible. To the extent I had one, the Esposito was my foundation.

The beggar's façade fell away like a snakeskin shed.

"You do understand I could do you good in this city, Darrow? Whatever you need. You want to own a chain of bars someday?"

I couldn't imagine anything I wanted that he could give me. I had my business, money in the bank. He couldn't do anything about my love life. My only problems were not knowing what happened to Susan and the truth of why Burton died.

"Such as?"

"Such as finding out who tried to barbecue your girlfriend. You care enough about her to know who that was?"

My vision went red. I grabbed the dashboard to keep myself from climbing back over the seat.

Mickey blew smoke, satisfied he'd found a lever.

"If you know something about that?" I spoke past the tightness in my jaw. "You ought to be talking to the police."

He flicked the butt past my ear and out the open window. Dain crushed it with his toe, picked it up, and put it in his pocket. Protecting Mickey from his own DNA, no doubt.

"I didn't say I knew who did it. But I could twist some arms, and so forth."

The "so forth" worried me. I didn't trust the little bastard as far as he could limp, but why would he want to own the Esposito? And for such a short time, though I didn't put much stock in that promise. Collaborating with him was jumping rope with a live wire, but if he could get answers? To the fire and where Susan was?

I thought of something else that might give me leverage.

"I do have a problem you could help me with. Other than the one you mentioned."

His intensity eased, as if I'd agreed to his request and we were now just negotiating the terms.

"What's that, bartender?"

"Someone—probably someone you know—kited a bunch of my checks. Maybe twenty grand worth. Think you can find out anything about that?"

His torso stiffened and he winced again.

"You saying I stole from you?"

I never believed he'd stolen the checks, and his reaction said he hadn't known about the theft. He seemed almost insulted, though Burton warned me many times that Mickey was a mood chameleon. What you saw was rarely what you got.

"I wasn't accusing you personally."

"I was a good friend to Burton." Here came his buddy delusion again. "I can extend the same hand to you, if you'll just take it."

"It probably happened the day you and your crew took over the bar."

He took out the pack of smokes again but didn't light up.

"I hate to think this because she was my daughter. But Synthia? She had an expensive habit."

"Not unless she could manifest from the beyond. It happened after she... left us."

He looked perplexed. If it was one of his guys and he didn't know it, the theft was a serious breach of discipline. You didn't take on a project without cluing in the boss. Mickey would also be pissed he hadn't gotten a share of the proceeds.

"I'll look into it."

I didn't expect to see my money again, but maybe this would divert him from his fantasy of owning my bar.

"How'd you hurt your foot?"

The question elicited an angry snort. He slid a Lucky out of the pack, tamped it against his fingernail, and lit it with a disposable lighter. Two long inhales and exhales preceded the answer. But injury was enough of a sore spot not to give a straight answer.

"Playing pickleball. What do you think?" He smoked some more. "We have anything else to talk about? If not…"

Suddenly he was eager to have me out of his cab. Because I'd asked about the cast?

"I don't know, Mickey. You called me out here. Did you get what you needed?"

Knowing he hadn't, if it was an agreement to sell the Esposito. I didn't believe for an instant the hand of friendship he extended was sincere, but I was less and less concerned about what he might do. He was vulnerable, to something or someone, and his power in the city was waning.

He flapped a hand at me, the emperor dismissing a serf. As if that were a signal, Dain pulled open the cab door.

I didn't want to leave him with a shred of illusion.

"Even if you find out who stole my money, Michael? This is my fucking bar. I built it up from a bucket of blood, and if I ever decide to sell it, you better believe it will not be to you."

I slid across the front seat and out the door. Was that a smile on Dain's ferret face? All the tensions and passions flying around were a mystery to me, ignorant armies clashing in Mickey's world.

"Darrow."

One last word from the reigning chief of the Boston underworld? Was his status in jeopardy? I stuck my head back inside.

"Mickey."

"I will find whoever stole your money." He inspected the burning end of his cigarette, a movie gesture, then butted it out on the leather upholstery. The stink of burning hide overrode the tobacco smoke. "And then you will have a serious decision to make. About the Esposito."

The certainty in his threat chilled me more than the words. Even weak, he was not without tools to hurt me.

"I make my own decisions."

"Whatever." He pointed the cigarette at Dain. "Ali, shut the damn door. We're done talking here."

Dain obeyed. He and I straightened up and he spoke to me quietly, as if he didn't want Mickey to hear.

"If I were you, I'd find a way to get clear of all this. There is a great deal of uncertainty in the man's world right now."

Which fit with my notion Mickey's star was falling.

"Your world, Alistair. I'm happy in mine."

His maimed ear turned red, his temper signaling. I started for the Esposito's door, more shaken than I wanted to show.

41

The next morning, Francesca was waiting on the sidewalk outside my building. I hadn't had time for coffee or breakfast, and I was trying to decide whether to go to Mr. Giaccobi's or Tootie's for some morning sustenance.

She was sitting on the fender of a dark blue Ford so aggressively plain it couldn't be anything but an unmarked unit. Her jeans were torn at the knees and the tight silky long-sleeved T-shirt matched the color of the vehicle. Oval cut sapphire earrings, large ones, completed the color coordination. I felt an unsolicited jolt of desire.

"Good," she said, not smiling. "Let's go."

"What's the big hurry? I need coffee."

She shook her head and slid her butt down off the car, her kneecaps winking through the rips in the denim.

"You can have some at the precinct. I got you in to see Martines. He's giving us half an hour, starting in…" She checked a diamond-encrusted watch. "Ten minutes."

Francesca called it an interrogation room, but it resembled the conference room at a scrappy startup: angular plastic contemporary furniture, a widescreen monitor mounted up in one corner, a whiteboard. The beige carpet was clean and smelled new. Oddly, there was also a shelf of plush toys and board games. I'd been conditioned by reading mysteries to think of an interrogation room as stinking of fear, sweat, and regret, but this room was as offensive as a hotel business center.

The coffee at D-4 was better than I remembered from visits with Burton. I was halfway down one cup and thinking about asking for another when the door to the room opened.

"Mr. Darrow? I'm Dennis Martines."

The man wore uniform blue, the assorted pins and patches telling a story about his career I couldn't read. He held out his hand as Francesca closed the door. He was medium height, pale-skinned, with thinning gray hair. If it hadn't been for the surname, I would have guessed he was Irish.

"I understand you have some information you think could be helpful."

I locked eyes with Francesca. Her neutral look said she wasn't about to jump in.

"You probably know Dan Burton and I were friends."

Martines bowed his head.

"I do. And I'm very sorry for your loss, of course. You can be sure we're doing everything we can to tie up the loose ends."

The pallid cliché irked me, as always.

"Really? Because it was my understanding you've closed the case. That you're assuming the robber fired all the shots that killed him."

Martines shot a look at Francesca that was easy to read: what the hell have you gotten me into here? Burton always described Martines to me as a corporate cop, more concerned with his place in the political hierarchy than committed to actual police work. He wasn't unique in that.

"I'm unable to speak to the specifics of an investigation." Smooth and mannered. "I'm sure you can appreciate that."

"Is what I said true, though?"

"As I said…"

"Spare me the grease job. I know not everyone loved Burton, but I'd have thought the brotherhood of blue would take better care of its own."

174

Martines pushed back his chair.

"If that was all I could help you with?" His hard glare at Francesca promised retribution.

"Hold on." I muffled my anger. "I wouldn't have come here if I didn't have evidence. There's a gangland connection to it."

Martines lifted an eyebrow.

"I don't know what Agent Gatoberri has been telling you. But this division does homicide. Not organized crime."

That was the problem. The police siloed itself: Burglary here, Gangs over there. Murder elsewhere. It made communication across the boundaries harder, maybe even nonexistent if you got a lazy or indifferent cop. Like Liam Macdonald, say.

"Even if one slops over into the other? Mickey's Barksdale's power base is under pressure from other forces, outside the state."

"Commonwealth." He corrected me, self-identifying as a pedant.

"And I'm pretty sure that triggered Burton's murder."

"You have evidence to support that?"

Mickey had someone on the inside here. Could it be Martines?

"What about the forensics? The angle of the kill shots being different?"

Martines whipped his head around to glare at Francesca. I jumped in.

"She didn't tell me. It's all over the street."

"You're saying Burton's death was a hit. Who told you that?"

I noted that he still wasn't calling it a murder. And I hesitated. The name of my source wouldn't impress him.

"A man named Maldonado. Intimate of Mickey Barksdale."

Martines hooted. Francesca cringed.

"Icky Ricky? He'd tell you green was gold if he thought it would do him any good."

"Who better to know than someone on the inside?"

"The man is not known for his, uh, probity. And he's not as

much on the inside as you might think. I wouldn't believe him if he looked at his watch and told me the time."

I had a card left, a weak one, which I played reluctantly.

"Liam Macdonald never liked Burton."

Stemming partially from the time Burton broke his nose. Martines put his hands on the arms of the chair, his knuckles white.

"No. Friend of a victim or not, you do not come in here and disparage my detectives."

Francesca sunk into her chair. I stared at Martines, letting the accusation stand.

"All right," I said. "I've done what I thought I should do."

Martines's mouth worked.

"I have to say I'm surprised you're paying so much attention to this, Darrow. When your girlfriend has disappeared? Your relationship with Burton was more important than that?"

The red wave threatened to drown me. I gripped my knees to keep from reaching across the table. He stood up.

"Agent Gatoberri. With me." He looked down his narrow nose. "Thank you for your input, Mr. Darrow. We always appreciate citizen involvement."

That was the last lie told in that room that day, at least while I was present.

42

Standing on Harrison Street, I wondered if Francesca remembered she was my ride. Humidity was piled up under the low black clouds and sweat slicked the back of my neck and under my arms. A pair of motorcycle cops exited the station, gave me a hard look, then mounted their bikes and blatted off, exhaust farting like bulls.

I was about to call a Lyft when Francesca stalked out the front door and down the stairs, her face a portrait in frustration. She passed me, walking in the direction of the lot where she'd parked the unmarked, not waiting for me to catch up.

"Well, that didn't go any better than I thought it would," I said as we climbed into the blue slickback.

"I'm not surprised. Martines is a big fan of Liam's. He dots his I's, crosses his T's, and files all his reports on time. And Dennis doesn't ever want to hear something that complicates his worldview. Especially if it means reopening a case."

As we exited the police lot, she left a streak of rubber on the street, ramming the shifter through its changes in a way that boded ill for the transmission.

"I appreciate your trying to make it happen." I braced myself against the dashboard.

"Yeah, well." The car bucked to a halt in front of the bar on Mercy Street. "And you can count it as a giant black mark on my career if this gets back to my bosses. Relations between us and the

177

locals are bad enough. Martines warned me off of Burton's case explicitly just now, in vivid terms."

Was his intransigence the default for a cop who worried about his place in the hierarchy, or was Martines hiding something?

"We're no further behind than we were."

"No. You aren't."

I took her message from the pronoun change.

"The reason they brought me on specifically to look at the car fire? Their chief chemist is in Hazelden, drying out. They wanted my expertise in chemistry, solvents, all of that. From testing paintings. Not for me to investigate anything else."

"So they don't want you to think for yourself?"

"I have to focus on what the Bureau pays me to do, and what BPD wants."

"You're saying you can't help out anymore."

"Not on Burton. I don't have an excuse. And if I do, I'm going to get yanked back across town to Maple Street."

The main FBI office in Chelsea.

"So you're quitting?"

She banged her fist on the steering wheel. The horn bleated.

"I loved that man. He could be a flaming asshole and he was stubborn as a rock. But I can't see that forensic story as anything but proof of an execution."

I was relieved she wasn't quitting, no matter what she couldn't do. She was my only partner in this.

"I'm not sure where we go from here," I said. "Any time Burton dragged me into something, I was support staff. He called the plays."

"But you have something going for you Macdonald doesn't."

"What's that?"

"Your connection with Mickey B. You can talk to him without getting your ass kicked. He'll talk back?"

"He has in the past. Doesn't mean he will."

"I'd work that as much as you could. If something is rocking his world, he might be looking for help."

Mickey had seemed tentative when we talked, less sure of himself than usual. Then there was the ankle, his pickleball injury. Maybe someone had broken it for him?

"Possibly." I still smarted from Martines's parting shot. "You think Martines was right about Susan? I should be more worried about her? I assumed she got frightened off. She has a history of running away."

"If she isn't going to talk to you, what can you do?"

"Burton's murder is the stone in the arch," I said. "We knock that out, the walls fall down."

"I think you're right. You knew Burton as well as anyone. There's always hope I can track what's going on on the sly."

"I did love Susan. I do."

"Maybe too much information?"

"I'm not saying this well," I said. "Both things are important. It's one ball of yarn. But I can't talk to Susan if she won't talk to me." I was tired of being passive. "Where to next?"

"Press on. As long as I stay focused on the car fire, I'll stay out of trouble. If nothing else, maybe I'll hear gossip if anything changes. And if you come up with something from Mickey, maybe I can act on it."

"Press on? What the hell does that mean?"

"Jesus, Elder, I don't know." Frustration made her whine. "There's nothing you can think of to probe him with? Open up a conversation? Would Mickey have put out the contract himself?"

I was already talking to him about the stolen checks. Could I leverage that?

"He'd have no reason to. He was always talking about what great pals he and Burton were."

I stared through the windshield. Alicia walked up the sidewalk, swinging a canvas bag.

"I have to get to work."

She stopped me with a hand on my arm.

"I'm still with you on this. I just can't be as obvious about it."

"I get it. And I do appreciate what you're doing. We will talk."

I climbed out of the car to meet Alicia and unlock the Esposito. Francesca chirped the tires of the unmarked away from the curb.

Alicia didn't say anything, but maybe she wasn't a morning person. At the bottom of the stairs, as I reached for the light switch, a voice rough as rock salt came out of the darkness.

"Leave those off for now, pal. Will you?"

43

Behind me on the stairs, Alicia gasped.

"Go into the kitchen," I said. "I'll handle this."

Though I wasn't sure who or what I was handling. Alistair Dain had been right about the Esposito's security, though, if people came and went at will.

She hustled into the kitchen, her back stiff with disapproval. The lights back there lit up, bright and white, and reflected out front to show the two-top at the far end of the bar was occupied. One man only, which was a relief.

I stepped in behind the bar and plugged in the string of small white bulbs that rimmed the big mirror. That extra illumination showed a man at the table with a tall glass of beer in front of him. I moved to his end of the bar, keeping the counter between us.

"Served myself. I hope you don't mind." He hefted the glass in a mock toast. "The money is in the register. I wouldn't want you to think I was a thief."

"I'm going to assume you have a reason why I shouldn't call the police on you?"

The man slurped his beer the way you would if your lips were numb with Novocain. He wore an open-collared white silk shirt under a dark suit, and the reflection from the bulbs glinted off his bumpy shaved skull. His skin looked sallow, but that may have been the light. He laughed my question off.

"Call them if you like. But it won't get you what you want."

He drank deeply from the glass. "I'm going to begin with the assumption you don't know who I am, but feel free to interrupt me at any point. I will point out that I came here to speak to you alone. No bodyguards, no entourage." He pulled back the lapels of his short black windbreaker. "No weapons."

His accent, faintly French and something lazier, clued me in. My throat tightened.

"If I had to guess, I'd guess you were Vinson. Come all the way up to Boston from the Big Easy."

His lipless mouth puckered.

"I wouldn't expect a Northerner to understand, but those of us who live there never call our city that. And my name is Frank. Please."

The radio turned on in the kitchen. Alicia had decided she didn't want to hear what was going on. Wisely.

"Frank. I think I would have remembered if you and I had any business to discuss. Do we?"

I searched my memory for what I knew about him, all of it secondhand through Burton. One of Vinson's associates, Edward Dare, had been tasked with recruiting Frank's female companions. Frank preferred young women who wanted a musical career. He'd use his connections in New Orleans to help them, in exchange for their company as long as he desired it. Dare must have exhausted the New Orleans options, since he'd come to Boston several years ago to recruit. Evangeline Turner, a singer I'd known, had survived the experience, but at least one other young woman had not, committing suicide when she came home to Boston. Burton had caught that case, too.

"Well." Vinson deepened his drawl. "I'm considering this more an introduction. I plan to spend more time in the city than I have up to now. I think it's only polite when you move to a new place that you introduce yourself to your new neighbors. Let them get to know you."

My general feeling of Mickey under pressure coalesced into this specific threat. Vinson was moving in on Barksdale, either trying to depose him altogether or chipping off some of his business. Likely the latter—a direct assault would mean blood in the streets and neither of them wanted the attention that would bring. Crime was a business. It ran best when it went smoothly and quietly.

Vinson read my thoughts.

"No. Nothing major's going on. I'm negotiating a partnership with your boss. I do know you're one of his familiars."

The slight upward lilt at the end of his sentence did not mean he was asking a question.

"Mickey is not my boss."

"As you know, there's always been a lacuna in Mr. Barksdale's operations."

He meant the drugs. Syndi, Mickey's only child, had been an addict since high school, so Mickey refused to sell drugs. That left a serious gap in his portfolio. But I had a strong memory of Burton telling me Vinson had killed Edward Dare for secretly funding a drug buy in New Orleans.

"I recall you were opposed to that trade also."

Vinson sipped his beer.

"The episode you refer to was a breakdown in lines of authority, not a business decision. And as a bar owner, you must understand that businesses grow and change or they die."

I wasn't going to argue capitalism with a gangster, but I'd never considered greed an ethical stance.

"And how does Mickey feel about this?"

Vinson coughed into his hand.

"We are coming to an agreement. But slowly. Change is always a challenge. But I'm confident we will reach equilibrium soon."

I surrendered to the impulse and poured myself a drink.

"I appreciate your coming by to introduce yourself, though I don't understand why, exactly. Since I don't work for Mickey."

"Oh, I understand you're not a part of his actual operations. But I'd like to offer you the opportunity to help me in a constructive way."

He raised a hand to forestall my protest.

"Nothing extralegal, you understand. Completely aboveboard."

"No. Just no."

"You're quick with the word, Mr. Darrow. Perhaps you should hear me out before you deny me."

I shook my head. It didn't stop his flow.

"I need a base of operations in the city, a place to meet with friends, have a beverage, listen to some music after an arduous day. I am quite a jazz fan, which you may not have known."

Pretty much the same pitch Mickey had given me, and just as believable.

"Not interested."

"I present this as an option, but it doesn't have to be voluntary. I will pay you a fair price for the Esposito. And if you would like to continue in your current role, I'd be happy to have you run the place." He nodded at the gallery of jazz photos. "I do approve the décor."

"As tempting as the offer is, I'm going to have to say no."

"Think about it." He picked up his glass and put it down without drinking. "Of course, when I don't achieve my goals, my disappointment can be acute. The people who work for me don't like to see me that way. They can react in quite a fiery manner."

He stared at me, making sure I heard the message. Before I could react, Alicia's voice sounded from the kitchen. She'd been eavesdropping, and the threat pushed her to acting.

"I'm calling the police."

Vinson stood up and zipped his windbreaker, in no hurry at all.

"I'm not a precipitous man, Mr. Darrow. Take a day or two to think about it. We will talk again."

And he slithered out through the kitchen, past Alicia's outraged squawk, heading, I assumed, for the emergency exit.

44

This was when I missed Burton the most, when there was a mass of conflicting and contradictory data and we could spin out the possibilities in a conversation. I'd always been a decent listener, a necessary talent for bartenders, and I used to listen to him spin out theories we could then discuss, shoot down, elaborate. A solution sometimes appeared that way, or at least a way forward.

But this strange desire of both Mickey and Frank Vinson to own a middling jazz bar in the South End made no sense. All I could think was it was a token in the conflict between the two gangsters. Because one of them wanted it, the other one did too. They were muscle-flexing over it, seeing who was stronger.

At least I had a better grasp of the stakes and the players. Vinson had come to Boston to take over the drug business in the city, either with Mickey's approval or not. Because Mickey had never organized it, that segment of the local crime scene would be diffuse, with many minor players, many territories. Vinson would collect the bits and pieces, organize them into a whole, and make it profit. On the other hand, Mickey would be paranoid about ceding any control in Boston, even over a business he didn't want. He wouldn't like the idea of anyone else with influence in his world.

None of it brought any clarity to what happened to Burton or Susan, other than the fact that when giants collide, other people get hurt.

I wasn't hearing any of the usual noises from the kitchen, the chopping, slicing, dicing. And the radio was off.

Alicia sat on a stool behind the sandwich board, her face in her hands. Her shoulders bobbed and soft sobs snuck out between her fingers, as if she were trying to hold them in.

"Ah, hell." I grabbed a box of tissues from the shelf by the door. "What's the matter?"

The inner rims of her eyes were red, her face the color of a fine linen handkerchief, as if fright had drained her color.

"I'm sorry." She hiccupped. "I just can't…"

"Don't worry about it." I wanted to hug her, reassure her it wasn't always like this, but I didn't know how she'd take it. "Talking to gangsters is not my favorite way to start the day, either."

Fresh tears. She covered her face again. I waited them out.

"I know it's scary. But this is not how this place usually is. It will pass."

"I can't do it, Elder. I'm a first-grade teacher, for fuck's sake. I can't work in a place where someone's running around trying to solve a murder and the cops and the gangsters keep coming and going. It's like a casting call for a bad movie."

She glared, daring me to contradict her. At least she'd stopped crying.

"Look, I'm sorry for the drama. This bar has a history. I have a history. All of it predates your coming to work here. I'm doing my best to stay out of it, but I can't keep other people from doing what they're doing."

She wiped her cheeks with a fistful of tissues.

"I love the cooking," she said. "The rest of the work. It's like I found something I didn't know I could be good at. But I don't think I can cope with the rest of it."

I was surprised by how much I did not want to lose her.

"I need you here, Alicia. I like what you bring, and you're good for business. I can't guarantee more weird things won't happen, but

I can try harder to stop them. I have friends on the police force. I don't like it any more than you do."

She shook her head, the springy red curls threatening to burst the hairnet.

"No, you don't like it. You love it. Anyone can see that."

It was more that I dealt with what showed up in front of me than that I enjoyed it, but I wasn't going to argue the point. If she wanted to leave, I couldn't make her change her mind. But truly, all I wanted was my bar, the jazz and the Scotch, and the pleasure of serving. And I wanted her here for that.

"I'm here to run the bar," I said. "The rest is noise. Stay. Please."

She raised her eyebrows. Was that pity in her look?

"Let me think about it. But no promises."

Asking if the lunch prep was ready would be pushing my luck. I nodded and headed back out front to the bar. Let things lie for now.

45

Having Frank Vinson insert himself into my life meant I didn't have a choice about being involved, in the short term at least. I was caught between him and Mickey, the Esposito a prize they were fighting over. Neither one gave a flying fuck about owning a bar—they coveted what the other one wanted.

And I was being acted on instead of acting again. Outside of the trip to Leon's Liquor Barn, which hadn't told me much except Leon was an asshole, I hadn't taken many steps on my own. All I had at the moment was a dim sense that Burton's murder and Susan's disappearance could be part of the same power struggle.

I finished setting up the bar, then kicked off a long playlist that would act as aural wallpaper. I didn't have the energy to curate tunes today. I checked back into the kitchen to see if Alicia had calmed down.

"What's for lunch?"

"BALT."

I smelled the frying bacon.

"What's the ALT?"

"Avocado, lettuce, tomato. Hot weather food."

The radio—Syndi's portable—was turned on low, Terry Gross's voice murmuring in the humid air.

"Sounds good. All set for a rush?"

People were descending the stairs out front, talking and laughing. I loved the sound.

"For now." Reminding me our discussion of her future was not over.

A foursome of tourists looked around the place nervously. I didn't post a menu outside, like a lot of places did. As the South End gentrified, more and more unfamiliar faces came into the Esposito. Tourists visited the SoWa Open Market, the photography museum, the Cyclorama. I handed out menus, took drink orders, and got behind the bar to work.

Today's lunch was an actual rush, a wave of business that lasted a solid hour and a half. Alicia and I did not have time to revisit our discussion. I hoped I wouldn't lose her. And if I did, I hoped it wouldn't hurt my relationship with her grandfather. Mr. Giaccobi was my sage up the street. I didn't want to lose that connection.

I bussed the tables from the last few meals and was down to two customers at the bar, a brass-blond woman in an unseasonable red sweater and canvas pants and a drywall guy who'd been in for lunch every day for a week. He must have had a job in the neighborhood.

Bill Evans, in one of his less experimental moods, played a straight-ahead version of "My Foolish Heart" when Francesca appeared halfway down the stairs.

The heat outside must have abated some, since she wore long pants, wide-legged, with cream and navy stripes, and an elbow-length ivory top with a scoop neck. Her hair was bundled up off her neck and a diamond tennis bracelet glinted from her wrist. I was struck all over again by her rich and effortless elegance, how she owned an innate ease with herself.

She carried a gray canvas folder trimmed in leather that she slapped on the bar, startling the drywaller from deep contemplation of his piña colada.

"You'd better have a quantity of very cold, very dry white wine back there," she said. "Or I will have to commit Eldercide."

I picked a glass from the hanging rack, held it up to the light to look for spots, and set it down on the bar. I poured her a bigger measure of pinot gris than I would have for anyone else.

She looked at the level in the glass.

"Try all you want. But you're not going to get me drunk. Or take advantage of me."

That was as near to flirting as anything she'd ever said to me.

Wes Montgomery swung into a syncopated version of "California Dreaming."

"You're in rare form. You hit the number? Scratch a winning lottery ticket? Score Taylor Swift seats?"

She took a healthy slug of wine and grinned.

"Ah. That is good."

She was playing me, but somehow I didn't mind. I nodded at the folder.

"Is there something in there I should know about?"

She sipped more slowly.

"Let me enjoy my wine a second, will you? But yeah. Maybe a break."

"Enough. What did you find out? What happened to Susan?"

"God, no. I wouldn't joke with you about that. I probably shouldn't joke about this, except it's opened up possibilities. Things are starting to make sense."

"What are we talking about?"

She flipped open the canvas folder to expose a sheaf of photocopies, stapled in three places across the top. She turned it around and pushed it across.

Autopsy Report—Barksdale, Synthia in dark black letters across the top.

The text was tiny and dense, the headings all words I didn't recognize, despite six years of Latin in secondary school.

"Is there a *Reader's Digest* version?"

"You should be impressed I know what you're talking about," she said. "Lots of people my age wouldn't."

"Francesca."

"Sorry. I wasn't supposed to be able to see this and I'm a little giddy. This may be my way back into investigating Burton. Your cook—the previous one—she was hotshotted."

"What?"

I knew what it meant, but I needed a minute to take it in.

"She was injected with a shot of heroin laced with fentanyl. Enough of it to drop the proverbial rhino."

"You're saying she was murdered? What if she didn't know what was in the drugs?"

"It wasn't a mistake. Bruises in places that make it clear she was held down."

My heart hurt.

"But why? A cook in a bar?" I was terrified Alicia would hear us talking about this. "She wasn't a threat to anyone. Who'd want her dead?"

Francesca shut the folder.

"I have a theory. Or at least the germ of one. Why this starts to make sense."

"OK."

"Whose daughter is Miss Synthia?"

"You think someone killed her because she's Mickey's daughter?"

"What else makes sense? It's a message to Mickey. Maybe retribution for something he did?"

Alicia came out of the kitchen with a plate in her hand, as if she were planning to eat her sandwich at the bar.

"Not now," I said.

She looked at my face and retreated, not without a poisonous glare at Francesca. Francesca snorted.

"What?"

"Woman has a thing for you."

"She's been spooked by all the to-ing and fro-ing. The cops and the gangsters. She'll get over it."

"Not what I'm seeing. She wants something else."

I didn't ask her what she meant. I was more interested in why Syndi had to die.

"OK. Two murders. They must be related somehow."

"That's what I mean about making sense. If Syndi wasn't an accident, Burton definitely was not."

"I thought we established that." Now I worried about something else. "It might even be three murders. When I find out what happened to Susan."

"But where's the connection? Two different ways of killing someone. What do they have in common?"

"That's why we call it investigating. If it was obvious, we wouldn't have to think about it. There is one thing they have in common."

"Mickey. But Syndi had nothing to do with her father."

"Is there coffee? If I have another drink now, I'll be on the floor by sunset."

Profit on brown water was negligible, which is why I didn't keep a machine out front. I went out to the kitchen and ran a K-cup through the coffeemaker. Alicia ignored me, pointedly.

Francesca nodded her thanks.

"OK. So Mickey is the link," she said.

"Yeah. But there's a different reason for each murder?"

"Drugs, in Syndi's case. And not pot, with dispensaries on every block. Someone sending a message to Mickey?"

"About what? He never trafficked in them."

"Icky Ricky used to be a pill pusher. Maybe he came back to start over."

"Is he that smart? Or ambitious? He was strictly a small-timer when he was in Boston before. What about Vinson?"

"Who he?" she said.

She'd been present for so much, I forgot she probably didn't know about Vinson. In fact, I might be the only one who remembered Vinson's first attempt to break into Boston. I outlined the story, including Burton's following up on the death of the young woman singer who'd committed suicide. I knew he'd never given up on holding Vinson accountable for that.

"Burton's notebooks talked about things the two of you got up to, but I don't remember that one."

"I'm still surprised he wrote things down. He was not the reflective type."

"How little we know who we love," she said. "Maybe he was going to write a book. So Vinson is the killer? Syndi's? Or the both of them?"

"He's upper management. The dirty jobs get farmed out to the working class. With layers of protection. But if he was in negotiations with Mickey, trying to create a détente, killing the man's daughter would have been counterproductive."

"Not to mention putting a contract out on Burton. Why muddy the waters if you were trying to do business?"

I walked down the bar. The woman in the red sweater had left a twenty-dollar tip and a phone number scrawled on a coaster. I made the drywaller another piña colada and returned to Francesca, tossing the coaster on the back bar.

She looked amused.

"That happen a lot?"

"More than you might think. A lot of people never get listened to. Bartenders are good at that."

"Either that or good at faking it." She tapped the canvas folder. "Where does this take us?"

"Doesn't take me anywhere. You're the cop."

"Yeah. But this is another case Liam Macdonald closed and Martines will fight opening up again. I might be able to nibble at the edges a little, but if I push it too hard, I'm going to get fucked. Again."

Coming from her elegant mouth, the curse surprised me. She glanced down the bar at the drywaller.

"I'm also hearing a rumor Mickey has someone on the inside."

"Inside the cops? I heard the same thing. Is it Macdonald?"

"Or Martines. Or someone else we don't know about."

"Another good reason to be discreet. For you, I mean."

"You really think Vinson had Syndi killed?" she said.

"Shit. I don't know. It feels pat. Too complicated."

"So what do we do? I'm still stuck on the car fire."

"What if I talked to Mickey about this?" I didn't love the idea, but it could kick something loose. "Without getting you in trouble?"

"You're going to tell him his daughter was murdered? He'll go apeshit."

"That he will. But in the chaos, we could find out what else is going on."

"Dangerous." She finished the wine in two swallows, her throat working. "You still close on Sundays?"

"Why?"

"Find out what you can from Mickey. I'll push on this autopsy report with Martines, but carefully. We'll regroup at my place Sunday. I'll cook for you."

I lifted my chin, surprised.

"OK."

"Noonish. No need to dress up."

46

Learning that Syndi had been murdered cleared my perspective. Events now aligned on a sort of continuum: Burton's murder, Syndi's murder, the car fire. If I could figure out the motives and connections, maybe the whole thing would make sense.

I had accepted that I was not going to hear from Susan again. I would have felt guilty about it, but I couldn't take responsibility for what other people did. I did have to wall off my rage at losing her again. I couldn't solve anything by flailing in anger.

Alicia carried the other half of her sandwich out to the bar and sat, looking defiant with Francesca gone. I didn't engage her. I was afraid to say something that would give her a reason to quit.

I had to be careful taking the news to Mickey that his daughter had been murdered, likely because she was his daughter. Mickey exploding would send shrapnel everywhere, and innocent people could be hurt. Like me.

"She wants something from you." Alicia took a large bite of her sandwich. Her observation floated in the air while she chewed. "And probably not what you're thinking."

"And what am I thinking?"

"You're thinking she wants to help you with your quest."

My quest. Jesus. I wasn't playing Knights of the Round Table.

"She doesn't?"

"She wants your body, Elder."

"Ridiculous. The woman was involved with my best friend, who died just a few weeks ago. That is not what's on her mind."

And it wasn't on mine, not that I didn't appreciate how beautiful Francesca was.

Alicia snapped a potato chip between her teeth.

"The guy is not always the first to know."

"And how is this your business?"

She wiped her mouth with a napkin, not hiding her flush.

"Just looking out for your best interests, boss."

A group of twenty-something women in softball uniforms racketed in the door and down the stairs.

"They're going to want to eat," I said. In other words, get your ass back in the kitchen and get to work.

She stood up, pouting.

"I was all done anyway. But thanks for asking."

* * *

I closed the kitchen at eleven and sent Alicia home. Back when I had live music, the Esposito was a late-night favorite of the Berklee students. The youngsters would come in, flash a fake ID, nurse a pitcher of beer, then get hungry. I missed their energy. I needed to bring back the music, reestablish my ties with the school.

With everything shut down for the night, I set the alarm, exited out the back door, pulled on the latch to be sure it caught, then locked it. The asphalt parking area behind the building, shrouded in dusty yellow light, was barely big enough for the car I'd rented. When the delivery came tomorrow, I'd have to park out on the street.

A three-wheeled motorcycle crowded in next to the Volvo, and a familiar figure in dirty yellow Keds, khaki walking shorts, and a T-shirt commemorating a Paul Revere and the Raiders concert sat on top of it. His leather jacket hung on the handlebars. It would be too hot to wear when you weren't riding.

His face, all planes and edges, reflected the light from a small tablet computer he held in front of him as if watching a movie. A bruise high on his right cheek made me wonder if someone had succumbed to the urge to smack him. Burton had put up with a certain amount of crap before breaking his nose, and it wasn't unbelievable that Liam Macdonald had pissed someone else off that much.

He didn't look up from the screen, though he knew I was there. Games.

"Macdonald. What the fuck?"

He swung his legs off the wide cushion of the three-wheeler and sat sidesaddle.

"Working late," he said.

Him or me? He looked taller and leaner out of his suit.

"You have something to say to me, you should have come into the bar." I pressed the fob and the rental Volvo peeped. "I'm heading home, as soon as you get your tricycle out of my way."

His eye twitched. It wasn't the first time someone had made fun of his ride.

"Lot of lowlifes running in and out of your place. Wouldn't be a good career move for me to be seen hanging out."

"And it is all about the career, isn't it?" I leaned on the car. "Now that you've peed on my shoes, why don't you tell me why you're here."

"I need you to look at something. Tell me what you think." He held up the tablet.

"Why here and why now? I could have come down to the precinct."

"No distractions here. No nosy people."

Was he worried about Mickey's inside source? Or was he the source?

I took the tablet from him, mistrusting his motives. This was a homicide cop who'd been happy to close out a fellow officer's death as essentially accidental, despite evidence to the contrary.

"What am I supposed to be looking at?"

He pressed the start icon on the video and leaned back.

The footage was security-camera quality, black and white, the image jagged and occasionally pixelated. The lens was focused on the back side of a concrete block warehouse.

"Industrial supply house, down next to the fish pier." His breath was beery. "Watch for it."

A figure in black pants and hoodie, head and face obscured, walked up to the rear entrance and pulled it open.

"Note the door was not locked."

"Who owns the warehouse?"

"Not important. A string of LLCs and shell corporations. Watch."

Nothing happened for a minute and a half by the counter in the lower right-hand corner of the screen. Then the hooded figure emerged through the door he'd entered by, carrying a small cubic container in each hand, each maybe three gallons.

"What kind of warehouse?"

"Industrial supply. Solvents, pipes, components."

"So those aren't gas cans."

Which you could buy at any auto supply store and fill at a service station.

"Same substance we found in your burned-out vehicle. Toluene. Much more flammable."

As the figure started to walk out of camera range, I noticed his shoes.

"Wait. Roll that back."

Macdonald stiffened.

"You see something?"

"I don't know. Can you go frame by frame?"

He rewound, poked the screen a couple of times, and the video slowed to a crawl.

"Best I can do."

"There. See the shoes?" I paused it with my finger.

The image was grainy, but you could see the figure wore black ballet flats. There was only one place I'd seen those recently.

"What about them?"

"That's Donald Spengler."

"Who?"

I handed back the tablet.

"Works for a guy named Ricky Maldonado. Who works, I think, for Mickey Barksdale. You never ran across him?"

"You're saying he torched your car on Barksdale's orders?"

That was what the video implied, but leaping to conclusions had already complicated my life too much.

"I don't know. Maldonado wouldn't go off and do something like that on his own. Mickey's people are usually pretty disciplined. But why?"

I didn't have a clue why Mickey would want to burn me out, if it had been his idea.

"Good question. Falling out among the principals? Including the amateurs?"

"I am not now, nor have I ever been, employed by Mickey Barksdale."

He stowed the tablet in a nylon bag hanging off the back of the three-wheeler.

"So you know. I never bought the fact that Burton's connection to Barksdale was innocent. But it doesn't mean I'm not doing a thorough job."

Martines had talked to him about my coming to the precinct, accusing him of nonchalanting things.

"If Burton was working for Mickey, why would Mickey want to kill him?" I said. "Or me? It makes no sense. That car fire was supposed to fry me. And if you put it next to Mickey's daughter being hotshotted? That guarantees Burton was more than a random shooting?"

Macdonald stood up off the trike like I'd goosed him.

"Where the...? Fuck. There's only one place you could have gotten that."

Shit. I'd dropped Francesca in it. But maybe the spirit of competition would get Macdonald's ass in gear. Any gear.

"I have a friend who works in the ME's office. Don't go making a bunch of assumptions."

Macdonald was slow-breathing, trying to calm himself. What else threatened him, other than I'd accused him of laziness?

"So give me a scenario, Darrow. How does this fit together? Because from where I sit, I have a cop shot trying to stop a liquor store robbery, a junkie dead from her own addiction, and a gangster with a thing against you who likes to play with fire. Literally."

"Look at the anomalies, for god's sake. You've got bullet angles that don't make sense, enough fentanyl in a single shot of heroin to drop a circus full of elephants, and video proof of a gangster connection to the fire that torched my car."

Macdonald's neck and shoulders locked up.

"Look. I know your buddy colored outside the lines. A lot. Off the edge of the page, even. And it got him what he needed. I don't—I can't—operate like that. Just because you once saw someone beat a dog, that's not the only way you keep it from biting."

"So you're saying you haven't quit on this? On Burton?" I let my disbelief show. "You just need more, what, certainty?"

"Evidence, Darrow. I can't cram random facts into a story just because I think it happened that way."

I was wrung out. I couldn't guess what other evidence he thought he needed. All I wanted to do was go home and think about why Icky Ricky, or Mickey, or both of them, would want me dead. And what that meant about Burton's death. And Syndi's.

"Whatever." I hadn't trusted him much before tonight. I wasn't going all in on him now. "Move your trike. I need to go."

He acted disappointed he hadn't convinced me. Of what?

"I will get there, Darrow. But in my own way and in my own time."

He threw his leg over the seat and faced front on the three-wheeler.

"And if I were you, I'd be careful who I trusted."

I was barely listening at this point. Donald Spengler could be in the wind.

"Terrific advice." I opened the Volvo's door.

"No, seriously. There's a rumor someone inside the department is talking to the wrong people. Information is leaking."

"As it does," I said.

Was he trying to divert suspicion from himself?

"If that's true, Liam, you better speed up your roll. Before someone rolls right over the top of you."

He shook his head and started the tricycle's engine. The blatting sound slapped off the brick and hurt my ears as he dropped the machine into gear and roared off up the alley. He was leaving me with more questions than I'd started the day with. And I'd started with plenty.

47

I drove across the city, up Comm Ave, and lucked into a parking space directly in front of my building. It was such a surprise that, as I locked the car, I looked around to be sure the city hadn't put up a new sign restricting parking in that spot to a full moon or only during Red Sox victories.

A heavy squeak, the door of a substantial vehicle opening, startled me. The noise came from inside a pool of shadow twenty yards up the street, where one of the streetlights was out. I was glad I wasn't carrying the pistol Burton left me. I was so jumpy I probably would have fired it out of reflex.

"Bartender."

Mickey was the last person I cared to chat with at three in the morning. He only called me "bartender" when he was pissed off about something, and I could only hope it wasn't me.

"Down here."

I sighed. Better to deal with him out on the street than to invite him inside.

I trudged down the sidewalk, aware of how little I understood how Mickey fit into all this. Spengler may have engineered the car fire, but it hadn't been his own idea. Had it been on Mickey's orders? Maybe Mickey had had enough of me poking around. Maybe he was calling me down Comm Ave to my death. I doubted it, but only because he would have made more of a melodrama of it. And made sure he had an audience.

I stepped past the outer rim of shadow defined by the burned-out—shot out?—bulb. A dark green Plymouth Fury with a white vinyl top, an enormous Chrysler product from the seventies, squatted at the curb with the front passenger's door wide open.

Mickey's voice, low but definite, carried from inside the car.

"Inside. And shut the door."

I shook my head at my own folly and slid onto the wide front seat of a vehicle from a time when steel was king and gasoline was thirty-five cents a gallon.

"I didn't know they made these things with leather seats." I pulled the door shut with a solid thunk.

"They don't. They didn't. It's a custom job."

Mickey sat behind the wheel and turned to the right so he faced me. The interior light stayed on. His cast was off, the ankle clasped in a thin blue plastic brace. The Fury was an automatic anyway. He could drive it one-legged.

"Very nice." Cost me nothing to compliment his taste.

I sank back into the soft seat, feeling the hour of the night in my bones. Then I heard a labored squawk from the back. I swiveled to look. Antoine—Twan—sat in the middle of the bench seat, seatbelt tight around his midsection, his hands in his lap mittened in duct tape, another gray patch over his mouth.

I looked back at Mickey.

"I hope I'm not interrupting something," I said.

I wanted no part of this. Twan couldn't be one of Mickey's favored underlings since he worked for Frank Vinson. Which made me wonder what I was here to witness.

"Did you ask me to help you out, bartender?"

"Yes."

"You weren't ever in the military?"

"No." Not only had my age group fallen between two major wars, the one time I might have been drafted, I was deferred on account of being rich enough to stay in college.

203

"I was. And it's how I run things. Now, I'm not one of those command freaks, understand." He reached behind him and patted Twan on the knee, making him twitch. "Am I, Antoine?"

Twan shook his head, as agreeably as he could under the circumstances.

"What I do expect out of people working for me is self-discipline. Restraint." He slapped Twan on the thigh, harder. "But you don't really work for me, do you?"

The accent, the *cher*—Twan was obviously one of Vinson's boys. I figured out why we were here.

"This is the guy who almost put me out of business? The check kiter?"

Mickey nodded as he took out a pack of Luckies, the red ball on the side shining in the dashboard light.

Twan's amber eyes above the duct tape were wide and pleading, if eyes can be that eloquent. I appreciated Mickey's finding the thief, but a knot in my chest told me something else was coming.

"I hope the money bought you something useful," I said.

"It was never about the money." Mickey laughed roughly and lit his cigarette. "Was it, Twan? Bartender, what do we do with people who try and fuck us over?"

I didn't want revenge, only my money back. Mickey needed to cool off.

"Main thing I'm interested in? As I said. Restitution. Other than that, I don't care."

Too late, I realized saying that gave Mickey permission to define his own vengeance.

And Antoine realized it. He whimpered. All three of us knew how volatile, violent, and vicious Mickey could be.

"He was trying to fuck me over to help his boss. Who also, I understand, wants to buy your bar."

Shit. We were back to that?

"It's still not for sale."

Mickey reached in front of me, opened the glove compartment, and slapped a thick envelope in my lap. A revolver gleamed under the tiny bulb.

"That was the easy part." He turned to address Twan. "What I'm talking about is a restitution of trust. My trust. I put a lot of effort into integrating one of your boss's people into my organization. Then you go off on your own. How did you think Mr. Vinson was going to react to that? Let alone me?"

He was addressing Twan, but it was also for my benefit.

"Michael, I'm tired. And just off a long night at the bar. Can we get on with it?"

He nodded, dragged on his smoke, then reached out the .38 revolver from the glove box. He set it, cold and greasy, in my hand.

"Take whatever you think is appropriate here, bartender. A finger or a toe? An ear? A life? Because there's restitution and then there's reckoning."

I wouldn't shoot anyone in cold blood, especially if they were tied up. Not to mention doing so meant Mickey would own me. Forever.

Mickey grabbed my hand and wrapped my fingers around the checkered handle, then bent my finger inside the trigger guard. I tried to pull my hand free, but his grip was strong as pliers. He forced the pistol over the back of the seat, making me twist my body, and slipped his forefinger inside the guard over mine.

He was too strong for me to pull away. He straightened our conjoined hands until the pistol pointed right into Twan's tearful face. Mickey started to squeeze.

* * *

I heaved with all my strength. A muscle in my rib cage tore. Everything slowed down as the pistol went off. Twan's black crew cut ruffled and the bullet ripped into the rolled and tufted seat behind him.

"Goddamnit."

Mickey wrestled the gun away, spraining my trigger finger, and pointed it into Twan's paper-white face, ready to rectify my mistake.

Twan whined again. Mickey laughed, harsh and ugly, and laid the revolver on the dashboard.

"Well, shit. You don't want to work against someone's good luck." He stared at Twan. "Which makes you one lucky son of a bitch."

I shook myself, my ears ringing. The aura of burnt gunpowder made me sneeze and a smell of urine penetrated the sulfurous smoke, an environmental hazard of its own.

"Hey, asshole. Those are real leather seats you're pissing on."

Twan's eyes were closed, leaking from the corners. I was relieved I hadn't shot anyone, with Mickey's help or without. But anger made me reckless.

"You'd kill someone over money?" I was shouting so loud my ears buzzed. "I was supposed to kill him over some bounced checks? That's something Mickey Barksdale does. Not me."

Mickey leveled a hard look at me and rolled down the window to flick out his butt. He nodded.

"Burton was a man who understood the power of revenge. And exercised it more than once."

"Fuck you, Mickey. You are a rabid fucking asshole."

I started to reach for him, blind in my rage. Bad enough Burton had been murdered, but for Mickey to transfer his own assumptions and desires onto someone who couldn't defend himself? Despicable was too weak a word.

Quick as a viper, Mickey grabbed the revolver and shoved it into my chest. The hard snout bruised me and my anger doused in an icy shower of fear.

"Look, bartender. I loved the man, too. Doesn't mean I'm blind to who he was and what he did."

I pushed the gun away. He would have shot me already if he was going to.

"Don't even start. He was a good cop and a good man. Let's leave it at that."

He set the gun down, well out of my reach. I felt light-headed and cold, as if all my blood had fled my body.

"Michael. Why are you trying so hard to make me your bitch? With buying the bar. All that."

I nodded at the gun, at Twan, whose occasional wordless sound attested to his being alive.

"What? I was trying to do you a favor." Mickey's innocence was as believable as Christmas cheer.

"Bullshit. You want me to owe you. What the hell for?"

He looked thoughtful. I prepared myself for lies. But maybe he would give away something I could use.

"It was clumsy, I guess. I've been trying to look out for you. Burton would have wanted me to."

His sheepish look was fake as pleather, his explanation as idiotic as the implication Burton would have asked him for a favor.

"By having me shoot someone."

"Well, if I asked you straight out to do it, you would have told me to go fuck myself, right?"

"To shoot someone? Yeah. And what is it you're supposed to be protecting me from?"

He shifted his injured leg as if it hurt.

"Everyone needs protection."

"What, you're my daddy now?"

Mickey glanced at the gun, as if it made a better argument than he could.

"People getting killed is bad for business."

That was rich, considering what he'd wanted me to do five minutes ago. But he was talking about Burton.

"So don't kill people."

"You don't understand. I'm reorganizing here, taking on a partner. I don't have control over everyone."

"Frank Vinson and the drug business."

He winced, as if talking about it hurt.

"It's not going so smooth."

"You're saying he's responsible for Burton? Collateral damage?"

"I wouldn't have gotten involved if I'd known how it was going to come out."

Was he telling me Vinson had put out the contract?

"You're saying Frank is responsible for all this? For Burton? For trying to fry me in my car? For Syndi getting hotshotted?"

Mickey went still as the Bunker Hill Monument.

"Say that again."

I hadn't planned to blurt it out, but here we were. The old saw about shooting the messenger crossed my mind. I kept a close eye on the revolver.

"Her overdose was not accidental. The heroin was laced with fentanyl, too much of it to be a mistake."

Mickey groaned and stared out through the windshield into the desert of Comm Ave. The smell of feces added to the close air in the Fury's cabin.

"Out." He pointed at the door. "I have to get this asshole out of here before those seats are ruined."

Too late for that, but the leather was not at the top of his mind right now. I was glad to breathe the clean night air.

Mickey ignited the Fury and drove off, so sedately I wondered how he was holding himself in.

I slapped the envelope of money against my leg and mounted the granite stairs for home.

48

Nothing happened for the better part of a week. At first, I worried what Mickey might do with Twan, but as things stayed quiet, I didn't care. Business was steady. Alicia calmed down when no one from the cops or the gangster world came into the Esposito for several days. I was curious how Mickey was going to deal with Vinson, but not curious enough to ask anyone. And I was stalled myself, with lots of shiny beads of information and no real thread to string them on.

Which meant, the following Sunday, that I was stuck again. If Vinson had had Burton killed, I didn't know what I could do about it. Liam Macdonald didn't want to hear from me, nor did his boss. And it was only barely possible Francesca could do something with the knowledge.

She lived in a small bungalow on Huntington Avenue in Hyde Park, a square yellow house set back from the street with a knob of granite ledge poking out in front of it. A gnarled white pine obscured most of the front porch. As I walked up the gravel driveway, a child-sized shape scrambled up the climbable trunk, but when I looked again, it was gone.

I rapped my knuckles on the wood frame of the screen door.

"It's open."

I pulled the door wide and stepped into the kitchen, where a floor fan moved air across the room.

Years of getting my calories from Scotch had dulled my taste buds and my sense of smell—I thought I didn't care about food anymore. But the cooking odors made me realize what I had been missing. My stomach growled.

"I was hoping you'd be hungry," she said. "I never get to cook this way."

She accepted the bottle of wine and inspected the label. I took in the kitchen, the avocado appliances from the Seventies, the patterned linoleum.

"Nothing like a nice Barolo with the Sunday sauce. Perfect."

It wasn't until she'd uncorked it and set it to breathe that she frowned at me.

"There's no polite way to ask. Do you mind if I drink in front of you?"

Because wine didn't do much for me, I wasn't worried about embarrassing myself.

"I may join you. I'm not really trying to quit. And thanks for the invitation, by the way."

She ducked her head and led me through the kitchen into a small square dining room on the other side of the house. The table was set with crystal, china, and genuine silverware. She poured wine into two balloon glasses and caught my look.

"I never get a chance to use my mother's place settings either. Let's sit for a minute."

She indicated two leather Stickley recliners in opposite corners of the living room. They were the expensive originals. My father had had one in his office.

"Nice place."

"This is the way they left it."

"Your parents' house?"

Because I couldn't imagine why else a young professional woman would choose to live out here in the sleepy suburbs.

"The price was right, which left me money to furnish it. And it's still inside the city limits, which my bosses prefer."

Even in the red-sauce speckled chino pants and denim overshirt, her face flushed with the heat of the kitchen and her hair messy, she was lovely.

She lifted her glass.

"Confusion to the enemy."

She pushed back the recliner and put her feet up. I sipped the Barolo and suppressed a grimace. I never drank wine unless there was nothing else. It took too much to get you where you needed to go, and I didn't really like the taste.

"It'll open up," she said. "It's a little dusty right out of the bottle."

I'd take her word for it. The paintings on the walls were familiar, artists I recognized from the freshman art appreciation course before they threw me out. Georgia O'Keefe of course, since I owned one; John Marin; Marsden Hartley; a few others I didn't recognize. They were originals and worth some money.

I wondered whether she had any new evidence to share. Had Macdonald shown her the video of Spengler buying firebomb supplies? That was supposed to be her case. The only new information I had to share was Twan's check-kiting, which didn't have any connection to the murders I could see.

We sat and drank wine. She looked out the bay window that fronted the porch, the lower branches of the pine hiding the street, until I broke the quiet.

"Anything new? On any front?"

"Outside of the fact I've been reassigned back to my office? Completely out of BPD?" She cradled her glass. "Nobody, but nobody, there has an interest in changing the story they signed off on. It's like they're afraid they'll have to take back the funeral, the twenty-one-gun salute. It's ridiculous."

"No doubt." I didn't think she could have done more from inside. Then I remembered Mickey's implication Burton might have crossed a legal line once in a while. "Did Dan ever talk cases with you?"

She held up her glass and looked at the wine through the light.

"Not very often, outside of the notebooks. He did like to hear about mine, which were usually about the lifestyles of the rich, the stupid, and the greedy."

"I was talking with Mickey Barksdale…"

"People think what they think," she said. "I got that from Macdonald, too. That Burton couldn't have broken all those cases without a lot of illegal help from his friends."

I sipped the wine. It was growing on me.

"One of the reasons they recalled me?" she went on. "The background noise about someone in the cops being in Mickey's pocket."

"My vote goes to Macdonald. He's been slow-walking everything."

"I knew you'd go there. I don't think it's him. He's lazier than a stoned ninth-grader, but I don't think he's bent. He is, however, a pluperfect asshole."

"Which we can agree on. So your thinking hasn't changed?"

"Not really. He seemed to work a little harder when he saw me around. Maybe. But he skips things. He likes to make the job look easy."

"I could see it if you were grateful to be out of it. Bucking bosses, even other people's bosses, is a career killer. But you'll lose the access."

She shook her head.

"I'm in it until we find out what happened—I just don't know what I can do. I'm starting to feel like this doesn't get resolved with legal remedies."

Was she hinting at vigilante action? I hadn't been thinking in terms of legal solutions at all. I didn't have to build a case to try in court.

"Knowing everyone involved? It's possible."

She took another slug of wine and sat up straight in the recliner.

"I'm probably going to lose my job. But I'm in it to the end, as long as you are."

"I am."

She reached out a hand to help me out of the chair. I wondered what I'd committed to.

"So let's eat."

* * *

It was as well as I'd eaten in years, restaurant meals included: meatballs, short ribs, the pasta. The sauce, which she called gravy, burst with the flavor of ripe August tomatoes and garlic. I even ate salad, not one of my usual food groups.

"Ah." I leaned away from the table. "You'll make someone a wonderful wife someday."

She broke into tears. Had she and Burton been close to marriage, and I hadn't known it? I was appalled at my clumsiness.

"Shit, Francesca. I'm sorry. Foot in mouth disease."

"We weren't going to do that. It's just the feeling, of losing him, comes in waves. It's so unpredictable."

What I could not have predicted was how, as we cleared the table, she made me aware of her physically: a hand on my arm as I passed her the dishes, a bump of the thigh. It confused me enough that, once we'd cleaned up, I decided to leave.

"This was lovely. Thank you. I'm heading home now for a long Sunday nap."

She held the screen door open for me. Did I detect disappointment? Or resignation? As I crunched down the driveway to my car, I thought it might be a good thing she'd been moved back to her old office. We'd see less of each other that way. And that felt like it might be a good thing.

49

Driving up Comm. Ave. toward my apartment building, I saw someone sitting on the stoop in the sun. I passed whoever it was too quickly to identify them, intent on an open parking space half a block up.

I backed in and shut off the engine, wondering if it could be Susan. But the hunched apparition on the stairs was too bulky to be her. He unwound his legs and stood up. It was Twan.

I yawned as I walked up the sidewalk, carrying the bag of leftovers Francesca pressed on me. I hadn't lied to her. The long nights were getting harder, and I did like to nap on Sunday afternoons. I hoped I'd be able to.

The last time I'd seen Antoine, he was quivering and shaking in the back of Mickey's Fury, messy pants and all. His bravado now had a desperate quality that recalled I'd seen him in that state.

"That fucking Barksdale. He's going to get his real soon."

He stood on the first step, eight inches or so higher than me, but I didn't feel threatened. He was dressed in lightweight black cotton slacks and a muted purple shirt over a gray athletic tee. I couldn't lose the image of him taped up and whimpering.

"If you say so." I watched his hands. He'd tried to rip me off for twenty grand—what else did he have in mind? "What are you doing here?"

"I didn't get a chance to apologize for stealing your money. That kind of thing isn't me."

I scoffed at the popular all-purpose excuse for someone caught in bad behavior.

"Look, sport. If you did it? It was you. You expect me to forgive you? You almost sank my bar. Did Mickey force you to come apologize?"

Twan's mouth screwed into an asterisk.

"I don't work for that asshole, and I never did. Look. I was in a jam. I needed cash fast."

"For something vitally important, no doubt." Gambling debts? Buying dope?

"I have a daughter."

"No. No sob stories. Tell me why you're interrupting my Sunday. Because I'm not believing any apology."

"I still need the money. She's—"

I cut him off.

"Take off."

"Look, can we go inside?" He looked up and down the avenue. "I'm exposed here."

"For fuck's sake. No. I'm not letting the guy who ripped me off come into my home. And I'm not giving you any money. So fuck yourself off right down the street."

"I know who killed Mickey's daughter," he said. "Does that hold any interest for you?"

I stared.

"And you didn't use that information to keep Mickey from beating the snot out of you?"

"I didn't know it at the time. Besides, the man was not in a mood to listen to anything I said."

"So why come to me?"

He hesitated.

"You and Barksdale obviously talk to each other. You have, like, a relationship. He'll hear it from you. And if he stays this pissed off at me, I'm not going to be able to work."

Which meant Vinson was irked with him for causing problems.

"What makes you so sure Syndi didn't OD by herself?"

"That's her name? Yeah. They gave her a hotshot. It doesn't take hardly any of that shit to put someone down."

"What shit? Is this what Vinson's bringing to town?"

Twan shifted from one foot to the other.

"Man, I have to pee. Can't I come upstairs?"

*　*　*

Twan came out of the bathroom, zipping up his pants. I was unsurprised I didn't hear him wash his hands.

"This is a nice place. What's the rent?"

Now we were going to make small talk?

"I own the building."

He dropped himself into one of the armchairs, as comfortable as if getting into the apartment was the whole point. I crossed to the antique highboy that was once in my childhood home on Louisburg Square, pulled open a drawer, and took out the Ruger Burton had given me. I'd never fired it at a human, but the sight of it might inspire Twan to get to the point.

"Whoa! Whoa!" He threw up his hands. "No need for that. What, did I sit in your chair, or something?"

I liked nervous Twan better than comfortable Twan. I twitched the pistol in his direction without actually pointing it at him.

"I'm tired, Antoine. And when I get tired, I get cranky. Is there any meat in this sandwich you're trying to sell?"

He was smiling, as if he didn't believe I'd shoot him. He wasn't scared the way Mickey had scared him.

I pointed the pistol at the floor between his feet and pulled the trigger. The crack of the cartridge led to a thump as the bullet dug into the hardwood floor. Twan yelped.

"OK. OK."

My ears rang. I'd surprised myself, but Twan needed to say his piece and get out. And I did not love the fact that he, and presumably Frank Vinson, knew where I lived.

Twan's amber eyes widened, catlike. I took the Harvard armchair across from him and rested the warm gun on my thigh.

"Point the cannon elsewhere. Please."

I shifted the muzzle to center on his chest.

"Can we move this along?"

He licked his lips. If he asked for a glass of water, I was going to shoot him.

"I have to tell you the whole story for it to make sense."

There was the criminal mind, in a nutshell, turning a murder into a story that somehow made sense.

"I don't know if you know this, but Frank has been to Boston before."

I knew the story. Were there details to it that Twan could tell me which made sense of all this?

"When Frank was here the last time? It was more personal than professional, if you know what I mean."

"Evangeline Turner," I said.

Twan nodded. Frank had fallen hard for her, and in a reversal of his usual practice, she'd dumped him. He'd come back to Boston to try and claim her.

"So you know."

"Keep talking." I waved the pistol.

"I don't know all the ins and outs, but it didn't go his way. Barksdale thought Frank was trying to move in on him, so he took him up to this little house in Maine and threatened to kill him."

"Mickey's not known for his forgiving nature. But your boss apparently survived."

"Your guy was there. The cop."

"Burton?"

Twan nodded.

"The story I got, Barksdale tried to get him to kill Frank. Something about Frank getting the cop's girlfriend killed."

Marina? My former cook?

"So Burton shot Vinson?"

"I don't know. He didn't kill him, obviously. But Frank's had a hard-on for him ever since. Also Barksdale, obviously."

And maybe a reason to kill Burton.

"Why is he partnering with Mickey now, then?"

"Frank's getting pushed out at home. He's too old-school for the punks coming up. When he remembered Barksdale didn't own the drug business, he decided to move in. Kind of forced him to partner."

"You're telling me Frank Vinson had Mickey's daughter killed?"

"It got his attention, didn't it?"

In an exceptionally cold way.

"You can't believe Mickey's going to let that go."

"He doesn't know."

"But he got the message."

"It's a done deal. Barksdale's whole thing blows up if he doesn't play. Frank's a smarter tactician."

Odd vocabulary for a hood, but I'd underestimated him before. Something about a Southern accent makes people think its speaker is slow.

"I suppose you were the one who gave her the shot." I wanted a reason to shoot him, even if I wasn't going to.

"Not me." But he looked away, lying. "I'm moving up. Management. My skills are better for that."

His embezzlement skills, maybe. He sounded proud of himself.

"So why are you telling me this?"

"Mickey and Frank aren't talking to each other. And Mickey doesn't know—suspects, maybe, but he isn't sure."

Though he did know Syndi's death was murder, because I'd told him.

"Frank wants him to know now. For the leverage. He wants to take over Barksdale's whole thing."

"And you want me to tell Mickey that Frank is responsible?"

"He's way more likely to listen to you than Frank. Or me."

"You guys are nuts. There's no upside for me. All it's going to do is make Mickey crazier."

Twan smirked.

"But you'll get to keep your bar. Frank's got a partner who wants it. But he'll lay off if you do this."

Which partly explained the conflict between Mickey and Vinson over the Esposito. I stood up and pointed the gun at Twan's left eye.

"You know what? You can get the hell out of here and take Frank Vinson with you." I wasn't going to be anyone's pawn. "Because I'm in a mood to mess up my walls with your brains, and in five more seconds, I'm going to."

Twan believed me, even if I didn't. He turned the color of eggshells and jumped out of the chair, discarding the pretense of cool. In the doorway, he turned back to say something, then shook his head and disappeared.

I double-locked the door behind him and watched out the bay window until he emerged downstairs and started walking east, toward Fenway Park. I put the pistol in the armoire and reached into my pants pocket to touch Syndi's sobriety coin. There had to be some way to make all these idiots leave me alone.

50

A good night's sleep tempered my enthusiasm for action, at least until I had a better sense of what it would accomplish. Mickey knew Syndi's death was murder, and he could find out Vinson had engineered it without any help from me. He would exact his own justice. But if that triggered a bloodbath, some of the blood might splash onto me. I tried to think of other options as I opened the bar on Monday morning. Mickey wouldn't like it if he thought I'd hidden something from him.

I groaned when I saw Liam Macdonald walk down the steel stairs around eleven-thirty. I was eating an egg and cheese biscuit and it tasted good and I didn't want to put it down. My appetite was better lately. Except for the glass of wine at Francesca's yesterday, I hadn't been drinking as much. I wasn't counting days, but it felt like more than a few since I'd needed the Scotch.

"Don't mind me." I held up the sandwich. "Breakfast."

He nodded amiably.

"This is Grant Green, right?"

Green wasn't a guitar player the casual fan could identify, like Wes Montgomery. I swallowed the last bite of biscuit, mildly impressed.

"Coffee?" I wondered if he'd come to gloat over Francesca being yanked back to the FBI office.

He nodded. His eyes were dark-bagged, his shoulders slumped, and he surprised me by slipping a ten-dollar bill across the bar. I would have given him the coffee.

"Maybe a little something in it? You have Maker's Mark?"

Interesting. He'd never unbuttoned this much before.

I brewed the coffee out back, doctored it, pushed the mug and the money back across.

"You need it that badly, I'm not going to nick you."

He took a sip. A light shudder rippled through him and he sat up straighter.

"Thank you." He pulled the stool in close to the bar. "You know a Richard Maldonado?"

The name woke me up. Francesca had reminded me of the story, but had she not passed it on to Macdonald? He probably wasn't in Homicide back when Burton dealt with Ricky, before he was exiled to Miami.

"I have heard the name."

If Martines hadn't told him the story, I wasn't going to tell Macdonald that he was in town or remind him that Ricky was my source for the information about the contract on Burton.

"I'm looking into whether he might have killed Burton," MacDonald said.

"Wait. I thought you'd closed the case. Now you've decided Burton's killing was deliberate?"

He looked down the bar.

"What changed your mind?" I said. "The funky forensics?"

"And other anomalies. Bits of information that surfaced. So, Maldonado?"

"Known to all three of his good friends as Icky Ricky," I said. "Burton ran into him some years back. He was a small-time dealer, mostly pills when that was a thing. Had a couple of minor league thugs enforcing for him. And one big guy, Native American, who got blown up by a car bomb."

And, I didn't need to remind him, Maldonado's henchman was apparently responsible for my car fire.

221

Macdonald nodded, as if checking what I said against his facts.

"But he was small potatoes when he was here. You think he had Burton killed? It was Mickey who ran him out of town."

"But before that. The fake pill thing. Didn't Burton unravel that?"

"Ricky didn't suffer from that. Legally, I mean. He just hauled his obese ass off to Miami."

"Maldonado came back to the city three months ago," Macdonald said. "Under Mickey Barksdale's protection. He was making a lot of noise about settling old scores. Of which Burton was one. Then, a month ago, he shut up."

Right around the time Burton had died. Where had Macdonald gotten all this new information?

"Sounds like you have someone on the inside of Mickey's organization." Or Mickey had Macdonald on the inside and was feeding him.

"You think Burton was the only guy who knew how to work a CI?"

"So Ricky made threats. Anything more solid than that?"

Macdonald hesitated. He didn't like giving up what he'd learned, which made me wonder why he was here.

"We're trying to back-trace a sum of money that ended up in the liquor store owner's business account, the week after Burton went down."

If he'd gotten this far, I might have to rethink my judgment about his laziness. Though I could not forget the rumors about a bent cop in the mix.

"It wouldn't have been Mickey. If he'd known about the contract, he wouldn't have let it happen. He thought Burton was his friend."

Macdonald grasped the handle of his mug.

"Maybe. I do know there's more going on behind the scenes than any of us knows about."

Was he asking for my help?

"You think Maldonado was trying to get back at Burton for what happened back then?"

"It's possible. What do you know about him? It was before my time."

"Donald Spengler was the last of Ricky's original crew. Looks a little like an old movie star?"

"The one who stole the toluene."

"Probably not the actual killer—he's general help. And not too bright." I thought. "You didn't come to give me an update. So why are you here?"

"We're just talking. You know things I don't know."

The upstairs door opened and Alicia walked down the stairs, carrying her tote bags.

"I made it to the farmer's market before everything was gone." She registered Macdonald's presence. "Sorry to interrupt."

I made my decision. With Francesca out of the investigations, I needed a contact in law enforcement. And if he was dirty, I wouldn't be telling him anything he didn't already know.

"Back in a minute."

* * *

I went back into the office for change and a bundle of ones. A lot of people still paid with cash, maybe so the credit card records didn't show where they'd been? One character had tried to pay me with something called Venmo, but I laughed him off.

"Is this guy a cop or a crook?" Alicia chopped onions, the big knife a blur. Her skills had improved.

I stopped beside her. She set down the knife and lifted the ski goggles.

"Cop. Look, I told you I'm sorry this makes you uncomfortable. It won't last forever."

"It's not me I'm worried about, Mr. Darrow."

"Elder. I told you to call me Elder."

She blushed. I walked back out to the bar, trying to guess what that meant.

I popped the paper strap on the singles and fitted them under the spring arm in the register drawer. Macdonald's cup was empty.

"Another?"

"Better not." He looked at his watch. "Lots to do today. You have time to tell me what you know, or not?"

I tried to sort out the plusses and minuses. Talking about it with someone who knew the details might help me see a way out of the confusion. But it could be a conduit right back to Mickey.

"Let's." I poured a short Macallan and set it on the edge of the bar sink, out of sight of any customers. "Here's what I know. Or at least I think I know."

Macdonald folded his hands on the bar.

"Frank Vinson is, or used to be, Mickey Barksdale's equivalent in New Orleans. And the two of them have history. A bunch of years back, Vinson poked his nose into Mickey's business here and got swatted back, pretty hard."

"Wait. He randomly decided to come into Boston?"

"More complicated than that. Frank used to pick up young women starting out in music careers, promising them help if they moved to New Orleans and lived with him. I guess he ran out of candidates down there. Average tenure? Four or five months."

Macdonald frowned.

"Why go hunting here? Not Little Rock. Or Houston or Tallahassee?"

"Unknown. He had a guy procuring for him, Edward Dare, who got killed later on. What happened was that Frank fell for one of the women from Boston and followed her here."

"OK. Explains the bad blood between Mickey and this Vinson."

"Another one of Vinson's 'conquests?' Came back and committed suicide. Burton caught that case, and it always bothered him. He knew Vinson was responsible, but he couldn't build it."

"Connection there. OK."

"Frank's back in town." I took a sip of Scotch. "It seems he was losing his grip on operations in the Big Easy."

"They hate it when you call it that, you know."

"Frank remembers, the one thing Mickey does not do is traffic in drugs. Real drugs, that is, not all the stuff that's legal now. This is because his daughter is an addict."

"Synthia. So Vinson decides to move in on this business?"

"How much drug traffic is there in the city?"

"It's fragmented. Mickey takes tribute but he refuses to manage it. So Vinson sees an opportunity to consolidate?"

I paused, aware I was moving into unsupported supposition.

"Here's where it gets fuzzy. I might be pulling this out of my ass."

Macdonald pushed his mug across.

"Changed my mind. Just the Maker's."

That made me trust him a little more. I splashed three or four ounces into the cup as the radio in the kitchen came on, NPR murmuring.

"The thinking is—"

"Whose thinking is this?" he said.

It was a mix of what Icky Ricky told me and Spengler's involvement in the fire. I wasn't sure I wanted Macdonald to know I'd talked to Ricky.

"Like I said. Mostly speculation."

The way Macdonald demanded evidence, reminded me so much of Burton, a ripple of grief caught me. Macdonald read it, looked away.

"What I think must have happened was Vinson came in hard. Mickey's no pushover. So he had Syndi killed. In a way that made it clear who'd done it."

"That's messed up."

"And now I'm into total la-la land. My guess is Mickey didn't fold the way Vinson thought he would."

Macdonald tasted the bourbon.

"That all makes sense. But where does killing Burton fit in?"

"That's where the whole thing collapses. Right or wrong, Mickey thought they were friends. And Vinson wouldn't want to complicate their negotiations by killing a cop."

"Nothing in Burton's caseload, the people he put away, popped."

"There must be a connection somewhere. I just don't see what it is."

Macdonald stood up.

"The brass is all done with this, you know. With Burton. We had the funeral, the honor guard. No one wants to open the can back up."

"And you do?"

I'd assumed he was sharing his bosses' certainty that Burton's death was random.

He knocked back the drink.

"I know Burton didn't think much of me. Which means you probably don't either. But I am a lot less certain about things I thought were settled. Interested, let's say."

I thought about broaching the rumor of a bad cop, to see how he'd react. He hadn't turned me into his fanboy yet.

"I'm trying to stay away from it," I said. "It messes with my business and it makes my cook nervous."

"Sure. I can see how hard you're trying to stay out of it. But if you come across anything else…"

I nodded, ignoring his sarcasm.

"Of course."

He turned and walked up the stairs, a man whose thoughts were too heavy to carry. I couldn't decide if I trusted him now, or if he'd only been trying to see how much I knew. So he could spike it.

51

Liam Macdonald's visit twisted me around. He'd been doing his job, if not in plain sight. And he seemed to have discarded the theory Burton's death was random, which was hopeful. None of it meant I trusted him more than before he'd come in.

"Good-looking guy." Alicia materialized at my elbow. "I wonder if he's dating anyone."

"I can find out for you, if you want. He does have a steady job."

That pissed her off for some reason, and she flounced back into the kitchen.

I put on some Keith Jarrett, which helped me think, and finished the drink I'd poured earlier. It left a metallic taste on the back of my tongue I had to chase with water.

I wondered if Mickey had found out yet that Frank Vinson had caused Syndi's death. That would put a crimp in their so-called negotiations. If he hadn't, I would have to tell him what Twan had confessed, if only to protect myself. If he thought I'd concealed it, he would take it out on me.

But if I was going to meet him again, it couldn't be here. Alicia was jumpy as a cat near running water, and she knew who Mickey was.

I pulled the landline out from under the bar. I didn't have a direct number, but I knew I could find him with a couple of calls. Fewer degrees of separation remained between us than I was comfortable with.

* * *

"Mr. G." The brass bell tinkled overhead as I walked into the coffee shop.

The old man looked up from cleaning the outside of the massive espresso machine and smiled.

"My friend. Have not seen much of you."

"Life of the small businessman. As you know."

"My granddaughter is working out?"

"Better than. She cooks like she's been doing it all her life."

"Being laid off like that hurt her heart, you know. You commit to something and they yank it away. I know she likes you."

"Likes working for me, maybe." She hadn't been that happy with me lately. "Is a quad shot possible? And may I borrow your back booth for a while?"

Tucked in the corner by the restroom door, that booth was where the old man rested between customers or did his paperwork. Giaccobi quirked up an eyebrow.

"A meeting? Of course."

When the subject of my meeting walked in, Giaccobi's expression went dark. Of course he'd know Mickey.

Giaccobi delivered my coffee and ignored Mickey as he slid into the booth opposite.

"Huh." Mickey watched the old man walk away, as if surprised that not everyone loved him. "It's good you reached out. I have some information you need."

"More or less what I was going to say to you. Who goes first?"

Mickey waved his hand at me. My heartbeat kicked up.

"Syndi's overdose was not her fault," I said.

"So you say. But any time a junkie dies, it's their own fault, right?"

This was like dancing with an untrained bear, one who might bite me at any moment.

"The amount of fentanyl in the heroin. Too much to be a mistake."

"People like junkies, they make their own choices. Am I right? Synthia was lost to me a long time ago."

He laid his hands palms down on the table, his fingers tinged yellow from nicotine.

"She was smarter about her habit than that. She wouldn't have done that to herself."

"She wouldn't?"

His reaction was cold, even for a man as bereft of parental instinct as Mickey seemed to be. Then I understood.

"You already know this. And who did it."

His cold green eyes gave me nothing.

"That's all? You called me here to tell me that?"

The flat reaction bothered me. Mickey was a hard man, but I couldn't believe he didn't care that Frank Vinson had murdered his daughter. He'd helped Syndi through rehab several times and now he was giving up on her?

"I thought you might want to know. If you didn't."

"OK. Thank you for your concern. So now I have something you need to know. But first, let me see if I can get myself something to drink."

He wouldn't let Mr. Giaccobi's snub pass. He walked to the counter, where Giaccobi was still polishing the machine with a cloth. I expected sparks, but Mr. G. held onto his temper.

Mickey carried back what looked like a glass of milk.

"Half and half. Stomach's getting worse."

As if I cared. He sat down. I wasn't sure I wanted to hear what he had to say. The last time he'd tried to help me, Twan had ruined Mickey's leather seats.

He stared at me.

"You had something to tell me?" I said.

He drank half and half, wiped his upper lip.

"I never liked you much, you know."

A couple of months ago, that would have chilled me, but Mickey was in a vulnerable state these days. His threats and intimidation were more automatic reactions than heartfelt, as if he were faking it until he made it. All I could do was ride with what happened, protect the people I cared about, and watch out for my own ass. 'No way out but through,' as the poet said.

"Feeling is mutual, Michael. If we didn't keep running into each other, maybe it wouldn't be a problem. But we do. So say what you want to say."

But he was in a mood to spread more poison.

"It isn't that you're a straight arrow. It's because you were such a shitty friend to Burton."

My mood caught fire. I wrapped my hand around the empty espresso cup, solid and white, and thought about crushing it into his forehead.

"Do it." He grinned. "But you better make it in one."

"Michael. I don't give a flying fuck what you think about me. Though I wonder why you try so hard to convince yourself that Burton loved you. You a little shaky about your feelings for him, maybe? A homoerotic feeling or two?"

He might not have been able to define the word, but he understood its first two syllables. The skin at the corners of his eyes tightened.

"Now that we've finished insulting each other. Maybe you'd like to hear what I have to tell you?"

"Please."

"First, let me apologize. Donald Spengler reports to Mr. Maldonado, who reports to me. And I did not ask either of them to do what they did."

"The firebomb in my car? I knew he did it."

"Is that a guess? Or do you have some outside information?"

"Closed circuit camera recording. Spengler carrying out two

plastic containers of accelerant."

"You've seen this video?"

"It's unmistakably him."

"I assume the police were your source?"

He didn't like the fact he hadn't heard about the video, which meant Macdonald was likely not his inside man.

"Random luck. I know the guy who owns the warehouse. And I learned what the substance was. Through legwork."

"I should have heard about this."

"I'm sure the Homicide folks will catch up with him sooner or later. I appreciate your thinking I needed to know."

"That can't happen," he said. "Spengler can't be arrested."

I held up my hands.

"Not my circus, not my monkeys. He might be in police custody right now." I released some anger. "And while I can't imagine why Ricky thought it was a good idea, I know he did it for your benefit."

Rage shortened my breath, but Mickey was barely listening, his mind far away from the coffee shop, spinning out possibilities. How to protect himself, foremost. Where I might have had a bare tolerance for the man before, a sour burning hatred replaced it.

He pointed a finger as he stood up.

"I would appreciate it if you didn't pursue this further. I promise you, I will take the appropriate steps."

"That's not up to me, Michael. It's in other hands."

The only sign he was troubled was when he set the empty glass on the counter on his way out, so hard it rang against the marble surface.

"*Stronzo*," Giaccobi said, loud enough for Mickey to hear as he exited.

The brass bell tinkled.

I didn't know what the word meant, but I could take a guess.

52

As I left Mr. Giaccobi's to return to the Esposito, the old man gave me an uncertain look, as if wondering whether Mickey and I were partners. Explaining it would have been too complicated. And I didn't want Giaccobi to be comparing notes with his granddaughter about how much time I'd been spending with the gangster.

I'd been gone an hour, but it felt like a day. Alicia had managed the bar fine.

"Thanks for jumping in."

She'd donned a white apron and stood with her arms folded behind the taps. Two solitary drinkers occupied opposite ends of the bar, both drinking draft beer. At least she hadn't had to break out the Mr. Boston Official Bartender's Guide.

"My mixology skills remain unstrained." She reached under the counter to turn off the music, some bass-heavy pop. "You look disturbed."

I didn't like her assumption she could analyze my psyche. We weren't that close.

"Just a little business I had to take care of, in person." The confirmation Icky Ricky had firebombed my vehicle was useful. I should let Macdonald know.

She unknotted the apron and hung it on a hook.

"How's Grampy today?"

I shook my head. Nothing Mr. Giaccobi told her about my

meeting would dispel her worries. All I could hope was that once this was done, neither a cop nor a gangster would ever set foot in the Esposito again.

The more I thought about it, the more I doubted Macdonald would do anything with the confirmation Ricky was responsible for the fire. Hearsay from a gangster boss didn't rise to his definition of evidence.

Francesca didn't pick up. I left a message that we needed to talk. She'd know what to do.

And then I turned my attention to my real job and got ready for a night behind the bar.

* * *

One of the things I loved about the bar business was its unpredictability. On a Monday night, when many places close for lack of business, the Esposito was slammed. There must have been an event at Franklin Square, because the dinner hour rolled through at full capacity, then after a short lull, we filled up again, with people in a mood to party. Neither one of us had a chance to draw a breath until after one.

Looking out over the crowded tables, Paquito Rivera driving the beat, I was pleased to see my bar reflecting what the neighborhood looked like now: different ages, different languages, different colors of skin. The business was coming together in a way I hadn't felt in a long time, without a hint of tension or argument anywhere.

The last three people climbed the stairs to leave, laughing and shoving each other. I followed them up, closed and locked the door, then breathed out in one long exhale as I sat down at the bar for a minute.

"Wow. That was something."

Alicia stood in the kitchen doorway, her fuzzy ginger hair awry except where it was plastered to her temples. Her smile was wide.

"Indeed. If it happened like that every night, I'd be a dead man."

"I don't know," she said. "It's kind of energizing."

"Tell me that after you're all done cleaning up."

She saluted me with a middle finger.

"Aye, aye, captain."

But she was right about the revitalizing effect. This was the first night in the bar since Burton was killed that had felt halfway normal. Whatever normal was these days.

Because Burton and Syndi were both gone. And Susan was still missing. I was stepping away from it all, I decided, letting the professionals handle it. I'd done what I could, and solving this was not my responsibility.

I checked my phone. Francesca's voice was hushed, as if she were trying not to be overheard.

"I'll meet you, late. Your place, after you close."

I assumed she meant the apartment, not the bar. What I wanted from her was advice, what to do with the information about Spengler and Icky Ricky. Then I could step away with a clear conscience, let the law take its course. This one good night of bar business reminded me what I was missing by chasing everything else. Being a half-assed detective was not who I was.

Because she'd stayed late, I dropped Alicia off at her apartment on Unity Street in the North End.

"Come in for a drink," she said. "I'm buzzing—I'll be awake for a while."

"Can't. One more thing I have to do tonight. In the name of getting rid of the cops and the crooks."

She tossed her head, her disappointment obvious.

"Your loss."

"Rain check?" It cost me nothing to say it, even if I didn't want it to happen.

"Maybe, maybe not." She poked me in the shoulder and climbed out of the car.

I waited while she keyed her way into the entrance of the brick building, wondering if I was reading her signals correctly. I wanted to be wrong. I could not deal with a personal relationship with someone I was working with. Not again.

Alicia flew out of my mind as I drove through the deserted streets to my apartment. What would Francesca advise me to do? Between her and Macdonald, they ought to be able to use the information to pressure Ricky.

Preferably in a way that didn't lead back to me. I was determined to let go of the sleuthing habit. The police were finally moving in the right direction. Motives? The guilty parties? Another question altogether. But also not my circus.

I was halfway up the outside stairs when Francesca appeared out of the shadows.

"Get me inside. Quick. I shouldn't be seen here."

53

The mystery act annoyed me. I ushered her into the building and bolted the street door behind us. She was vibrating with worry, adrenaline, or something stronger. Upstairs, I made her a cup of herbal tea and we settled in the living room. She shook her head as if trying to clear water from her ears.

"As of today, I'm undercover Francesca."

What was I supposed to do with that?

"Not much to hide from in this part of town."

"You never know who's watching. Your information is half the reason I'm undercover. But don't tell anyone."

She was giddy with the new role.

"Undercover for what?"

"You know we're charged with investigating cases of municipal corruption. Which includes those inside a police department."

I'd thought the FBI was mainly about thwarting terrorists these days.

"That's a pretty broad interpretation. So you're supposed to find the trout in the milk?"

She frowned at me, not getting the reference.

"Martines and my boss got together. I got reassigned back into BPD. The murders and the gang aspect, ostensibly."

"Macdonald's going to love that."

"Whatever."

"Martines must be sure the dirty cop's in Homicide. Anyone in the frame besides Macdonald?"

She blew past the question.

"You know, this is what I volunteered for. You have no idea how boring fraud is. And if some in-house asshole has been hiding Burton's death, I want to be the one to bring him in. Or her."

"There's only one cop in Homicide who's involved in all three investigations," I said.

"You have anything to eat? I'm starving."

We moved into the kitchen. As I put together a platter of fruit and cheese and crackers, she stayed close to me, radiating warmth and a scent that mixed lemongrass and coconut. I won't say I disliked the attention, but it distracted me. And made me wonder what she intended. She'd never struck me as someone who acted unconsciously.

She laid a square of cheddar on a wheat cracker. I decided not to dance around the question anymore.

"Do you think it's Macdonald? Or not."

She shook her head and swallowed.

"Martines thinks so. But I'm not sure. It's too obvious."

Before talking to him yesterday, I'd thought Macdonald was either incompetent or lazy, and slow-walking the investigations. I had a bit more confidence in him now. Also, some of the poor impression I had of his work ethic was based on things Francesca had said. So why did she now think he was OK?

"Who else could it be?"

She speared a chunk of Manchego with a toothpick.

"Martines himself, maybe. He could have brought me back in as a feint. Or someone who's not directly involved in either case? I know Liam didn't love Burton, and he's enough of a prick to tank the case. But to be part of killing him? I don't see it."

I almost forgot why I'd called her in the first place.

"Had a conversation with Mickey. He confirmed that Icky Ricky, using Spengler, firebombed my car. Probably trying to help Mickey out. Mickey claims he didn't authorize it."

She held up her hands.

"I can't do anything with that now. Tell Macdonald."

"Can you feed it to him? He won't take it seriously if it comes from me."

"He'll snap at a chance to bring someone in. And I can't drive outside my lane right now."

She was taking herself seriously as an undercover cop. I hoped it wouldn't put her in danger.

"OK. I'll talk to him again. But reluctantly."

"You've been talking to Macdonald?"

"He wanted me to know how hard he'd been working. That he was making progress."

"Classic diversion. Maybe he is the bad guy." She wiped her hands on a napkin. "I better get going. I have another meet."

"At this hour?"

She grinned. "Midnight riders. One more thing."

She stepped around the butcher block table and laid a finger on the placket of my shirt.

"You know how much I cared about Dan. But he's gone, and that part of my life is over." Her breath smelled like mint. "You don't need to do anything with this right now, but I think you're a nice man. And I would like us to spend some time together. Eventually."

As I dealt with the surprise, she turned and walked out of the kitchen. A moment later, my apartment door clicked shut.

I reached in under the sink and pulled out a fresh bottle of Macallan.

54

One day after all that, Donald Spengler was dead. The *Globe* was taciturn about his murder, as it tended to be unless the crime included municipal corruption, clerical abuse, or racial conflict. A two-paragraph mention in the Metro section contained Spengler's name, called him a known criminal associate without saying whose, and sidestepped details of how he'd met his end. I found out later the weapon was a commemorative bat from the Cape Cod Baseball League.

It was lunchtime on Wednesday, and the brisk business put everything else out of my mind. Alicia made a clam chowder that, despite the hot weather, went over well with the tourists craving local color. No one asked why there weren't tomatoes in it. If things kept up, we'd have to serve beans and brown bread on Saturday nights.

I'd delivered fried chicken sandwiches to a group from the South End Senior Citizens' Center and was standing behind the bar, tapping my fingers to a barrelhouse version of "You Can't Take That Away From Me" when the landline buzzed.

"Esposito."

"You see the paper?"

"Francesca? See what? Spengler?"

"The same. If you haven't yet, you need to talk to Macdonald."

I'd been putting it off. My desire was to be out of this, not deeper.

"I don't know. If he's the bad cop..."

She blew a raspberry into the phone.

"You can't believe anyone but Mickey did this. If you don't bring Liam what you know, he's going to think you're in cahoots with the thug. And if Liam is the rogue cop, you'll force him to do something. If he doesn't act on what you tell him, he exposes himself."

"You want me to rat out Mickey Barksdale."

"What is this, *On the Waterfront*? This takes Mickey off the board. Assuming Macdonald builds a solid case, which you can help him do, Mickey's in Cedar Junction a hella long time."

"If he builds a solid case. Mickey's not stupid."

"Are you taking his side, then? Maybe because he killed the guy who torched your car and your girlfriend?"

I had to admit to satisfaction at the turn of the karma wheel, though not enough to condone a murder. But she was taking it as proof that Mickey had killed Spengler. I wasn't so sure.

"You're right. I suppose."

"I'll text him. So he'll expect you."

"You don't trust me to do it?"

I heard her smile.

"You wouldn't be the only person in the world conflicted about who the villains are."

* * *

Macdonald wanted me to come to the precinct and make an official statement. I demurred.

"I'm trying to run a business here, Liam. And I don't want to be seen there, on the off chance the wrong person notices me."

He huffed.

"You're buying that crap about a bad cop?"

"No comment."

"And you're not going to tell me any details. Other than the fact it has something to do with Barksdale."

"It will be worth your time. I'll buy you lunch."

"I can't get there until after three. Meetings."

One of the major reasons I loved being my own boss. No meetings. Ever.

"Sorry to hear that. See you at three. It'll be quiet."

* * *

"You dragged me crosstown for this shit?"

He looked thin and drawn, as if the investigations were leaching the juice from him. He didn't turn down the offer of a drink.

"There's only the evidence of the videos, right?" I said. "Of Spengler stealing the material. That's not going to convict him. This ties him to Mickey."

He pinched his nose.

"Doesn't help that Spengler can't testify. Do you know how hard it is to build a case against these assholes? The upper-level ones like Barksdale? Witnesses recant or disappear, evidence gets misplaced. I'm not sure the department wouldn't rather back-burner this one, too. Let the assholes kill the assholes, as a deputy chief said to me yesterday."

"So you don't think it helps."

"The unsupported word of a known gangster? Who may also be a murderer his own self?"

"Liam. The fire wasn't him. He's a business guy. Someone in his organization colors outside the lines and it hits his bottom line. Of course he's going to react. He's been working for years to legitimize his operations. You don't do that by firebombing people."

"So this same businessman goes out and beats his subordinate to death with a baseball bat?" Macdonald smiled as if he'd trumped my ace. "Mickey has a fishing shack in Chatham. The bat was a giveaway at an Anglers' game."

"That's too easy. He's not an idiot."

"It's what I have," Macdonald said. "Evidence, not supposition. Not pulling things out of my ass."

I didn't think I was wrong. Mickey was too calculated to do what Macdonald thought. At worst, he would have had Icky Ricky do the deed, maybe as penance. If he'd killed Spengler himself, it would never have appeared in the newspapers.

"Flimsy shit." I turned around to change the music—I'd never gotten Flora Purim.

"Easy to see which side you're on," he said.

"It isn't that."

"Then what? That Burton could have done it better? Maybe you should get one of those wristbands—WWBD. The *champeen* detective."

It had never occurred to me Macdonald was competing with Burton, especially *ex post facto*.

"Fuck that noise, Macdonald. Do the right thing. Or at least do a little more work than you've been doing."

55

Alicia emerged from the kitchen five seconds after Macdonald left. I still harbored doubts about him. And if he arrested Mickey, some of Mickey's rage could splash onto me. I'd have to look out.

"What?" I said.

She frowned. "Nothing."

"Sorry," I said. "I'm still tangled up with those people you hate to see in here."

"I could hear you two all the way back in the kitchen."

Shit. Now I had to smooth things all over again, reassure her nothing weird or violent would happen inside the bar.

"Look."

"That's never a good way to start a sentence." She stepped around me and squirted a glass full of ginger ale from the soda gun. "Sounds a little like 'Now look here, missy.'"

Her laugh was brittle. Maybe she'd come out front to quit.

"Mr. Darrow. Elder. I've been thinking."

Double shit. She was going to quit. Well, I'd survived without a cook before her. And aside from the clientele she didn't like, she probably thought the bar was on its last legs financially.

"Thought I smelled wood burning."

She punched me in the arm.

"Not funny. Though it's good to know you're not always doom and gloom."

"What is it you want to say to me?"

She squeezed lime into the glass and sipped, her brown eyes steady above the rim of the glass.

"I'm changing my mind. About what it's like to work here."

Here it came. I shrugged away a minor sense of bereavement.

"You have to do what makes you comfortable." I would regret losing her. She'd brought lightness to the place.

She read my face, did a sputter-take, and set the glass down. Grabbing a napkin, she wiped her mouth.

"Oh, hell. You thought I was quitting."

"You've talked about it before. You're not?"

"Hell, no. I've been talking to Grampy."

I poured myself a shot. God knows what Giaccobi had told her.

"He's known you for a long time."

"That's true. So?"

"Look." She chuckled. "My grandfather is like the unofficial mayor around here. Same as he was in the North End. He knows more than you'd think a little old man behind a coffee machine would."

That didn't surprise me. Bartenders were in a similar position, halfway between an appliance and a sentient robot. We listened and we remembered.

"What is it you think he knows about me?"

"More than he told me, I'm sure. But he says you and this Burton were close friends. That you treated your last cook with respect, even though she was an addict. He told me that a car fire might have killed your last girlfriend." Her voice snagged. "I can't imagine what that would feel like, losing someone you loved."

I was torn between embarrassment at how much she knew about my troubles and irritation with the old man for exposing them.

"Appreciate the concern. I don't see how it has anything to do with you. Or how you do your job."

"You don't have much of what educator types call emotional intelligence, do you?"

I closed my eyes. Talk like that tired me out.

"How does that have anything to do with anything?"

"After I talked to Grampy? I get what you're doing. I'm not as worried as I was."

"OK."

"I'm trying to explain why I'm staying around, Elder. You need someone like me for the balance." She shook her head when I flinched. "Not that way. In the bar. Dark and light. Thinking and feeling."

"I appreciate your saying that. But none of this is your problem."

"It is if I'm going to keep working here. Do we work together well?"

"We make a decent team."

"All right, then." She dumped the half-empty glass in the sink, ice chiming against the stainless steel. "That's all I have to say. I'm here, I'm working for you, I'm on your side."

My eyes stung. I hadn't felt as if anyone was on my side for a while.

"Thank you."

She turned serious, as if a bird had flown over and shadowed us. Her mouth set in a line and she tucked stray hairs back under the hairnet.

"You don't have to answer this right now," she said. "But maybe you could give some thought to whether you might date a laid-off first-grade teacher."

Then, as if surprised by her cheekiness, she turned and fled into the kitchen.

I shook my head—more complication. So I did what I always did to help me think, turned to the music and found a playlist, anything to change the air. A drink wasn't going to help me figure this out.

56

The rest of the day passed uneventfully, or at least no more eventfully than Alicia's declaration of interest made it. Pedey Thomas, one of my customers from the days when the Esposito was a dive bar, got in an argument with a professor from UMass Boston over the proper use of a pronoun, but after everything that had happened in the last month, the heat and light around something that trivial felt comical. I settled them down by making them sit with a stool between them and buying each a drink.

I'd been assembling a playlist of music that evoked the old movies, all the noir classics, and it was starting to come together. Enough so that when the phone under the bar buzzed, I was tempted to ignore it. But the Esposito was open, and I was here to serve. I turned the music down and picked up.

"Esposito."

"I know it is," Mickey snarled. "And I understand the bartender there has been taking my name in vain."

His god complex surprised me not at all.

"Don't know what you mean, Michael."

Except I did. Somehow he'd gotten clued in to the fact I'd carried his connections with Spengler and Icky Ricky to Macdonald. And he'd learned about it stunningly fast. If Macdonald wasn't the one working for Mickey, it was someone as close to the investigation as he was.

"Well, that's bullshit. You're not man enough to own up to your own shit?"

I was relieved he was on the phone and not here in the bar or out in the alley. I'd seen him in full red rage, and it was the kind of memory that stuck with you, tightened your sphincter.

"You told me yourself. Elements in your world want to see you fail. It was probably one of them."

Convincing him someone else had betrayed him might make me safer. A little.

"I hear the weasel in your voice. And I have what you might call eyewitness testimony you were there in the station."

"Doesn't mean it had anything to do with you." Unless Macdonald was the rogue, all Mickey knew was that I'd talked to him, not what was said. "They called me in to talk about some case of Burton's, six or seven years ago. It might have to do with his murder. They're saying it is a murder now."

I was churning, like one of those college kids who pedaled the Swan Boats.

"More bullshit." His fire did not abate.

I looked down the bar, where a couple of my customers appeared ready for another drink. Letting Mickey yell at me wasn't worth irking them.

"You weren't there, Michael. You have no idea what was said."

"I might as well have been. I have ears as well as eyes. And I'll say this clear enough that even a bartender can understand. Don't be accusing me of things. Or there will be consequences."

It felt like he was fishing, trying to verify a suspicion. And I'd reached a point that he didn't scare me. What concerned me more was confirmation of his direct line into BPD, one he was confident enough to brag about.

"Mickey. What you do, right? Is there anyone in this city who doesn't know you're a hoodlum? That people get killed if they so much as ding your car door? I have no incentive to fuck you over.

All I want is to be left alone and run my bar."

And in the back of my mind, I cursed Francesca, who'd insisted I go to Macdonald. Somehow the word slipped out.

Mickey blew out air, charging the line with static.

"You know, bartender. I've been trying to treat you right. Because we were both friends of Burton."

"I appreciate that."

"People only fuck me over one time. Ask anyone. You could ask Donald Spengler, if he was still around to give you an answer."

My breathing checked. That sounded like a confession.

"And if I had to deal with Spengler myself, it was because of you. You should be able to defend yourself, not rely on me."

So now Spengler's death was my fault.

"Don't push this on me, Mickey. I didn't say anything to anyone they didn't already know. Get hold of your people and find your traitor. You really trust Frank Vinson? Or Icky Ricky? You yell at me, you're barking up the wrong oak."

"For someone who says he doesn't care, you know an awful lot about my business."

"Most of which I've had shoved down my throat."

"I am not fucking around anymore, Darrow. If nothing comes of this, fine. I'll leave you be. But if you flapping your gums causes me trouble, I'm going to rip your head off and piss down your neck."

What I'd told Macdonald would cramp Mickey's style. And if they ever arrested him, I would get the blame. My bravado blew off like dandelion fluff.

"Goodbye, Mickey."

He was on a landline too, because the sound of a receiver being slammed hurt my ear. Alicia walked out of the kitchen with a plate of French fries. Her face turned pale as newsprint when she saw me.

"What just happened?" she said.

57

The next morning, before I was awake enough to remember Mickey had threatened my life, the doorbell down at the street-level door bonged. An indistinct voice, gender and age indistinguishable, rattled through the ancient intercom.

I wasn't so adventurous that I hit the release automatically, but grabbed the .38 from the drawer in the foyer and started downstairs. The other two apartments were still vacant. At least I didn't have to worry about tenants being in danger.

Francesca peered in through the wavy antique glass of the door. I opened up. She frowned at my pistol as I slipped it into the back of my waistband.

"Expecting someone else?"

"Not expecting anyone."

I started upstairs.

"Armed and dangerous and grumpy, too."

"Unless you're carrying coffee on your person, do not speak to me for the next ten minutes."

She sucked her teeth in annoyance, but I wasn't the one who'd interrupted the peace of a Thursday morning at this ungodly hour.

Two cups from the percolator later, I thought I might make sense.

"You ready to talk now, sunshine?" she said.

"It's still too early for someone with my hours. I notice you didn't bring breakfast, either."

"Are you always this much of a bear?"

I wasn't, but I'd lost sleep thinking about Mickey's threats. And why did she care what I was like in the mornings?

"Sorry," I said. "Tough night. Is this important?"

If I hadn't been so sleep-fogged I might have appreciated her more, in the expensive sleeveless peach-colored shift, flared at the knee to highlight her long tanned legs. Her shoes looked handmade. She caught me looking, that sixth sense women have that someone's watching them, and sat down, crossing her legs with a soft whoosh of cotton.

"Mildly. Maybe. I was off yesterday. Did you get to Macdonald?"

I played dumb, not sure why that was so important to her.

"Macdonald. You mean what Mickey told me? The connection to Spengler?"

Her patience was too deliberate. Had she really shown up at six in the morning to see if I'd done what she asked me to do? She couldn't have called?

"I did get in to talk to him." I got up from the kitchen table to refill our cups. Now that I was drinking less, I was hungrier in the morning. "You want to go out for breakfast, talk about it?"

She frowned as if I were avoiding the question.

"And what did he say?"

"Not a whole lot. He was going to add it to the mix of things he was looking at. He didn't act like it was a smoking gun."

"Did you tell him Mickey more or less confessed to killing Spengler?"

That threw me off. Mickey had only implied that to me in our conversation last night. After I'd talked to Macdonald.

"No. But a couple of hours later, Mickey was on the phone to threaten my life. So that was one solid result of what you asked me to do."

She cooled me off with a look.

"I'm sorry if you felt threatened. Mickey is fighting to keep his place in the world, or so I keep hearing. He doesn't have time to bother with you. Hang in. I know you want to do the right thing."

She wasn't convincing. I had enough history with Mickey to know how persistent he was when he felt wronged, how utterly he believed in vengeance.

"What bothers me," I said. "Is how fast he found out I'd talked to Macdonald. Not even a full day passed between my going in and Mickey on the phone threatening me with bodily harm. That's pretty solid evidence of an inside man."

"You know those guys in Homicide are like old ladies, right? The way they gossip? It might not be sinister. Just someone shooting off his mouth."

"Mickey as much as admitted he had someone."

"That's different. Did you tell Macdonald that?"

"This was after I talked to him." She was confusing the timeline. She leaned the chair back on two legs. Her knees flashed.

"That is a problem."

"You think? In addition to the fact that Mickey's after my ass?"

"It goes in the other direction," she said. "If there is a rogue, we can't rely on evidence coming out of the cops any more than what's going in."

"Almost has to be Macdonald."

She twisted her mouth.

"Maybe. I still think it's too obvious. We need to figure out who's safe to talk to."

"I thought you were undercover. Who are you going to talk to?"

Her smile made me glad we were on the same side.

"I have my ways, Mr. Darrow. I do have ways."

58

Icky Ricky Maldonado walked down the stairs like the fat man he used to be, light and high on his toes. His companion surprised me—Alistair Dain. Alicia was sitting at the bar with a cup of coffee, reading the sports section of the *Globe*, waiting for our first customers of the day. Ricky was not who I'd had in mind.

When she looked up from the paper, she recognized his type and sighed.

"Here we go again, huh?"

She refolded the newspaper and slapped it into my midsection as she bailed out for the kitchen. At least it didn't scare her anymore.

"Gentlemen." They approached the bar, Dain a pace behind, as if he were Ricky's underling. "And I use the term loosely."

Ricky had a leather and canvas satchel slung across his chest, spoiling the drape of his purple-patterned Tommy Bahama. As he fumbled with the bag's catch, I dropped my hand below the bar. I kept the .38 close, though mostly for deterrence. I doubted I could shoot anyone. The movement startled Dain, who reached inside his seersucker jacket. He was back to the blue pinstripe.

"Go easy," he said.

Ricky looked surprised. Dain stared in through the kitchen door as the radio turned on.

"I've got something for you to look at," Ricky said.

"I'll bet you do." I looked at Dain. "Whose side are you working today?"

One of the questions Macdonald hadn't been able to answer was what benefit Ricky saw in returning to Boston. He'd been retired, or whatever the nonfatal gangster equivalent was, on South Beach in Miami. I had to assume he'd had a sweet life down there.

Dain ignored me. Ricky extracted a bulky eight-by-ten envelope from the satchel and slapped it on the bar in front of me. A small white label in the center read **Mr. Elder Darrow in re: Esposito**.

"What's this?"

"Open it."

The legal-sounding label worried me. Nothing to do with lawyers was ever a positive experience. I unfolded the metal ears holding down the flap and spilled out banded packs of hundred dollar bills on the counter, fifteen of them by my quick count. Foreboding cramped me.

"What's this supposed to be?"

"A down payment. Mr. Vinson would like to express his appreciation of your good work."

Ricky's tone was formal as a judge. This settled the question of who he was working for. He must have changed horses midstream.

"Creep!" Alicia shouted and drew the curtain across the kitchen doorway to block Dain's leering.

"I don't want anything to do with this."

The former fat man cocked his head.

"I don't believe you're in a position to turn this down. Nor should you."

"In my world, Rick, someone hands me a wad of money, they expect something in return. There is not a thing in the world I want to owe to Frank Vinson."

Ricky sighed as if I were his dumbest cousin.

"I don't partake of alcohol anymore, but a glass of ginger ale would be welcome. Ali. A drink?"

Where Ricky had developed his lord of the manor tone? Too much public television, maybe. Dain cleared his throat and pointed at the top tier of bottles.

"Shot of that. It isn't the Diamante, but any tequila is better than none."

Because it bought me a moment to think, I filled their orders.

Ricky sipped ginger ale and patted his lips with a paper napkin.

"As I said, Mr. Vinson appreciates your efforts. Bringing Mr. Barksdale to justice for his misdeeds."

Shit. Had they arrested Mickey?

"I didn't bring anyone to justice for anything."

Which I fervently hoped Mickey understood.

"On the contrary." Ricky grinned at Dain, who toasted him and sank the fifty-dollar-a-shot tequila in one. "Your reporting on Mr. Barksdale's treatment of my subordinate was instrumental in bringing him to justice."

So Ricky also knew I'd told Macdonald about Mickey's confession. I still couldn't make the timeline work. And I didn't feel good about making life easier for Vinson. Francesca owned some of that.

I restacked the money on top of the envelope.

"I am not accepting this. It makes it look like you paid me to fuck Mickey over. To help Frank."

"Mr. Vinson, please."

Ricky reopened the satchel and pulled out a white envelope with the return address of Carter and Mundale, a white-shoe law firm in the financial district. Frank had wasted no time putting down business roots in Boston.

"This is not a bribe. It's completely aboveboard."

The flap was unsealed. The single sheet of paper was headed Bill of Sale. I scanned the paragraphs of close type and found it conveyed the Esposito to one Richard Maldonado, for a sum I estimated was ten times what the bar was worth. A blank line at the bottom for my signature sat above my typed name. Frank Vinson had signed as the purchaser.

I pushed the money and the papers back at Ricky. Deprived of his view of Alicia, Dain watched us with a disinterested calm.

"This bar is not for sale."

"You don't understand." Ricky held up his hands. "Mr. Vinson is purchasing the establishment on my behalf. As a reward."

For turning on Mickey and helping Vinson take over Boston?

"All it requires is your signature."

"Not going to happen."

Ricky lifted a shoulder.

"You'll have to negotiate that with Mr. Vinson. I'm simply the messenger."

And he headed for the stairs, Dain covering his rear. As the upstairs door closed behind them, Alicia came out of the kitchen, drying her hands on a towel.

"Is today's gangster ensemble gone yet?" She stopped short at the sight of the money. "Holey moley. Is that for us?"

I ignored her assumption, packed the bills and the unsigned bill of sale back into the manila envelope, and sealed it shut.

"Someone's idea of a joke. It's Monopoly money."

"Looks real to me."

I tossed her the package.

"Would you drop that on my desk for now? Please?"

I'd put it in the safe later and figure out how to return it.

"Sure thing, boss."

And she carried the $150,000 and the papers into the back. Out of my sight.

To say I was confused was understating it. First, Mickey had wanted to borrow the bar, but now Vinson was trying to force me to sell. But why did Icky Ricky want my place? Stealing it from me was the hard way to get a business to launder your cash. It was clear Ricky worked for Vinson now.

I poured a maintenance-sized shot of Scotch. My options were murky and I wished Burton were here to talk them through. Did I have any way to fight back against a hostile takeover, even one that paid me a premium price? And if I did give up the bar—not that I was considering it—what in the hell else would I do with my life?

Voices coming in through the street door pulled me up out of the worries. I kicked off a playlist of instrumental piano that wouldn't challenge anyone's musical taste too much and stuck my head into the kitchen.

"Customers, Alicia. The lunch rush cometh."

59

I was pleased to see Francesca amble down the long steel staircase around three-thirty that afternoon. The lunch rush fizzled early and I was mired in a mud puddle of overthinking. Everything in the bar was clean, bright, and ready for the next wave of customers. Assuming there was one.

"What are you doing in my neighborhood? Somebody's cleaning lady boost a John Singleton Copley?"

I had no idea what she did with the FBI, though my best guess was that the fraud squad covered things like Ponzi schemes and using art objects as collateral for arms deals and the like.

She was working a beach-town vibe this afternoon, a red polka-dotted halter dress that left her shoulders and collar bone bare, a hem that barely reached her knees, and woven straw flats. Her forearm was layered with gold bracelets, a dozen of them, and she wore a ring with a large sapphire ringed in small diamonds.

Her body moved as if unencumbered under the dress, and I wondered what message she was trying to convey. The idea of being with her was not as hard to conceive as it had been a month ago. I didn't owe Burton's memory that kind of deference.

She turned down my offer of a drink.

"Depositions today." She spun so the skirt flowed around her, then sat at a two-top and crossed her legs. "Distractions are us."

"Hot day, again."

"What the hell? Maybe a spritzer. And could you come over

and sit for a minute? I don't want to have to yell across the bar."

She glanced at the kitchen door, the implication being she didn't want Alicia to hear what she had to say. I poured chardonnay into a glass with ice and added soda.

"Not drinking today?" she said, as I sat down across from her.

"Not at the moment. What's up?"

Her neck was tense. She sipped.

"Ahhhh. That takes the edge off."

"Francesca. Don't play with me."

She set the glass down.

"Sorry. I didn't mean to make it a moment. Mickey Barksdale's been arrested. For murder. Of Donald Spengler."

That hit me like a crowbar across the middle. Fuck. My first thought was how Mickey would take this out on me.

"And he's blaming me, I have no doubt."

She looked uneasy, as if she felt responsible.

"I wasn't there," she said. "But I understand he did not go peacefully."

"He resisted arrest?" That didn't sound right. Mickey didn't do panic. "He would have had lawyers and a bondsman waiting at the precinct."

She shook her head.

"Murder charge. Bail's a nonstarter."

"So, the good news is, he's locked up. The bad news is, he thinks it's my fault. Even though it's not."

The tiny bubbles of her drink rose and dissipated in the air. She looked worried, but she wasn't the one Mickey would come after.

"More or less correct." She put a hand on my arm. "I apologize. If I hadn't pushed you to go to Macdonald…"

"It was the right thing to do. But why does everybody think I told Macdonald Mickey confessed? That's not what I said to him at all."

"You didn't?"

"No."

"I assumed."

Something was off. I couldn't see it.

"None of this solves the Burton question," I said. "Or Syndi's death. But at least Mickey off the streets will help keep the peace."

"Your mouth to God's ear."

Which meant I was safer than before, for the moment. Mickey's minions wouldn't come after me without his approval. And if Icky Ricky's abdication to Vinson meant anything, Mickey would lose more power while he sat in jail.

"Thanks for coming to tell me. I might have freaked if I'd heard it on the news."

She wiped up the wet ring her glass had made.

"He's in isolation. Threats against him in the jail population."

"Lion goes down, the hyenas converge."

"One other thing. Unrelated."

"Sure."

"You consider the possibility of a night on the town?" Her dark brown eyes sparked with reflected light. "We've been sharing this weird road for a while. Might be fun to do something completely social."

"That would be lovely." I felt as if I were stepping off a high diving board. "Let's make a plan."

60

It wasn't closing time, but close enough that Alicia was gone for the night. I paid for the Uber to take her home, and she only protested a bit. At least she wasn't there to witness my second visit by cop that day when Liam Macdonald showed up.

As befitted the hour, the music was low and the lights were dim, love the dominant theme. Two couples sat at opposite ends of the floor, heads close, holding hands. And two college-aged women—I'd checked their IDs—sat at the bar sipping fizzy drinks and trading sultry promissory looks. Which made me think again about Francesca asking me out. Maybe it wasn't as innocent as I thought. Did she think we could have a connection? I had to admit the idea gave me a charge.

Macdonald looked as if he needed someone to love him. What remained of his faded ginger hair was mussed and his face drooped with fatigue and worry. He'd built enough of a case to have Mickey arrested, which should have made him happy. I wondered what was bothering him now.

He sat down and the stool creaked underneath him.

"You're OK, then."

"Why wouldn't I be?"

"Let me have some Jameson's. No ice, a few drops of water."

"I can't let you drink the tourist crap."

I pulled the bottle of Black Bush off the top shelf and free-poured into a rocks glass, water on the side. His affect was so dead, it was dragging me down.

"So why wouldn't I be OK?" Tension laid a wall in my stomach. He tasted the whiskey.

"Someone from the precinct was supposed to call and tell you."

"Fuck, Liam. Spit it out."

Instead of spitting, he took another solid bite of the Irish, shuddering like a man who didn't like whiskey.

"He's out."

"He. Who? No. Fuck. I thought they didn't allow bail for a murder charge."

"Not bail. He broke out. I should say, got broken out. They were transferring him from one part of the jail to another."

"This was at Bradson Street? How the hell does a murderer get broken out of jail?"

Macdonald's face pinked.

"Because a couple of minimum-wage corrections officers didn't know who they were dealing with. One of whom is currently in Mass General in a coma."

"This is not good."

"And the other one is dead." Macdonald rubbed his brow. "The guy in the hospital comes to, we might find out how it happened. But right now, in that elegant phrase, Mickey Barksdale is in the wind."

"He must have had inside help." Maybe the rogue cop who supposedly resided inside BPD?

Macdonald shook his head, pushed the empty glass toward me.

"Never attribute to malice which is adequately explained by stupidity."

So he knew Hanlon's Razor. It didn't mean he wasn't covering for himself.

"I don't know, Liam. Mickey's been ahead of everybody the whole way. Hard to believe he didn't have help."

Ahead of everyone but Frank Vinson, but then Vinson had no reason to help Mickey escape.

Macdonald shook his head, not wanting to believe it. Then he checked.

"Wait. You think I helped him escape?"

I turned my back to refill his glass. I didn't want a confrontation, but he needed to understand how little I trusted him.

"Didn't say that, did I?"

"Didn't have to. But you never had an opinion of me that you didn't get from Burton, either."

The way he spit out Burton's name confirmed an obsession. But could a bent cop bend far enough to kill another one?

"I don't think you're dirty, Liam." If I was lying, it was only to keep the current peace. "But who else but someone in the cops has the clout to break Mickey out?"

"Jail personnel." He accepted a second measure of Irish. "If it is a cop? My money's on Martines. Nobody in the jail's going to argue with a captain. He's a career climber, though. I don't see why he'd risk it."

Unless Mickey had a hold over him. I hadn't seriously considered it might be Martines, and it didn't escape me Macdonald was proposing an alternative to himself.

"Someone better figure it out. Mickey didn't levitate himself over the walls."

"Suspect me all you want. But answer me this: if it was me, why the fuck would I be here warning you? And why the fuck would I have arrested him in the first place?"

Questions I couldn't answer. He slammed back the rest of his drink. Was he sly enough to double-bluff me? Cops could be consummate liars.

"So fuck you," he said. "But watch your ass. You know Mickey has to be upset with you."

He stormed up the stairs, leaving behind the curious looks of all the lovers. Fucker hadn't even offered to pay for the drinks.

61

I wondered if my desire to drink was leaving me altogether, since the first thing I thought of when I took a break on Friday afternoon was to go out and have an espresso. I hadn't been in to see Mr. Giaccobi since the day Mickey and I met there, and I might have been avoiding the old man's disapproval. Alicia was happy to cover for me. She thought my visiting him made her grandfather happy. She did love that old man.

"It's fine." She washed her hands in the bar sink and tied on a clean apron. "Never much happening at this hour anyway. And it'll give me a break from you."

I let that slide.

"Bring you something?"

"If he has some of those pignoli cookies. And only four of them."

"Done."

Summer hadn't divested itself of heat and humidity, but its grip was softening as we moved toward September. The angle of the sun was lower, it was darker in the early mornings, and I welcomed it. Fall was a much calmer time than summer in the city.

I checked over my shoulder several times as I strolled up Mercy Street toward the coffee shop. Mickey was not stupid enough to escape from custody and then expose himself by coming for me, but the man's temper did not always incline him to intelligence.

The bell over the door tinkled as I entered. Mr. Giaccobi sat in his booth in the back corner, reading a tabloid newspaper spread out on the table. The print was in a foreign language, Italian, I assumed.

The old man's face, seamed like an old baseball glove, lit up.

"Mr. Darrow. A pleasure. What can I get you?"

He hustled behind the counter.

"Four shots? A little macchiato? That's not too much for you this late in the day?"

He let steam blow through the metal wand and packed coffee into the gruppa.

"It's early in the day for me, Mr. G."

I thought about the long night to come and hoped that people came into the Esposito with the same anticipation, the same expectation of welcome, I felt here.

He pulled out a larger-than-usual china cup and saucer and warmed it with hot water. Then he pulled the shots with complete attention, steamed some milk, and spooned a small amount of the foam on top of the crema. From an unmarked bottle he took from under the counter, he poured a small amount of a transparent liquid down the back of a spoon into the cup. He carried it back to the table, two miniature biscotti balanced on the saucer.

"Come sit with me," I said.

He reseated himself. I dunked one of the biscotti, ignoring his gasp.

"You're taking a midafternoon break?" he said. "Or do you have something on your mind?"

Mickey Barksdale was on my mind, but I didn't want to burden the old man with that.

"Don't you ever need to get out of here and walk around? Clear your head?"

He tipped his head, bemused, as if wondering why someone would need to do that. I looked at his hands, big-knuckled with arthritis, and wondered if I would still be tending bar when I was his age. Assuming I lived that long.

"Everything's all right at your bar? My granddaughter's not causing you any trouble?"

Only in the sense she seemed to have a crush on me. I wondered why the old man worried about her so much.

"Both her parents are gone, you know." He must have been reading my mind.

"I didn't."

"Stupid stuff. They were hippies."

Late-stage ones, given Alicia's age.

"What happened to them?"

He moved his mouth as if he wanted to spit, reminding me one of the two had been his child.

"Stupidity, as I said. They tried to grow their own food, raise pigs for the meat. Something to do with *e coli*."

My coffee had a sharp lemon flavor that cut against the fat of the milk. Giaccobi nodded at my look.

"Limoncello. I make it myself."

Not everyone got a taste. I felt honored.

"So you look out for Alicia now."

He made an offhand gesture.

"Long time. That girl is a gem."

"She's been terrific in my kitchen."

"She'd a good person who's had some bad luck." He frowned. "I don't want her to have any more."

I felt his worry, and it abashed me. I hadn't paid much attention to her as a person, more as a worker in my business.

"I hope I'm treating her well enough that she stays on for a while."

"I understand you're still getting yourself into trouble. Even without the help of your friend Burton."

Every time we talked, I was reminded how deeply he was tapped into the city.

"Nothing I can't handle."

He puffed up his chest, mocking.

"Big boy now, huh? Nothing scares you?"

"I can take care of myself."

He grabbed my hand, like one of those claw machines at the amusement park.

"And the people around you, too? Because your other cook. Synthia? I understand she did not take her own life."

"No one's going to threaten Alicia."

"Your girlfriend didn't think anyone was threatening her. Do you understand what you're in the middle of?"

I shifted in the booth. I'd thought of the coffee shop as a retreat, not another place to confront my problems.

"Then tell me."

"Your cook Syndi. She was clean. The drugs were forced on her?"

"There's no evidence." I couldn't discount the fact she had slipped a few days before she died. But there was the story of the high amount of fentanyl. And I believed what he was saying. "But yes."

"You have to ask yourself why someone wanted her off the earth. She was hurting no one. And you know whose daughter she was."

"You're saying you know she was killed because she was Mickey's daughter? Is there evidence?"

He ducked his head.

"I hear a lot of things. What you're saying, I heard from several places."

"Who did it? Frank Vinson?"

"I'm not a policeman," he said. "I hear things like that. But I have no proof."

All of which confirmed my notion Mr. Giaccobi was more than an aged coffee purveyor.

"So you see why I worry about my granddaughter."

I moved pieces around in my mind, suspicions clicking into likelihoods.

"I do. And I promise you. Nothing is going to happen to her."

"I'm trusting you to make sure of that." His tone would freeze vodka.

I drank my coffee before it got cold. What was one more brick on my load?

"The two of us will be fine.

"You will." It was a command, not a hope.

He slid from the booth.

"You have a business to run. And so do I."

He picked up a small bag off the counter and handed it to me as I walked toward the door.

"Cookies. I know she told you she wanted some cookies."

62

Things stayed quiet for the rest of Friday and onto into Saturday night, no visits from cops or criminals, and so, nothing to worry Alicia. I enjoyed the respite from my focus on everything: Mickey, the murders, all the associated shadowy threats. The only notable event was that Francesca made good on her hint and asked me out. After a fashion.

"Come for Sunday brunch again," she said on the phone. "I never get to cook anymore. We can curl up after and do the puzzle."

She might have meant something other than the crossword, and the idea didn't bother me a bit. Burton had been a practical man. He knew life moved forward, not back.

I hired a guitar player for Saturday night, my first venture back into live music in months. The Esposito's business was starting to stabilize again. No rumors of Mickey's whereabouts surfaced, which made me think he had disappeared. Vinson might take everything over, but his tenure wouldn't be different from Mickey's. The weak tie between Mickey and me would be severed, which was fine with me. And all the noise about buying my bar should go away, too. Vinson only wanted it because Mickey wanted it—he'd have to find another way to compensate Ricky for turning on his old boss.

Al Pianto, the guitar player, was a local veteran, the kind of sideman a bigger traveling act might pick up for a gig in Boston. I'd known him from the earliest days of the Esposito—he'd been a friend of Cy Nance's at Berklee—and he was a pro. No hand-holding required.

He closed out the set with a bouncy version of "Body and Soul" that shouldn't have worked, but it did and gained him a round of applause. He damped the strings and leaned into the microphone.

"Back in twenty, good people. And don't forget to tip your bartender."

I handed him a tall glass of gin and ginger ale.

"Decent crowd," I said, as he sidled into a space by the service bar and drank.

"Really glad you're back with the music, man. But really? No one listens."

That was the perennial lament of the performing artist, that no one took them seriously.

"I was."

He shrugged as if my opinion didn't count. His curly hair was a little too black for the lines and gullies on his face. He wasn't old, but definitely well-seasoned.

"I almost didn't take the gig, you know."

I mixed a pair of whiskey sours and delivered them along the bar.

"Why's that?" I said when I came back.

He gave me a sideways look, rolling a guitar pick back and forth across his knuckles.

"Word is your bar is in someone's crosshairs."

Pianto was a cousin to someone on the fringe of Mickey's organization.

"I doubt it. Best bet is Mickey's on a fast train out of town. Or head-down somewhere, waiting for the noise to die down. I'm not worried about him."

The guitar player eyed me.

"You'd like to think so, right? Except someone's coming in right after him."

"New boss, same as the old boss. You're talking about Vinson?"

Al whipped his head around to see if anyone was listening.

"Better not to be throwing names around."

"You're saying I have to worry about him, too? Listen, if you know something…"

Pianto drained his glass, the ice rattling against his teeth.

"I know nothing. Other than the fact that Frank Vinson likes your bar."

He turned his head toward the stage as if he wished he hadn't said that much.

"That again? What the hell does he want the Esposito for?"

Though Icky Ricky's desire was as believable as any other story. Pianto set a callused fingertip to his lips.

"Forget I said anything, Elder. I don't know a goddamned thing."

Of course, I chewed on it the rest of the night. That and the fact Mickey's arrest had not untied the big knot of everything. Vinson had killed Syndi, trying to bully Mickey into giving up, but I'd still heard no evidence. And no one knew what had happened to Susan. The cops were still working on the firebomb, but with Spengler dead, that would get shelved. And I still didn't have a solid motive or a suspect for Burton's murder, other than it had something to do with the clash between Mickey and Vinson.

I told myself to stop perseverating. If Vinson wanted my bar, I'd fight him for it. Or maybe I would take it as a sign my bartending days were done, the way I'd looked at Mr. Giaccobi and thought about doing what I was doing twenty years from now.

Pianto finished his set to lighter applause. He was right tonight—people weren't listening.

I paid him off in cash and a bottle of Jack Daniels. He hustled off up the stairs without any further comment on the bar or my vulnerability. Last call came and went.

I turned up the lights, poured myself a big drink, and started the cleanup, trying to suppress all my worries in the anticipation of a Sunday brunch with the lovely Francesca.

63

I've never been a believer in omens or portents, but Sunday
morning was so cool, clear, and dry, I couldn't help feeling
upbeat. The humidity receded into hints of autumn, and a pleasant
tightness sat in my stomach as I pulled the rental into the driveway
next to Francesca's house in Hyde Park. The insurance company
was dicking me around on paying for the immolated Volvo and I
was tired of not having my own vehicle.

I grabbed the bottle of Sancerre, knowing I wouldn't drink
much of it, and climbed the front stairs to the porch. The screen
door was closed, but the inner door was open, and I wondered
what it would be like to live out here in the quiet suburbs, where
you apparently didn't need to lock your doors.

"Beware of geeks bearing gifts." I stuck my head around the
screen door, not wanting to walk in without an invitation.

"In here."

I stepped around a small exquisite Oriental rug made of silk,
not wanting to get my shoes on it.

"You can take them off if you want."

She appeared in the doorway to the kitchen, wearing a black
apron with painted fireworks and the legend THIS COOK
BANGS, over a long-sleeved black T-shirt and khaki Capris. Her
feet were bare, toenails a lemon yellow. She blushed when she saw
me read the apron.

"Gift from a girlfriend."

I toed off my loafers.

"Nice and cool out there this morning. For a change."

"You came to talk about the weather, you can go home right now. But come into the kitchen. I've got a pot boiling."

I stopped to inspect a small rectangular painting, dark-toned, of a green leafy background with a cut limb in front. Even I could recognize the style.

"Georgia O'Keefe? That's an original?"

She looked uncomfortable.

"My aunt lived in Taos in the Seventies. Pretty nice, isn't it?"

The word didn't do it justice, though it surprised me to learn any more of O'Keefe's paintings were still in private hands. I owned one. The ex-Microsoft guy had owned a bunch of them.

"Looks like it should be in a museum. I hope you have it insured."

"It's not much of a risk if no one knows you have it. I don't have people over much."

We trekked into the kitchen, where she plunged the bottle of wine into an ice bucket.

"I knew I could count on a bartender to bring a good bottle."

She sounded nervous, which made me feel better. A relationship shifting to a new phase is always fraught.

She picked up a wooden spoon and stirred the bubbling saucepan, then rapped the spoon on the edge of the pot.

"Shrimp and grits. Or if you don't like that, I'll make you an omelet. But who doesn't like shrimp and grits?"

"Sounds delicious. What can I do?"

"Keep me company while I stir." She pointed to a small café table in a nook by the window, set with silver and china. "Drink? Or is it too early on a Sunday morning for that?"

Delicately bypassing the fact I was a drunk and would drink almost anything at any time. Confession time.

"I'm not that much of a wine drinker." I would have welcomed a stiff shot to tamp down my nerves.

"Cupboard over the sink. There's Scotch in there."

There was—a bottle with a purple label that read Macallan, Edition Number 5. I'd never heard of it.

"This all right?"

"It's open, isn't it? And you're someone who'll appreciate that kind of thing."

I poured a modest amount into one of the wine glasses.

"Maybe you could open the wine for me?" she said.

I blushed at my hurry to pour my own drink and picked up the corkscrew. The tiny blade peeled away the lead foil and I pulled the cork. I was pouring when I heard her curse.

"Shit!"

The large saucepan was leaning off the edge of the stove. Her other hand held the lid. I grabbed a towel and helped her wrestle it back up onto the stove.

"That is one heavy sucker." I dropped the corkscrew in my pocket and refolded the towel.

"Thanks. That stuff gets on your skin, it's like napalm."

She picked up her wine glass and clinked mine. I took a swallow.

"We're almost ready. Why don't you go in the living room and check out the crossword? I'll call you when it's ready."

"You're sure it's safe for me to leave you here alone?"

She pretended to swing the spoon at me.

"I will move no more pans without your supervision."

I carried my Scotch into the well-appointed living room. The original Stickley recliners would be six or seven grand apiece today. More original paintings adorned the walls, a Western landscape I thought might be a Bierstadt. Francesca had a highly developed aesthetic sense, and apparently the money to feed it.

The recliner held me like a soft hand. All the anticipation—of a good meal, good company, maybe something more intimate—was delicious. My dormant feelings, not the least of which was simple lust, stirred.

I opened the magazine to the crossword puzzle and looked around for a pen before thinking it would be rude to start in on someone else's puzzle. I started to call out to the kitchen to ask if that was all right, but suddenly my eyes bleared.

I shook my head. I'd been sleeping better now that I was drinking less, and I'd slept very well the night before. I took a slug of the Scotch to let its pungency jolt me, the bite of the alcohol, and then wondered why the room seemed to fade away.

64

I woke up, embarrassed about falling asleep until I realized my hands were zip-tied in front of me.

"Not in my house you're not," Francesca said, out in the kitchen.

Her voice was strained, but adamant. I thought she was talking on the phone until I heard another voice, all too familiar.

"If I kill him and take him out of here right now, in daylight, all your neighbors are going to see me," Mickey said. "You want that to happen? And your house to be the last place he was seen?"

But if he was going to kill me, wouldn't this also be the last place I was seen? I tried to shake the fog from my brain, feeling deep disappointment for being played by her. I didn't have the whys, obviously, but Francesca was the last of the whos. She had to be the cop on the inside who was working with Mickey.

"Look," she said. "I know he's been a pain in the ass."

Many thanks, Francesca.

"But you're radioactive right now. You shouldn't even be here. If you get caught again, it spills onto me."

Mickey laughed, a guttural cough.

"Should have thought about that before you 'acquired' all those pretty things. The man fucked me over. You did the right thing to call me."

"I cleaned your cash through every one of those deals, Mickey. If I get slimed with this, you lose me as an inside source."

"Then, what? We leave him in your cellar until it's dark?"

Mickey sounded unhappy. I was frozen, hearing myself talked about as if I were already dead.

"Do we really need to kill him?" she said. "That's just going to add more pressure."

Good thought, Francesca. Let's run with that. The chair squeaked under me and I hoped no one had heard.

"You still don't get this, do you?" Being out of jail hadn't softened Mickey's rage. "Burton and this guy have been pains in my ass for years. Decades. If Burton had left Vinson alone, if the bartender had kept his nose out of my business? I wouldn't be out here twisting in the wind. Maldonado wouldn't have done something stupid like torch his car. I wouldn't have had to hide his girlfriend out in that rehab place. Everything would have worked out fine."

Shock penetrated worry over my own fate. Susan was alive? But why had Mickey taken care of her?

"If we kill him, it ratchets up the pressure on you," she insisted. "Which puts more pressure on me. I can't launder your money into the art world if people know I'm working for you."

So this was his prize. Mickey always and forever needed places to launder his cash. Francesca would have access to art sales, maybe even illegal ones, through her work with the fraud squad, and he could hide his capital in them. And she could indulge her own fine tastes. Except that with Mickey on the run now, something else was more important.

"We could make it a medical thing," Mickey said. "There's no one left I need to send a message to."

"The way you sent a message with Burton?"

She sounded bitter. Maybe she had had honest feelings for my friend.

"You're not supposed to know that. No one is. That was between Maldonado and me. Where did you hear that?"

"I don't know. A rumor going around."

"Well, your rumor is wrong. Maldonado put the contract out."

That didn't mean Mickey hadn't wanted it.

"Medical means what?" she said. "Like a suicide?"

There were YouTube videos that showed how to break free of zip ties. I wished I'd ever been interested enough to watch one.

"You have pills, right? Ali brought you a package a while ago."

That must be how Mickey trapped her originally. He might not sell drugs, but he wasn't averse to using them as leverage.

"So?"

"So the bartender likes his Scotch. Let's mix him a cocktail."

"I already ruined one bottle of expensive Scotch putting him to sleep. I could have killed him then, if I knew that's what you wanted."

She'd accepted Mickey's solution. I wedged my hands down into the pocket where I'd dropped the corkscrew and tried to push it up toward the opening. If I had to die, maybe I could do it with my hands free.

"Well, load it up," Mickey said.

"Not until we figure out where the body goes. If it's supposed to look like suicide, why would he do it in my house? Can't we leave him in the bar? Or his apartment?"

She sounded unsteady. Maybe she hadn't bought the idea.

"That's one story," he said. "He loses his best friend, gets depressed, offs himself."

"I suppose."

The corkscrew was out of my pocket, but the angle of my bound wrists made it impossible to get my nail into the groove of the blade.

"You know what? I'm tired of this," Mickey said. "I have a much better story."

"Wait. Put that down. You don't want to kill me. What happens to your deal then?"

"I can find another way to clean the cash. You think I don't know you gave me up? This closes the loop: bartender gets depressed because his friend dies, then more so when his girlfriend turns him down. If he can't have you, he doesn't want you to live."

"That's crazy. You've already seen what happens when a cop goes down, the way the force reacts."

"Well, you're not really a cop's cop, are you? And if I already killed one, what's the difference?"

Even though I expected it, the crack of the gun made me flinch. The air smelled like fireworks. The solid thump was Francesca's body hitting the floor.

* * *

I had no time left. The corkscrew kept slipping from my hands, which were stiff from the lack of blood flow. I slammed my heels down to bring the recliner upright and levered myself to my feet. The ties around my ankles were loose enough that I could shuffle, if I didn't keep losing my balance. I managed to get the screw part of the corkscrew out of the handle and wedge it between my fingers. It wasn't much, but I wasn't going down easily.

Mickey stepped into the doorway to the living room and broke into laughter at the sight of me falling over myself. I wrapped the hand with the corkscrew in the other hand, to hide it. He pointed a pistol at me.

"You're not going to get far on foot," he said.

I pushed down an urge to vomit.

"You know, Mickey. Burton never thought of you as a friend. And I never bought your bullshit about it, either."

His face rippled. Actual regret? But a sociopath has a thousand ready faces.

"He was getting too close. I needed this thing with Vinson, but Burton was still after him."

"For what? The last time Vinson was here was a decade ago."

"One of Vinson's girls. She didn't end up well. And you,

bartender. I asked you politely. But you couldn't let things go."

He made it sound as if I'd planned to screw him. All I'd been doing was wandering around bumping into things.

"But you didn't have the balls to take Burton on yourself, did you?" I was trying to provoke him, but why? Other than to buy time?

He perched his ass on the wide oak arm of the recliner and sighed. His gun hand was steady as a lighthouse. I'd seen the ends of a hundred movies and knew this wouldn't end well.

"Burton and I helped each other out a little, over the years. But I was trying to protect Vinson, the asshole. And our business. If he'd stayed home in New Orleans, none of this would have happened."

"Vinson killed Burton? I thought you did."

"Maldonado set the contract for me. Back when I thought I could work things out with these assholes."

He was trying to excuse himself. As long as I kept him talking, I had a speck of hope. Not much more.

"You had Burton killed because Frank Vinson came to Boston?"

"He was supposed to organize the dope business. I'd keep everything else. But that wasn't enough for him."

"You skipped over the why."

"I told you. Burton had a hard-on for Vinson from way back. He wasn't going to let it go."

I remembered the story Burton had told me, about the young singer from Roxbury who'd gone to New Orleans to be a star, but came home and killed herself. From shame.

"Burton was going to arrest him for a ten-year-old crime?"

"Frank's been doing that shit for years. He had the girl killed. And Burton was building the case. No statute of limitations on that shit."

"So Maldonado took it out for you."

"None of it matters, bartender. The man is still dead."

He straightened up and gestured with the pistol.

"Talking time is over, boyo. We need to wrap this up. Out in the kitchen."

"Maybe you should shoot me right here." It would mess up his scenario, at least.

With his free hand, he took out a knife and cut the zip ties around my ankles and wrists. My hand was still closed around the puny chance the corkscrew gave me. He poked the knife at my chest.

"I have to do that, it won't be as clean as a shot to the head. And you'll still be dead."

I worked the point of the corkscrew back between my fingers, hoping he'd turn his back to lead me into the kitchen. But he wasn't that stupid, prodding me through the doorway from behind.

Francesca's body lay on its side, blood from a gaping head wound pooled dark on the checkered linoleum. Her torso was curled in, as if, at the end, she'd been trying to protect herself. My stomach lurched at the smells of fresh death, mingled with the odors of what she'd been cooking.

"One last thing." Mickey pointed the pistol at my mouth. "You understand that I hated to see Burton go, right? He was a good friend to me, and you don't…"

My rage took me. I slashed at his eyes with the point of the corkscrew, throwing my other hand against his gun arm and pushing it to one side. The pistol went off with a crack and the window at the far end of the kitchen dissolved.

Mickey ducked away. I grabbed his wrist, but he was stronger and yanked himself loose. I slashed again, just missing his nose.

He growled, forgetting the gun in his own rage, and lowered his shoulder, driving me deeper into the kitchen. I lost my grip on the corkscrew and slammed into the side of the stove. My ribs cracked.

The stove was hot against my back as if the burners were still on. I reached up behind my head, seared my hand on an open flame, and grabbed the handle of the saucepan. As Mickey brought the gun around to bear, I sloshed the contents into his face. Like napalm, Francesca said. Hot grits.

The gun fired wide, then clanked on the floor. Mickey screamed and scrabbled at his eyes with both hands. I gagged in breath past the pain in my side and picked up the gun, panting as if I'd just run the Marathon.

65

Mickey moaned and rubbed at his eyes as he lay on the floor, his pale green Hawaiian shirt sopping up Francesca's blood. Before he could recover from his hot grits facial, I located the rest of the zip ties in a canvas bag on the counter and doubled them, tight, around his ankles and wrists. I picked up the knife, then tossed him a wet towel. His expression promised death, but I no longer cared.

I sat down in a kitchen chair among the carnage and contemplated the end result. I was sad: for Burton, of course; for Syndi and Susan: even for Francesca, betrayed by her own greed. And I wondered if my life could get back to normal. Publicity around Mickey and his recapture would mean people coming to the bar on account of my notoriety, not for the food or the music. And that wasn't why I'd invested myself in a dive bar all those years ago.

But putting the story together, solving what had happened to my friend, felt like an accomplishment despite the losses, a capstone on my memories of the man.

Macdonald arrived in Francesca's kitchen at the same time as the medical examiner and the forensics team. Since Hyde Park was part of the city proper, there were no jurisdictional issues.

The medical examiner confirmed what all of us knew, that Francesca was dead. ME's assistants zipped the remains of her corporeal self into a bag and heaved it up onto a gurney. Figures in white Tyvek suits moved through the kitchen like crackling ghosts, measuring, lining angles, bagging bits of evidence in paper bags.

Macdonald tilted his head toward the living room. I reached under the sink, pulled out an unopened bottle of Scotch—cheap stuff—and grabbed two glasses. No one commented on my tampering with the crime scene.

We sat in the recliners. I poured two glasses of whiskey, knowing it wasn't going to do me any good.

"You're clouding the evidence trail," Macdonald observed.

I toasted him.

"Arrest me."

"We could do this tomorrow. At the precinct."

"You're thinking of detaining me?"

"Not even close. We'll do the GSR, but they already fluoresced Barksdale's hands. Easy to tell he fired the shots."

I spun him the story of the day, not sparing the fact Francesca had me thinking with something other than my brain.

"Never happened to a guy before," Macdonald said. "You didn't witness Barksdale shoot her?"

"I didn't see it. Why would that make a difference?"

My adrenaline ran high. I was hateful enough to enjoy the blisters rising on Mickey's face.

Macdonald wrote something in his notebook.

"So she and Barksdale were going to kill you."

One of the reasons Mickey hated me so much was that I had been Burton's friend, not something Mickey could truthfully say of himself. I closed my eyes. I needed to sleep.

"After Burton, came my cook. Syndi?"

I tipped the bottle at him, a question. He nodded and I poured.

"The OD. Barksdale's daughter."

"Frank Vinson killed her."

"Who's he again?"

I didn't have the patience to wonder how he knew so little. Or whether he was playing dumb.

"Gangster from New Orleans. Trying to move in on Mickey."

"OK. So Vinson killed your cook."

"Mickey's daughter, Macdonald. To put pressure on Mickey."

"Vinson was trying to hijack Mickey's interests?"

Light dawned on Marblehead, as we used to say in grammar school.

"Which he can do now," Macdonald said. "So Vinson killed Burton?"

I shook my head.

"The original plan was for Vinson to organize just the drug business. But he wanted everything. Mickey did it to try and placate Vinson."

"Mickey had to know killing a cop was going to bring more heat."

"Which is why Icky Ricky put out the contract, at Mickey's request. Burton was building a case against Vinson."

"So Mickey didn't kill him."

Leon probably did the actual deed, but we'd never know.

"And your missing girlfriend? Collateral damage?"

I wasn't going to tell him about Susan being in rehab somewhere, until I could find out where.

"I can't tell you how much I hate that term. Like the damage was incidental. But yeah—I'm not sure if Maldonado was trying to help Mickey out or sucking up to Vinson."

"Doesn't matter which."

"Does not." I set my glass down, deeply fatigued. "Is that enough?"

"For now. Tomorrow's fine, for the formal statement. You need a ride home?"

"I'm fine."

A sense of unreality enveloped me as I walked down the long hallway toward the front door. What would happen to the paintings, all of Francesca's beautiful things?

Out in the rental Volvo, I turned on the engine and the wipers. As if to mimic my state of mind, a thick layer of fog had crept in from the ocean and grayed out the sky. I turned on the A/C to deal with the humidity. I should have felt relieved, but there was more to do, more places I needed to go. The story wasn't entirely over. Susan.

66

"So, it's all over," Alicia said.

We were drinking coffee in the bar before opening, a way to gird ourselves before the day rolled over us. A week after Mickey was rearrested, business was better than ever, but it wasn't because I was famous. The newspapers had made very little of the fates of Francesca Gatoberri and Mickey Barksdale and I spied the fine hand of the FBI protecting its reputation.

We were back to live music on Fridays and Saturdays, and I had been more or less sober for the better part of a month, confident enough that I carried Syndi's sobriety coin for good luck.

"It would appear so."

My last task was finding where Mickey had stashed Susan, but that wasn't Alicia's problem.

"I mean done, as in all done."

Mickey was in an isolation cell this time, the penal system having learned from previous experience. Rumor was that an ambitious young ADA—was there another kind?—planned to charge him with every offense they could find evidence for, the object being to imprison Mickey beyond a time when parole would free him. Any of the murders should have been sufficient, but evidence tying him to those was still murky. There was always going to be a difference between the law and justice.

"To the best of my knowledge."

No one had heard from Frank Vinson. Liam Macdonald

indicated things in the criminal world were temporarily quiet, likely as Vinson consolidated his position. He would be a subtler foe for the cops than Mickey, but I couldn't have cared less about that.

"Good. Because I've been waiting for a quiet time to ask you something."

I tensed. She'd made it clear in a dozen ways she had a crush on me. I liked her well enough, enjoyed her energy and the way she cared about the world, but I'd misread Francesca so badly, I was skittish. And I'd known since the first days of the Esposito what a mistake it was to sleep with your cook.

"I thought we'd closed that discussion. Because of the boss thing?"

She tapped her fingers on the bar to the rhythm of Wes playing "Unit 7."

"If I didn't work here, would you think of dating me?"

That was blunt enough. OK. Back at you.

"I'd rather have you cook."

"One weekend at the Balsams." Resort in northern New Hampshire. "We can eat some good food, get a massage, talk this out. Maybe there's something there, maybe not. And if not, I'll drop the subject."

It took a minute, but what the hell. We could afford to close the Esposito for a weekend. And at the moment I had the attention span to pay heed to my own life.

"OK. Deal. Separate rooms."

She grinned and pulled a sheet of paper from her apron pocket. "The details."

I shook my head, outplayed, but not really minding.

"Super. Now let's go run this bar."

67

Right around four, cocktail hour, Icky Ricky Maldonado strutted downstairs into the bar, the taps on his shoes ringing on the steps. The scattering of afternoon customers paid him no mind.

My stomach tensed. I'd predicated the Esposito's future and mine on Vinson leaving me alone.

"What the hell do you want?"

He oozed to the bar, a paunch starting to show under the knit shirt.

"Amstel light. And the keys."

I wiped the bottle, popped the top, and set the beer in front of him. I didn't bother with a glass.

"Five seventy-five. What keys?"

"The keys to my bar. Though after everything that's happened, I'm thinking of renaming it the Clusterfuck."

I considered shoving the bottle down his throat.

"Just kidding," he said.

"I told you it isn't for sale. In fact, wait here."

I went back to the office, my heart banging, and carried out the money and the phony bill of sale and shoved them across the bar. Ricky shrugged, unconcerned as a cat.

"Frank gave it to me. For helping him out."

"I thought you were helping Mickey out. With the contract on Burton."

"Better options for me this way. Mickey thought he was in charge, but Mr. Vinson held the cards. I helped him find Mickey's pressure points. His daughter, for example. And Leon worked for me. So where are the keys?"

"You can't force this."

"Look at the paperwork, Darrow."

I unfolded the phony bill of sale. My signature filled the line over my typed name. I felt as if a hammer had been driven into my skull. Someone had broken into my office and forged my name.

"I didn't sign this."

Ricky plucked it from my fingers.

"I suppose we could go to court to find that out. But I'm not sure Mr. Vinson would like the publicity. As noted, your security system sucks."

I would regroup, call my attorney to see if I had options. Until then, I'd pretend I was going along.

"I need to clear out my personal stuff. Pictures, my belongings. Sunday afternoon. I'll turn it over then. And bring the rest of the money."

"What you got is what you get."

"You do not want a cloud on the title, Ricky. Bring the million nine."

He frowned, not understanding my legal threat. I didn't either, but it sounded believable.

"Five PM Sunday. That will give me time to find a decent bartender." He leered. "Maybe your cook wants to stay around."

Maybe not. How would I explain this to Alicia?

"I understand your pain." He smiled nastily. "I had a place of my own once, before Burton chased me out of town."

He pulled a small envelope out of his shirt pocket.

"A show of faith here, from Mr. Vinson. Your girlfriend." He passed it across. "Her current location. She's still in a coma. But otherwise all right."

My first priority was getting her safe.

"I can see why they call you Icky, Ricky. And come Sunday? Don't forget my money."

Ricky pointed a finger at me.

"You betcha, bartender. Just be here on time."

68

It amazed me what you could learn on the Internet. By Friday morning, I had assembled what I needed. I had Susan transferred to a facility out in Dover where she could stay, anonymously, until things resolved.

Alicia and I drove up to the Balsams on Friday afternoon, and the weekend was going better than I'd expected. Away from the Esposito, out of our usual roles, we had a lot in common: a wicked sense of humor, a deep affection for the city of Boston, and an appreciation for high-end dining. We also shared an unspoken acknowledgment that no one in the world was looking out for us except ourselves.

She'd reserved separate rooms on the same hall, not adjacent, which made things much simpler.

After dinner Friday night, I walked her back to her room, her face flushed with the wine she'd drunk. I'd had a glass with dinner and hated it less than I thought. At the door, she turned her face up in an unmistakable invitation.

I still wasn't sure how far I wanted this to go, but it would have been churlish to ignore her.

"You could come in," she said, after the kiss broke.

I shook my head, thinking of the long drive ahead.

"Let's take it slower than that. You've been imbibing."

She hiccupped, which made both of us laugh.

"You're right. We'll talk tomorrow. I promise to be sober as a judge."

Given some of the jurists I'd known, that was not a high bar.

"I'll meet you for breakfast in the atrium. Maybe nine?"

She put a hand on my shoulder and got up on tiptoes to kiss my cheek.

"You're missing out."

"No doubt. Mañana."

* * *

The idea presented itself as Icky Ricky stomped up the stairs and out of the Esposito, the taps on his shoes ringing Taps for my life in the bar. I could not afford a legal battle with Frank Vinson, and I wouldn't be able to prove I hadn't signed the bill of sale. So here I was, two hundred miles south of the bed I was supposed to be sleeping in, making sure no one else would own the Esposito.

The first thing I did was disable the sprinklers. Then I shoved the tables and chairs into a pile in the middle of the floor. I draped fabric softener strips soaked in kerosene over that, choking at the stink. Then I lit the hurricane candles from a theme party last year and tucked them in and around the pile, so the flames licked at the heavy furniture.

In the kitchen, I turned the fryer up as high as it would go, also the grill. The peanut oil blackened, then started to smoke. Even if the place wasn't destroyed completely, suspicion would fall on Ricky or some other gangsters. No one would believe I had torched my own place.

I set the photos of Dizzy and Miles by the emergency exit, ready as I could be for the grand finale.

I carried the crate of glass bottles from the kitchen, hearing Louis Armstrong in my head singing "Kiss of Fire." I lit the fuse on the first one and fired it into the pile of tables and chairs. The shattering triggered a fierce joy that only increased as I threw two more. The fire's low voice moved from a growl to a roar.

As I backed away down the hall toward the exit, the long tongue of heat chased me. Passing through the kitchen, I tossed the last of the Molotov cocktails against the steel hood, shedding ribbons of flaming gasoline down into the fryer and igniting the hot oil with a whoosh.

I quick-stepped to the rear, picked up the photos, and slammed the emergency door behind me.

Regret would take me later, if at all. I walked down the alley to Mercy Street, where I'd parked the rental, stored the pictures in the trunk. Because the bar had no windows, I couldn't see how well it was burning. Maybe it was a childish response: if I couldn't have it, no one could. But it felt necessary. And it was time for me to go.

As I drove north out of the city toward New Hampshire, I did not think about what might come next. I had money in the bank; a new friendship, maybe a new relationship, with Alicia; and no more weight on my neck. As a bonus, I appeared to be leaning toward sobriety.

I touched Syndi's pink coin in my pocket as I pushed up 93 at close to a hundred miles an hour, feeling an unaccustomed hope for the future. For change. And, at least temporarily, an end to the sadness.

Acknowledgments

For Anne, without whom, what? I couldn't fathom. Steadfastness, love, and wicked humor. Thank you for being here.

For bringing Elder into the world in the first place and supporting him through these seven books, massive gratitude to Deirdre Wait, Eddie Vincent, and Cynthia Brackett-Vincent of Encircle Publications. I'm tempted to quote Jerry Garcia in full here, but suffice it to say it has been a long strange trip. And worth every turn of the wheel.

Jule Selbo gave *Closing Time* an incredibly close beta reading and provided some on-point advice that made this a much better book.

No writer survives long without a community. The souls needn't all be like-minded, nor do they all necessarily know what they've contributed, but without them, the days are that much longer and the work very much more severe. In no particular order, with blessings on all your heads:
- Bill Carito and Barbara Ross
- Barbara Kelly
- Diane Kenty and Brenda Buchanan
- Gayle Lynds and John Sheldon
- Tim Glidden and Kathy Lyon
- Matt and Susan Powell
- Craig and Muffy Deslauriers
- Chris Holm and Katrina Niidas-Holm
- Gary Lawless and Beth Leonard
- Jeri Theriault and Philip Carlsen

About the Author

Richard J. Cass graduated from Colby College in Maine and earned an MA in Writing from the University of New Hampshire. His short fiction has won prizes from *Redbook*, *Writers' Digest*, and *Playboy*.

The Elder Darrow Mystery series—*In Solo Time, Solo Act, Burton's Solo, Last Call at the Esposito, Sweetie Bogan's Sorrow, Mickey's Mayhem*, and *Closing Time*—features an amateur sleuth who owns a jazz bar in Boston. *Solo Act* was a finalist for the Maine Literary Award in Crime Fiction, and *In Solo Time* won that award. *Mickey's Mayhem* was a finalist for the Nancy Pearl Award, given by the Pacific NW Writers Association.

Cass is also the author of *The Last Altruist*, which won the Nancy Pearl Librarian's Prize for Genre Fiction and was shortlisted for the Maine Literary Award for Crime Fiction. He has also published a book of short stories titled *Gleam of Bone*.

He studied with Thomas Williams, Jr. and Joseph Monninger

at the University of New Hampshire, and has also studied with Ernest Hebert, Ursula K. LeGuin, and Molly Gloss. He has been an Individual Artist's Fellow for the State of New Hampshire, a Fellow at the Fishtrap Writers' Conference in Oregon, and served on the board of Maine Writers and Publishers Alliance. His fiction and nonfiction have appeared in *Playboy*, *Gray's Sporting Journal*, *ZZYZVA*, *Best Short Stories of the American West*, *Tough*, and *Shotgun Honey*. He lives in Cape Elizabeth, Maine.